Karen grew up in a small town in north-eastern Victoria, Australia where she rode horses through a beautiful landscape of eucalypts, lakes, and snow-capped mountains. Her love of country continues to influence both her fiction and nonfiction writing. She built a career in a range of educational settings culminating in heading Australia's first writing and publishing degree. She holds a Ph.D. and M.Ed. (Hons) in the areas of myth and fantasy as well as a range of post-graduate qualifications in Education, ESL, and Literacy. Karen travels extensively overseas but enjoys nothing more than camping in the Australian Outback. She is the author of two travel books that use poetry to explore the power of journeying and of 17 fantasy novels.She lives in Melbourne, Australia and writes full time. You can find out more about Karen and her books on her website.

Connect with K.S. Nikakis

Amazon: https://www.amazon.com/author/ksnikakis
Twitter: https://twitter.com/KSNikakis
Facebook: www.facebook.com/ksnikakis
Goodreads: www.goodreads.com
Website: www.ksnikakis.com
Email: author@ksnikakis.com

WORKS BY K S NIKAKIS

Non Fiction
Travel and Poetry

Journey: Seeking the Sacred, Spirit and Soul
in the Australian Wilderness
In the Company of Birds: Poems from an
Outback Odyssey

Fantasy Novels
Series

Angel Caste series:
Angel Blood
Angel Breath
Angel Bone
Angel Bound
Angel Blessed
Angel Caste – Complete 5 Book Series

The Kira Chronicles trilogy:*
The Whisper of Leaves
The Song of the Silvercades
The Cry of the Marwing
remnant hard copies only

The Kira Chronicles series:
The Whisper of Leaves
The Silence of Stone
The Secrets of Stars
The Thunder of Hoofs

The Crying of Birds
The Music of Home
The Kira Chronicles – Complete 6 Book Series

Fantasy Novels

The Emerald Serpent
Heart Hunter
The Third Moon
Messenger
I Heard the Wolf Call My Name – *Finalist -*
Best YA Novel Aurealis Awards, 2019

Fantasy Novels – YA

The Dragon of the Drowned World

Fantasy Short Stories

The Gift
The Tale of Prince Anura
Dragon Sprite
Glass-Heart – Finalist –
Best YA Short Story Aurealis Awards, 2019
Ghost Stream
The White Stag
Rite

THE DRAGON OF THE DROWNED WORLD

K.S. NIKAKIS

First published by SOV CONSULTING LLC - SOV
Media Australia 2023 Amazon: www.amazon.com.au

Publisher: SOV CONSULTING LLC - SOV Media
Melbourne, Australia.

Cover by AS Nikakis: http://asnikakis.com
Image: Elena Zakhariya/Shutterstock.com
Typography: Philipp H. Polk/Linux Libertine (Regular)

National Library of Australia
Cataloguing-in-Publication entry:
Nikakis, Karen Simpson
The Dragon of the Drowned World
ISBN 978-0-6451927-1-1

For those who like their fantasy deep

CONTENTS

THE DRAGON OF THE DROWNED WORLD

When over lands the oceans sweep
a Kraken rouses in the deep,
a dragon circles ever higher
a phoenix rises from the fire,
a serpent wakens from its sleep
a griffin shrieks with tearing beak.

What's washed away cannot return
the older ways must be relearned.

There is no hope except in flame
the ashes where a phoenix came,
there is no glue for things that fail
except the shine of dragon scale,
we are the griffin made complete
by all the parts we choose to keep.

Forget the twins of right and wrong
the world is legend, myth, and song,
throw off your fear and crippling doubt
to start your journey, first set out.

To heal the world and make it whole
you first must mend your broken soul.

CHAPTER 1

Jojo scanned the horizon, desperate for things to have changed, but the ocean remained its usual vast rubbish tip of bobbing trash. He doubted he'd ever get used to it. He remembered the rubbish tip at home with its stink and circling gulls, and he remembered the sparkling blue sea, yellow sand, and gulls of his family beach holidays, but now the two memories had somehow got all mixed up.

He used to hope this was a dream he'd wake from but the world had changed into something terrible and showed no signs of changing back. He eased his weight off his bad foot and wind-milled his arms as he almost slipped from his rock. A single dunking in the filthy water could put him in the Infirmary and while the waves might be gentle now, they could change in an instant and he was six slippery rocks from shore.

He licked his lips and spat. Even the salt tasted mouldy but at least the beach was empty of Finders. The sun had yet to rise behind the usual blanket of cloud and the dull sky painted the sea and its cargo of trash a gloomy grey. Not that it was any cheerier when the sun was up but at least the grey made the bigger lumps of trash less obvious. They could be dead animals, or dead people, or a thousand other dead things ready to wash up. Broken pieces of timber were tossed on the shore along with the twisted remains of machines, and endless bits of plastic wrapped about branches and tangles of rope, and chunks of highways in sticky, sand-covered lumps.

Sometimes storms delivered whole slabs of buildings which made the Uncles happy as they built the Town, but even without storms, Finders scoured the beach for anything useful the tides delivered and Jojo was desperate to be gone before they appeared.

He wedged his stick into its usual crack in the rock and shifted his weight to his good foot. He'd named this rock *the peak* because it was higher than the stepping-stones he used to reach it, but it was more like an island than a peak given the surrounding sea of muck. Yet despite the trash, there was a patch of calm, clear water in the peak's shadow like a window into the world of Before, which was why Jojo loved it.

He'd found a bottle there that had somehow escaped the sea-rust and smash of other things, and he'd held it to the light and been made breathless by its sparkle and the memories of when the world had been whole. He still held the bottle to the light when he was alone and it still made his belly flip. It proved there had been a Before even if the Uncles discouraged people from talking about it.

Jojo glanced back to the beach, relieved to see it empty of everything except last night's trash-lines, then peered down into the clear patch of water. There was something there! Not a bottle, but something grey and finely ridged, that shone despite the lack of sunlight.

It looked like a dinner plate but the rim was snapped off along one edge and his stomach dropped in disappointment. Just another piece of trash, he concluded, but there was something about the way it glimmered that held him. He poked at it with his stick, surprised by how heavy it felt, then wedged his stick under to raise it, but it slipped off no matter which way he tried. Sand fogged the water then settled again, leaving the plate as shiny as before.

A quick scan told Jojo he was still alone but gold glowed to the east and waves slopped higher against the peak. A breeze had sprung up too. He needed to get off the beach before the Finders arrived or worse, the waves rose, but he refused to abandon his new-found treasure.

Nothing floated nearby to help him but at least there were no sea snakes or eels and he took a deep breath, plunged his arm into the water, and hauled the plate to the surface. He should have rolled up his sleeve because the wet material kept the filth close to his skin but it was too late now, and he clamped the plate to his chest, and started back. His stick slipped and he almost dropped the plate but he reached the shore then limped off as fast as he could along the beach.

Sand was always hard going and the heavy plate made it worse as did dodging the great ropes of seaweed-tangled rubbish and blood crabs in search of food. There was plenty to be had. The bloated carcasses of cattle, sheep, and pigs still washed up and there were always dead seabirds and fish. The Uncles said the birds were poisoned by the fish they ate but nothing seemed to poison the crabs.

The Uncles called them *blood* crabs because they were red but Jojo thought it was a good name anyway given their massive pincers were always covered in blood. He gave the crabs a wide berth, worried that once the carcasses had stopped washing up, the crabs might start on the likes of him.

The Uncles had too much to worry about to be bothered with blood crabs, although they and the Aunts made sure dead people were quickly removed from the beach. For *proper burial*, they said, but Jojo wondered if the blood crabs had something to do with it too.

Proper burial meant those like Jojo had no idea whether their families had washed up too, but dead, and since been buried. Not knowing allowed Jojo to hope that his mum, dad, Davy and all his friends from Before lived on and it was only a matter of time before they found him or he found them.

Something caught his eye and for a horrible moment he thought it was a sea snake but it was a bird tangled in plastic. The Uncles warned against touching the creatures that washed but the bird's beak opened and closed in a mute call for help and Jojo stopped.

'This isn't a nice place to be,' he muttered, as he tore the plastic away. He feared the bird would peck or scratch him but it stayed huddled on the sand. 'Good luck, little bird,' he said, and went on but it wasn't long before he stopped again. At first he thought the movement he saw ahead was Finders but it was something worse. A seething mass of blood crabs had stretched themselves like a wall across the sand to block the way he must go.

There must be something really big there to attract so many and Jojo nervously licked his lips. It could be a cow but it could also be the body of someone he knew, and whatever it was, even the smallest *Flotsam* knew you *never* disturbed blood crabs when they fed.

CHAPTER 2

Jojo scanned for other routes to his cave but the ocean pounded trash high onto the beach to his left and the cliffs soared skywards to his right. To make matters worse, the cliffs here were so crumbly they were almost impossible to climb even with two good feet, which he didn't have, and with two free hands, which he also didn't have.

Birds screeched above the clouds and the breeze swept the hair from his face as he wondered whether he should bury the plate and reclaim it later but while the ocean stayed low one day, it crashed against the cliffs on others, and he might never find it again. Now there was more light, the plate actually looked like the crab backs he and Davy found on their summer holidays but *if* it were a crab back, the crab must have been enormous.

The Uncles and Aunts spent lots of time warning against the dangers of the beach, and the forests, and the Marshes, and the Stream, in fact, about the dangers of everywhere except the Town and Jojo understood why. The oceans that had risen to smash, crash, and wash away the time of Before, had poisoned many of the creatures that survived, so that they lived on in strange shapes or in gigantic or miniature versions of their former selves. And no one knew how dangerous they were.

'Well, young Joseph, what have we here?' Jojo started as a shadow enveloped his. The *blood* crabs had made him forget about the Finders and of all the Finders he tried to avoid, Axel was top of the list. At fifteen, Axel might only be a couple of years older but he was a lot taller and broader, and he was a Boater, having arrived by boat, not by raft like Rafters, or by clinging to rubbish as Flotsams like Jojo had.

Jojo saw the other Finders strung out along the beach but Axel always led because, according to some of the other Flotsams, Axel wanted first pick of whatever washed up so he could impress the Uncles. 'You know the rules, Joseph. Only Finders decide what's taken from the beach and only Uncles decide what's kept. Hand it over.'

There was no avoiding the order and Jojo reluctantly held out the plate. Axel's sandy brows knotted theatrically as he weighed it between his hands, held it to the light, and tested its flexibility by trying to twist it. Jojo could scarcely bear to watch. The plate was as shiny as his bottle and he was terrified Axel would break it. Axel now held it edge on, one eye screwed shut as he judged whether it was straight enough to use on some building or other.

'Just a piece of rubbish, Joey,' said Axel at last, 'and we already have enough rubbish in the Town.' Axel's pale blue eyes bored into Jojo's and it was clear he suggested Jojo was rubbish too. Jojo didn't care, all he wanted was his plate back, but Axel hurled it towards the cliffs instead. The plate sliced through the air like a discus, hit the cliff, and exploded. There was a burst of music, a flash of fragments in the air like blue fire, and then the whole lot were gone.

Axel smirked as he sauntered back the way he'd come, but Jojo remained rooted to the spot. The blood crabs still waved their bloodied pincers and the ocean still crashed its wreckage on the beach, but Jojo felt like he'd been sucked into another place. There was anger there and frustration at his weakness, and the horrible grief that came whenever he thought about his family.

A hand touched him on the shoulder and he jumped. 'Axel always was an arse,' a voice said and Jojo managed to look up. The hand belonged to Raj, his dark eyes narrowed in a scowl. 'Brave enough to smash up other people's things, but not brave enough to face the blood crabs.' Jojo became aware of the crabs again and of the surge of dirty water up and down the sand. Raj obviously noticed too. 'Tide's on the turn, Jojo. Let's see what we can salvage.'

Raj led the way between the piles of rubbish towards the cliff and Jojo followed reluctantly. The task seemed pointless. The plate was gone, smashed to smithereens before his eyes. It was probably only trash anyway, as Axel said, and Jojo still had the bottle. He wanted Raj gone too, and the crabs, so he could crawl into his cave and hold it, knowing it was safe. But Raj hunted amongst the rocks at the base of the cliff and had already collected several large fragments. He stacked them on a clear patch of sand and Jojo used his stick to hook out more from tangles of stinking weed. They looked bigger than those he'd seen fly through the air and he wondered if there were any way to stick them together.

Raj seemed to be thinking the same. 'It's a shame we don't have glue in the Town,' he said, as he brushed the sand from his hands. 'Maybe some will wash up,' he added, with a smile. 'Anyway, at least you've got the pieces.' Jojo nodded, his gaze on the pile. 'I have to get back to Finding,' said Raj eventually, and headed off. 'Try to keep your things away from Axel,' he tossed over his shoulder.

'Yes,' called Jojo. 'Thanks.' Raj raised his hand but kept walking and Jojo wondered how to get the broken pieces back to his cave. Carrying a single plate had been hard enough and now he had lots of bits to juggle, and he still had to get past the crabs. 'First things first,' he muttered and faltered. It was what his mum always said.

He knotted his shirt tails tight around his waist and slipped the fragments inside next to his skin. They were lighter than the plate which meant lots of pieces must be missing. At least the broken edges felt silky so he didn't have to worry about being cut.

The crabs were still busy feasting and he considered whether he could sneak past them if he stayed hard up against the cliff. It would be difficult, given the piles of broken rock, but the alternative was to beat a passage *through* them with his stick. Even the idea of it made him sick with fear. His stick was only good for taking weight off his bad foot which meant he'd need something bigger and heftier, *and* two free hands, *and* to be able to run if the crabs turned on him. It all seemed pretty hopeless. Every surge of dirty water reached further up the sand and that told him this tide would be one of those that reached all they way to the cliffs.

He glanced back along the beach and gasped. The Finders had disappeared! Axel might be an *arse* but he was a smart enough arse *not* to get wet and Jojo licked his lips. He had to do *something* and he had to do it fast, but before he could move, a rogue wave crashed onto the beach, knocked him off his feet, and dragged him into the sea.

CHAPTER 3

Jojo thrashed about as the wave turned him over and over, and choked as dirty water rushed down his throat. Plastic bottles, drink cans, cloth, and shards of wood glanced off him as they churned about with him. It was like being in a giant washing machine but then he glimpsed light and kicked with all his might. He broke the surface, coughing and spluttering, and sucked in air as he trod water. He was already a long way from shore and the next few waves would drag him even further out *if* the plate didn't down him first! But the plate felt super light rather than heavy.

He was too busy keeping afloat to worry about why. His bad foot gave him a painful limp but he'd won swimming competitions at school which was why he wasn't just another nameless boy in the cemetery. It was also why he feared eels and sea snakes turning up more than drowning.

He knew that to escape the water, he needed a big wave that would break high on the beach so he could get clear of it before it dragged him back in. He dodged rubbish while he scanned for sea snakes and eels, and finally saw the water hump along the horizon. Jojo swam hard as the wave drew closer, swerved around a sheet of tin, and then rode the break all the way in. The last push of dirty foam left him up near the cliffs as he'd hoped, and he thrust his hands deep into the sand to anchor himself but the wave dragged him back anyway. His hands left desperate furrows in the sand, and then blessedly the wave was gone and he scrabbled up the beach and collapsed panting behind some stone.

The waves made it dangerous to be *anywhere* on the beach but to stow the plate with his bottle, he either had to retrace his steps along the beach to the Town and come all the way back through the thorn trees, or risk the sea *and* the blood crabs.

He didn't want the plate *anywhere* near the Town, especially near the Boys' Dorm, where there was nowhere to hide *anything*. The other boys would demand pieces or smash those he had left like Axel had, and he shivered at the prospect, then shivered again as he stared at the blood crabs. Even Axel's company seemed preferable and he reluctantly turned back towards the Town and stopped.

There was no beach left! Waves surged past last night's trash-lines to smash against the cliffs and unless he moved *now*, waves would claim him again, this time for good. Jojo limped off as fast as he could in the direction of his cave, water sucking at his heels like a monster determined to devour him. He'd lost his stick in the sea somewhere which made the soft sand almost impossible to cross, and to make things even worse, he rushed towards a horde of hungry blood crabs!

The smell hit him first, then the sound of their claws rattling like dead wood against stone. There were so many of them, they all but covered whatever they fed on, but Jojo glimpsed the purple suckers of a huge tentacle and a great seep of sludgy oil that inched its way down the beach. The stink was so bad he had to clamp his hand over his nose.

There was no way the crabs would abandon their feast and they were crowded hard up against the cliffs, as if they were keen to avoid the waves too. They tore at the tentacle, making it shake like rotten jelly, and Jojo watched in horrified fascination, then a wave crashed right behind him and he grabbed a nearby plank and hastened forwards, holding it like a sword before him. And then something

11

weird happened. The crabs stopped eating and turned their black-stalked eyes on him.

Jojo stopped. He could scarcely breathe but the crabs remained motionless, the only movement the strips of putrid flesh that dangled from their claws stirring in the breeze. Jojo crept on, knuckles white on the plank, plate pieces cool beneath his soggy shirt. Movement rippled through the crabs and Jojo gave a choking cry, expecting an attack, but the crabs heaved sideways instead to open up a passageway. Jojo was terrified it was a trap but had no choice but to continue on through the crabs and putrid slop.

Ooze clung to his sandals, then sand clung to it, so that his feet were soon many sizes bigger. He cleared the crabs and every instinct told him to run like mad but his bad foot and boots of goo made it impossible and he limped on as fast as he could. A scuttling sound erupted behind him and he whirled, fearing the crabs were after him, but it was just them going back to their gorging.

Jojo tossed the plank away and hurried on. Nothing made sense but he was desperate to get as far from the crabs as possible and it was a long time before he stopped to scrape the stinking mess from his sandals. His feet smelled worse than roadkill on a summer's day but there was no way he was risking the waves to wash them.

His bad foot throbbed from his struggle through the sand but it throbbed even on a good day. He'd broken it somewhere in the maelstrom that had washed everything away and there was no one here to fix it. All sorts of people had washed up, even a couple of nurses, but no doctors, or X-ray machines, or anesthetics. There wasn't much sympathy either. There were people in the Town who couldn't walk at all or whose wounds still festered, and some who had staggered ashore only to die soon afterwards. Jojo knew he should be grateful to be alive but he secretly hoped his foot would heal by itself and he'd be normal again.

He grabbed a new walking stick from a tangle of the trash, which made him faster, but the breeze grew to a wind which brought stinging showers of sand. Luckily his cave was just around the next jut of rock but when he finally cleared it, he saw somebody was there.

CHAPTER 4

Jojo swore under his breath; his cave was secret and he wanted to keep it that way. At least it was Lee, another Flotsam, and not a Finder. The cavern's opening on the cliff-face was hard to see from below but Lee had perched exactly where he needed to start his climb. She didn't speak and Jojo recalled he'd never heard her speak even in the Kitchens. The wind blew the heavy fringe from her face reminding him of Chen, his friend from Before, and he had to stare at the sea until his breathing steadied.

'You can't stay here,' he said eventually. 'The tide's coming in.' Nothing. Jojo grunted and licked his lips. 'You need to climb the cliff.'

'You've climbed it?' she demanded, looking at him suddenly.

'Some of it,' he muttered, which was true. But there was a shaft at the back of the main cavern that exited into the thorn trees behind. It was an easier climb than the cliff but he wanted to keep that secret too.

'The cliffs break like rotten wood,' she muttered, her gaze back on the ocean.

'They're okay here, you just have to be careful. They're a lot safer than the beach at the moment,' he added.

'*You're* on the beach.'

'Not for much longer,' he retorted, and scrambled onto a rock. 'Come on,' he ordered, and began his climb up the cliff, not stopping until he reached his first perch, a flatter area where there were bushes to cling to. He expected Lee to wedge herself in beside him but he was alone. He peered down. She hadn't even moved! He could see great swells rolling in and his heart bolted to his throat. It was the sort of day the Uncles warned of, where the waves smashed high on the cliff to sweep everything away.

'Big waves are coming,' he screamed down in panic. 'You *have* to climb!' She didn't seem to hear him and Jojo swore and scrambled back down. He must be mad going towards the waves rather than away! The first of them roared closer and his stomach somersaulted. 'Climb or you'll drown!' he shrieked.

'We'll drown anyway,' she said dully. 'Like all the others.'

'Lots of people drowned but lots of people got washed up too,' he gabbled, his horrified gaze on the approaching wave. It was almost here but Lee still didn't move. 'There must be places with lots of people, family even,' he added wildly. He'd never voiced his hopes aloud his family lived, even when alone. The Uncles discouraged such talk. *By God's grace we are alive and we must make a new life in the place He has gifted us. To do other, is to insult His gift.*

Jojo's head filled with the wave's roar and he fled back up the cliff. He had no time to look behind him and was relieved when Lee joined him on his perch. He clung onto a bush as the wave smashed just below him, showering him with foul-smelling foam.

'The cliff's too dangerous to go any higher,' panted Lee. 'We'll drown!'

'The waves won't . . .' began Jojo, but then a second wave crashed so close its foam dragged at their ankles. Jojo snatched a glance seawards. Even bigger waves were rolling in! 'Climb!' he yelled. 'There's a cavern just above!'

He scrambled on, thinking only of where to put his feet and hands, sensing Lee hard on his heels. The cavern loomed darkly above and he hauled himself over its lip. 'Get inside!' he panted.

'We'll be trapped!' she gasped, not moving.

'There's a shaft at the back which leads to the clifftop,' he said hurriedly, then grabbed her arm and yanked her inside. It was dim and the enclosed space amplified the wave's roar. 'We need to get higher!' he shouted, above the din. They scrambled up the wall of stone that divided the cavern's front from its back and crouched on top as an ear-splitting crash heralded the wave's arrival. Water gushed in through the cavern's opening and Lee clutched Jojo's arm. He barely noticed. *Please stop, please stop*, he entreated, but the water kept on coming.

'We're going to drown,' whispered Lee.

'There's another way out,' repeated Jojo mechanically, and gasped as he noticed the water's churn. It was full of eels and sea snakes!

CHAPTER 5

The rush of water finally slowed and then was sucked back out as the wave retreated, but lots remained trapped between the cavern floor and the bottom of the opening. It swirled about, awash with rubbish and the shine of eels and sea snakes. The wall they crouched on acted like a dam, with the seawater on one side, and the cavern's usual darkness on the other. It was so dark there Jojo had only stumbled on the hole in the side that led to the shaft by accident. He wanted to escape up the shaft now, before the eels and sea snakes slithered onto the wall, but first he must stow the plate.

'Where's the shaft?' whispered Lee, obviously wanting to be gone too.

'Behind us on the right hand side. There's an opening low down in the stone. You'll have to feel for it. You'll need to wriggle through it on your stomach but it soon opens up and you'll see the shaft. It's an easy climb up.'

Lee half stood. 'Aren't you coming?'

'I have to do something first. I'll follow.'

'That's what they said but they never did.'

Jojo couldn't think of anything comforting to say but the approach of another wave was unmistakable. 'This whole place's secret,' he said hurriedly. 'No one else knows about it.'

He wanted Lee to promise to keep it secret too but she said nothing and he scrambled away along the wall. He was terrified the eels or sea snakes would lasso his ankles but they slid back under the water at his approach. The cave was the same level as the wall and he stumbled in, deposited the plate pieces with his bottle, and hastened back.

17

The wave's roar was deafening but Lee was still on the wall! 'Go!' he yelled, and together they scrambled down into the darkness. He heard the wave smash into the cavern behind them and Lee shriek but he was already on his stomach, skinning his elbows and knees in his haste, aware of Lee behind him and of the slosh of water that followed. And then he was clear of the stone and climbing.

He hauled himself up, horribly aware of how close Lee was to the surging water, and then blessedly he was out, and lying on his back under the thorn trees. Lee was too, lying on her back as he did, gasping for air. Jojo expected the water to gush out carrying its horrible writhing cargo but nothing happened and he struggled upright, his bad foot almost too painful to use. 'We need to get away from here before … the eels and sea snakes join us,' he panted.

'Sea snakes … can't live on land and eels … don't want to,' said Lee, still struggling for breath.

That might have been true *before* the world had been flipped on its head, thought Jojo, but he said nothing. A wind whined through the thorny branches above and he shivered. All he wanted was to get away from the shaft and out of his sodden, stinking clothes. 'Let's get back to the Town,' he said.

He could tell from Lee's face she was less enthusiastic than him but they set off through the trees. A thorn inflicted a stinging scratch on his hand and Jojo swore as he sucked the blood away. He consoled himself that at least the thorn trees hid the shaft's opening and their long, hooked thorns discouraged anyone else from wandering about in them but the wind made them more dangerous than usual. 'These thorn trees are worse than the sea,' he muttered, as he fended off a branch that headed for his face.

'*Nothing's* worse than the sea,' said Lee dourly.

Her head was down and Jojo struggled to think of something to say, but then birds screeched, making him jump. 'Crows,' he said, glad of a distraction.

'Ravens,' corrected Lee, as she watched the birds wing away.

They all looked the same to Jojo but he forgot about them as the thorn trees gave way to the sweep of open, tussocky grass that ran away to the cliffs. The cliffs were too high to see the horizon from the trees even on a good day and today was not a good day. The sea sent up a fume as thick as fog which meant the waves must be enormous and Jojo faltered as he wondered whether they would overwhelm the Town.

The Uncles had built the Town high above the shore, he reassured himself, and while it made it hard to haul up things from the beach, Jojo had felt safe there from the first day he'd washed up. But now, as giant waves sent their spume high into the air, he began to fear that nothing was truly safe.

'We should get back,' he muttered, worried people would notice them loitering near the thorn trees, investigate, and discover the shaft. Lee said nothing but she slowed her pace to his as he hobbled off, still keeping parallel with the trees. He knew she'd be a lot quicker on her own but he was grateful she didn't stride away or worse, ask why he limped.

Flotsams were tossed about with everything else in the sea and he wasn't the only one to have washed up injured. Lee had obviously been luckier than him but then wondered if she really had escaped injury. Her head was down again so that her hair hid her face and not knowing what to say, he stared at the thorn trees instead.

Despite their spicy smell, they were the same dull colour as everything else. Grey ocean, grey cliffs, grey-green grass, grey hills, and dark grey Mountains in the distance. At least the Stream was clear and the Marshes a deep emerald green, and there were blue-sky days too, although not very often, and not today. Today was grey and if the wind had colour, Jojo dourly concluded that it would be grey too. And then, even as the thought crossed his mind, the wind dropped, and the waves fell silent.

CHAPTER 6

The change was so sudden Jojo stopped. 'It's happening again,' whispered Lee, and Jojo's heart wedged itself in his throat. He wanted to tell Lee what the Uncles had told him: that the earth had ceased its shaking, breaking, and up-ending and that the ocean would stay where God intended and leave the land to them, but even breathing was difficult.

He stared at the cliffs as she did, knowing it was pointless running. In a moment, a great wall of glass-grey water would rear up over the land and with a stupendous blow, sweep them into oblivion. Time seemed to still and then something rustled behind him and Jojo whirled.

He feared some creature had burst from the trees but there was nothing there either and then, with lightning speed, the rustling morphed to a roar and he was hit by a storm of leaves and twigs, and a wind that knocked him off his feet and sent him rolling over the ground so fast he became airborne. He hurtled towards the cliffs, striking the ground in bruising thumps, his head filled with terrifying visions of plunging into the sea, but then he smacked up against a boulder and stopped.

The air was thwacked from his lungs but he managed to fling out an arm and grab Lee's ankle as she was swept past. The wind threatened to tear her from his grip but then it stopped and she crawled into the boulder's shelter beside him. There was a tingling hiatus and then the wind reversed and roared from the ocean's direction instead.

'I think it's a *wind-flip*,' said Jojo when he had breath enough. The older boys told tales of wind-flips and of strange creatures that haunted the Mountains, but Jojo never knew if the tales were true or just intended to scare Flotsams like him.

Lee said nothing and Jojo peered towards the cliffs. There was less fume and the sound of the waves was softer. 'We need to get back to the Town before the wind does something even worse,' he muttered.

'I don't want to go back,' said Lee in a small voice. 'It's awful there.'

Jojo opened his mouth to disagree and shut it again. The wind might try to blow them off the cliffs but the Town's crooked, sea-rusted buildings were hardly inviting either. They had seemed like heaven after two days alone in the sea clinging to roofing iron but they were made from the grey and broken things the sea tossed up and so were grey and broken too.

'It's not that bad,' said Jojo, reluctant to criticise the Uncles who spent their days hauling things from the beach to make what they needed, or the Aunts who spent theirs finding food and clothing for everyone.

Lee made no reply and Jojo struggled upright and groaned. He'd hit a lot of rocks on his trip towards the cliffs and felt every one of them. The wind was still gentle but he had no idea when it might turn into a murderous monster again. 'Let's go back to the trees where it's safer,' he said.

'*Safer* unless they fall on us,' said Lee darkly, but she followed him back up the slope. At least the wind had given Jojo plenty of walking sticks to choose from and he selected a nice straight one and stripped off its leaves. The stick helped with his pain but he was no faster and he would have been well behind had he been with anyone else.

His mum would call Lee *considerate* but Jojo guessed it was probably Lee's reluctance to return to the Town that slowed her steps. Screeches erupted above the clouds and he tightened his grip on his stick. There were more birds about but at least the crows, or *ravens*, he'd seen earlier looked and sounded like Before, unlike the birds that sounded like rusty gates but looked like yellow sparrows or the big birds with tearing beaks that squealed more than they chirped.

Jojo started as he noticed a bird with reddish feathers and enormous yellow talons perched nearby. It watched them pass and Jojo looked over his shoulder often to make sure *Big Talons* hadn't followed. 'The birds here are really strange,' he muttered.

'Changed, like everything else,' said Lee. 'Father says …'

She stopped and Jojo knew it wasn't just because the Uncles warned against insulting God by criticising His gift of new lands. It was because, like him, she avoided talking about her missing family.

'I wonder what other animals have changed,' he said, to fill the silence. 'I saw a gigantic squid on the beach this morning, or at least, a chunk of one. It was purple and I don't think squid are ever purple or ever that big. Maybe there're blue and yellow ones in the ocean now too,' he rattled on. 'And maybe there're unicorns and pegasuses in the Mountains,' he continued, starting to enjoy himself, 'and griffins and phoenixes. Everything's so odd here, you never know what's possible.'

'And *loongs*,' said Lee, unexpectedly joining in.

'Loongs?'

'Dragons. They have different names in different places. They're called worms and serpents too.'

Jojo licked his lips nervously. He had hated anything wriggly since a snake had slid into his sleeping-bag while camping. And anyway, *dragons* were always *dragons* in his comics: scaled, winged, fire-breathing and *always* super ferocious. Things might be strange here but not that strange. 'You only find dragons in myths and myths aren't real,' he said, to reassure himself.

'Myths are real to the Uncles,' said Lee, so heatedly Jojo stared. 'They go on and on about how brave Noah was in the Flood and how we have to be brave, but the story of Noah and his Ark is just a myth.'

Jojo had never heard Lee say so much in one go. 'I don't think the Uncles mean that,' he began. 'I think—' Twigs cracked and Jojo spun, fearing Big Talons had followed them after all and something *did* move in the trees.

'It's only one of the stupid Finders,' muttered Lee. She was right, saw Jojo in relief, and even better, it was Raj.

'The Aunts sent me to look for you,' he said, as he came level. 'It's been a bad day on the beach.'

'And here too,' said Jojo. 'We got caught in a flip-wind,' he added, wanting to distract Raj from asking how Jojo had got from the *flooded* beach to the thorn trees. He hoped Lee would add to his story but she'd dropped her head again.

Raj's eyebrows rose. 'A flip-wind?'

'You know, when the wind blows really hard from one direction and then suddenly blows really hard from the opposite direction,' said Jojo. Raj still looked puzzled and Jojo's face burned as he wondered whether the older boys had tricked him after all.

'I suppose that explains today's smoke,' said Raj. Jojo stared at Raj blankly and Raj beckoned him into the open. A faint streak of black was visible across the sky. 'It was darker before and went all the way to the Mountains,' said Raj.

'The Mountains?' echoed Jojo.

'Yes,' said Raj quietly. 'It means there's people there.'

CHAPTER 7

They continued along the edge of the thorn trees but Jojo barely noticed their direction. *It means there's people there.* Mum, dad, Davy? School friends? Neighbors from Before? 'The Uncles won't care,' intruded Lee's voice.

Jojo started, surprised she's spoken at all as well as by her words. 'They'll send someone to check, won't they?' he asked Raj anxiously.

'They haven't before. They reckon building the Town's more important than sending people off on wild goose chases.'

'*Haven't before*?' repeated Jojo hoarsely.

'I've been here a fair bit longer than you, Jojo,' said Raj. 'There's been smoke other times.'

Jojo's stomach clenched as it did when longing for his family got mixed up with feelings of helplessness. 'How many other times?'

Raj shrugged. 'Mainly when the wind's blown from that direction. The Uncles say it's probably smouldering rubbish. Lots of things caught fire when everything changed.'

'But what if it isn't *smouldering rubbish*? What if it's people like us?'

'It won't be,' said Lee sarcastically. 'We're the *chosen ones*, like Noah, remember.'

'I don't know about that,' said Raj evenly. 'But the Uncles work hard to make the things we need like houses and furniture and it would be a lot harder if they had to make things for a whole lot of new people too.'

'But they could be people we know,' cried Jojo.

'It'd still be a lot more work,' said Raj. 'The Uncles reckon we have to make a place for *us*, and other people, *if* they exist, have to make a place for *them*.'

Jojo's head filled with visions of Davy's round face, split with a grin as Jojo high-fived him and left for school, and it took him a moment to notice they'd reached where the land dropped away to the Town. Voices drifted up along with the sound of hammered metal, but he stared away beyond the Town's motley roofs to the Mountains.

'Why did the Uncles put the Town here?' demanded Lee.

'Obviously because of the Stream,' said Raj. 'It's got fresh water and fish and we're less than a day's walk from nut trees and berries which are important for food too. The Uncles also reckon that as the land hasn't changed here, it won't in the future.'

'It doesn't look very natural to *me*,' said Lee

It didn't look very natural to Jojo either but nothing looked natural compared to Before. The cliffs looked like they'd been sliced with a knife, the Mountains resembled a sawblade, and the Town sat on top of giant steps, with the Aunts' Gardens on the next step down, and the Stream on the bottom one, and the whole lot connected by paths made by people as they went up and down.

Jojo's gaze shifted to the Town's sea-rusted buildings. The Girls' Dorm, the Boys' Dorm, the Aunts' Dorm, the Uncles' Dorm, the Kitchens, the Washrooms and latrines, the Infirmary, and the Store lined up along a single straight street. The Kitchens' chimneys were smokeless which meant the ovens had been closed off for the day and that meant nothing to eat till Last Meal.

Jojo's stomach growled right on cue and he peered upstream to where the berry bushes grew. Only the Aunts were supposed to harvest them because, according to the Uncles, the Aunts knew the good from the bad, but Jojo would risk them if he got hungry enough.

'The Aunts asked me to remind you of your Activities,' said Raj eventually.

'*Chores*,' corrected Lee tartly. '*This* for girls and *that* for boys. What kind of silly rule is that?' Jojo kept his gaze on the ground. Lee seemed to be making up for all her silences by suddenly saying lots of uncomfortable things.

'You'll have to ask the Aunts that,' said Raj equably, and with a nod, headed off down the path to the Town.

Lee stayed where she was and Jojo moved restlessly. 'What are your Activities?' he asked.

'Sorting the clothes the Finders bring up from the beach and saving the buttons and zips off the really rotten stuff. What about you?'

'Collecting driftwood for the ovens.'

'I'll swap.'

'I don't think the Aunts would agree,' said Jojo awkwardly.

'Oh, forget the Aunts,' tossed off Lee. 'It's the Uncles who call the shots.' She flicked the fringe from her eyes and looked sideways at him. 'Are you *always* going to do whatever they say?'

'I don't know,' said Jojo slowly. It'd been the Uncles who'd carried him from the beach and put him in a bed made by them, in an Infirmary built by them, and now he slept in a Dorm built by them too. 'We all need to help.'

'Of course we do, I didn't mean that,' said Lee impatiently. 'I guess I was asking whether you want to stay here forever.'

'It won't be forever,' said Jojo quickly.

'Won't it?' said Lee, her gaze on the rusty-coloured buildings below. 'The Uncles want to finish the Town so we'll always have somewhere to live, and to put in gardens, so we'll always have something to eat, but they don't want anything else. God gave us this place and we must be *grateful*, she mimicked.

Jojo still heard the clang of hammered metal but it was Raj's words about the Uncles' refusal to search the Mountains that filled his head. If Raj were right, his mum and dad and Davy might all live out their lives far away in the Mountains, while he lived out his life here.

Shouts sounded from below and he blinked hard to clear his sight. 'They've found something in the Stream,' said Lee, craning her neck. Jojo's heart quickened. He wondered if it were something to do with his family but it was hard to see anything from his vantage point. 'Let's find out,' said Lee, and set off down the path.

Jojo followed more slowly and not just because his foot was painful. He told himself that bodies washed up on the beach not down from the Mountains but then he recalled Raj's reminder that Jojo hadn't been there very long. Jojo really had no idea what'd happened before he'd washed up.

A crowd had gathered on the Stream's muddy bank and he squeezed through them with lots of *excuse me's* until he got to Lee's side. The Uncles were some way from the shore, thigh deep in the water's swift flow, busy lifting something onto a sheet of iron. The bigger boys leaned closer blocking Jojo's view and he heard a hush fall over the crowd. For a horrible moment he imagined a body, perhaps even of his mum or dad or Davy, but the Aunts would have taken the younger children away and they still stood there, wide-eyed, grubby fingers in mouths.

The Uncles came into view again as they hefted the sheet of iron onto their shoulders and, as the crowd parted to let them through, Jojo glimpsed a flash of gold, startling against the Uncles' grey clothes. Some of the crowd followed the Uncles in solemn procession but most of them went off in other directions, probably back to their Activities. 'Did you see what it was?' he whispered to Lee.

She shook her head. 'Someone said it was a cross but it looked more like a bit of tree branch.'

'But it was gold.'

'So, it was a bit of *gold-painted* tree branch, not that it matters. The Uncles will claim that God's sent them a sign and you know what that means, don't you?'

'No,' admitted Jojo.

'It means we'll all be here forever.'

CHAPTER 8

Jojo stared down at the Stream. He supposed he
wouldn't mind staying in the Town if his family were
with him or *if* he knew for sure they never would be.
There was warmth here, and food, and company. It was
better than being all alone in the ocean.

'Still alive I see,' croaked a voice behind them. It was
Mary, the ancient Aunt who'd cared for Jojo when he'd first
washed up, and she'd obviously heard their conversation.
'Whatever the Uncles decide the Stream's given us, you've
got your Activities to do.'

Mary was scarcely taller than Jojo with a mop of
grizzled hair that waved about even on still days, and
with bent knobby fingers which never fully uncurled. Jojo
thought she'd broken them in the water but Mary said it was
rheumatism, whatever that was.

'I'll start now,' said Jojo quickly, his face burning at
the possibility Mary thought him lazy. He hoped Lee would
speak too so he wouldn't have to bear Mary's scrutiny alone
but *talkative* Lee had been replaced with *silent* Lee again.

'You're not much use to the Town on empty bellies,'
continued Mary. 'Best come up to the Kitchens. I put some
bread aside from First Meal in case you two made it off the
beach.'

Mary grinned but Lee still said nothing and Jojo shot
her an irritated look. 'Thank you,' he said, having to speak
for both of them. Mary led the way up the path and for once
Jojo had no trouble keeping up. The rheumatism that curled
Mary's fingers made her legs crooked as well so that she
rocked like a boat when she walked.

Jojo guessed she was a Boater or Rafter because there were no Flotsams as old as Mary in the Town and he guessed the smaller children and older people were Boaters or Rafters too. Flotsams had to be young and strong enough to keep on swimming or to keep on hanging onto something. The very young and the very old who'd ended up in the water had drowned.

His breath caught as his thoughts jerked to his mum and dad. They were good swimmers but Davy had never learned. It wouldn't have mattered, he countered wildly, because his mum and dad would have held onto Davy, *except* it was impossible to swim *and* keep someone else afloat for hours or even days on end. And there was no way they would have let Davy go which meant …

Jojo felt like someone had pulled a plug deep inside him and everything that gave him hope had drained away. He stumbled into Mary and his face fired. 'S-sorry,' he stuttered, mortified by his clumsiness.

Mary's shrewd eyes considered him and she briefly touched his arm. 'You both need to wash, and you, Jojo, smell like you've gone for a dip. Get some clean clothes on before you come to the Kitchens and be quick about it. I have my own Activities to see to.'

Jojo and Lee hurried off to the Washrooms and Lee disappeared into the nearest entrance. The boys' entrance was at the other end and while the building wasn't big, it was draughty with its high set windows open to the weather. The Uncles had decided that shutters could wait until winter *if* there were a winter because nobody knew whether the seasons had been turned on their heads too.

Wood wasn't wasted on heating water and the water carted from the Stream and deposited in a big tub was always chill. Jojo scooped out a bucketful, quickly sorted through the boys' clothes for the right size, grabbed some rags, and hastened to a cubicle. He was used to camping so washing from a bucket was nothing new unlike using rags for flannels and towels. Real towels had yet to wash up but loads of plastic buckets had and while many were smashed, there were still plenty to cart water and stow the smaller things like nails and screws in the Store.

He gasped as he sloshed the water over himself, roughly rubbed himself dry, threw on the clothes, and tossed the water into the gutter at the cubicle's back. He deposited his sodden clothes on the dirty clothes pile and rushed back to the Kitchens.

The big room still smelled of First Meal and his mouth watered. Lee already ate, head down, at one of the long wooden tables and Jojo slid onto the bench beside her and tucked into his meal. Mary had saved them some tea and reheated the bread in the coals. The *tea* wasn't really tea, just fragrant leaves in boiling water, and the *bread* was a sort of cake made from ground up nuts but it was still delicious.

It had been the nut trees that had saved the first wash-ups from starving before they'd learned to build fish traps and worked out which greens were edible. Add in the berries and the Town ate well enough although not *often* enough for Jojo.

First Meal began the day and Last Meal ended it and there was nothing in between. *God has given us enough*, the Uncles said, and they were probably right, but Jojo still longed for the fruit and oatmeal biscuits his mum had set out for snacks *every* day.

Mary's knife made regular *chop-chops* in the background as she cut up greens but Jojo's attention was on Lee. He willed her to raise her head so he could whisper a reminder not to talk about his cave, but she finished her meal, rinsed her plate and mug in the bucket, and left.

Jojo took bigger bites of bread, keen to leave too, but then Mary's chopping fell silent. 'Glad to see you've taken up with Lee,' she said, as she wiped her hands on a cloth. 'She needs a friend and so do you.'

'She was on the beach,' said Jojo, hoping to convey the idea they'd met by accident.

Mary nodded. 'Lots of interesting things on the beach, Jojo, but best to avoid the sea. Too many nasty things still floating in it.' It was Jojo's turn to nod but he kept his eyes down as he rinsed his utensils, mumbled his thanks, and left.

The grey morning had turned into a grey day but at least the breeze was gentle and he went to the Store to collect rope for his Activity. He needed ten pieces for the ten bundles of driftwood he must send down the Stream to the Town. Digging noises beyond the Dorms told him the Uncles put in the foundations for something new, which seemed odd given the Store's roof was still only bare beams at the front. Roofing iron continued to wash up and there was even a big stack of it in the Store but the Uncles seemed keener to start new buildings than to finish older ones.

The rope he needed was heaped in the furthest, gloomiest corner and Jojo picked his way past the things the Uncles decided were worth keeping. Metal brackets, wire and mesh, straight-sawn timber now securely wrapped in reclaimed plastic, buckets of screws, nails and bolts, stacks of plastic buckets, fishing nets and buoys, and a jumble of broken tools. The Uncles said they would net for fish in the small inlets once the ocean had cleaned itself up, but Jojo couldn't imagine the ocean ever being a sparkling blue again.

The whole Store stank of sea water but the rope pile positively reeked, and to make matters worse, the rope had tied itself into a giant, vile-smelling knot. Jojo propped his stick against the wall, grabbed a coarse, hairy loop, and heaved. Enormous grey, many-legged things scuttled over his hand and Jojo yelped and leapt back. The whole pile was home to a pack of giant spiders!

CHAPTER 9

Jojo feared even tiny spiders and these were enormous with huge, bloated bodies the size of his palm. They certainly weren't natural and must have changed when the world had flipped on its head. He wanted to go back to the Kitchens and beg Mary for a different Activity but the idea was almost as scary as the spiders and he wiped his sweaty palms on his trousers and tried to think.

Maybe he could use his stick to hook out some rope but he'd still have to cut it with something. He returned to the tool pile and cautiously poked about with his stick, worried that spiders lived there too. Sea-rusted files clanked against hammer heads and screw drivers with brittle plastic handles, but there was nothing to cut rope and time slipped away. Lots of boys collected driftwood for the fires so there must be *something* to tie the bundles with, and that *something* had to be rope.

The front of the Store was light, thanks to the missing roof, but he could see no rope there either which meant it must be back near the spiders. He reluctantly returned to the rope pile and there, on the very top in the dimmest part of the Store, he saw a small bundle of rope. He guessed that whoever had used it last had simply tossed it there, probably in a hurry to get back for Last Meal, but it meant Jojo had to retrieve it without disturbing the spiders.

The spiders had scuttled *away* from him, he recalled, which meant they were probably more scared of him than he was of them. He smiled shakily. It was what his mum said whenever he ran from a spider but she had still taught Davy not to play with them.

'Get on with it, Jojo,' he muttered. He took a deep breath, propped his stick against the wall, and planted his good foot on the rope pile. The whole lot shivered but nothing appeared and hardly daring to breathe, he followed with his bad foot and felt the pile sponge-down under his weight. Then he stretched out his arm, snatched the bundle, and fled.

His heart still rattled as he hastened down the path to the Gardens, his speed not helped by leaving his stick in the Store. The grey sky looked the same but he sensed Noon had passed and he was late to his Activity. The Gardens echoed with the *thud-thud* of Aunts clearing the ground and the chatter of the youngsters who helped by stacking the stones along the boundaries but he didn't pause.

The path down to the Stream was steeper and having to juggle the rope bundle made things worse, but he managed to find another stick to steady himself the last of the way. The Stream splashed along as usual, broad and clear, and his heart lifted as he hurried off towards the Mountains, but he hadn't gone far before he saw a Finder crouched on the bank.

It was Ben busy cleaning sea-rust from some cooking pots, and not happy about it, by the look of his scowl. 'You'd better get driftwood faster than you walk,' he said. 'There's no way I'm missing Last Meal 'coz you're too lazy to turn up on time.' Finders had several Activities and one of Ben's was obviously to stop the driftwood bundles Jojo sent down from sailing past the Town over the waterfall into the sea.

'I can finish by dark,' said Jojo quickly.

'No you can't. The nut groves are too far.'

Jojo blinked in confusion. 'The Aunts said I could collect driftwood anywhere.'

'Well, the *Uncles* say you've got to get it at the nut groves where it's clean. Even the most useless of Flotsams could collect it here.'

'I'll get going then,' said Jojo, keen to get away from him. Finders liked to throw their weight about but the Uncles' orders made sense. Even the timber on the beach was stacked out in the weather to let the rain wash the poisons out before being stored.

The path Jojo followed had been made by the Aunts' treks to and from the nut groves and he stared at the water as he limped along. The Stream shone despite the lack of sunlight and was so clear Jojo felt like he could touch the stones deep on its bed. Their soft golds were like a healing medicine after the ocean's filth, as were the Stream's clumps of lime-green waterweed, and flash of tiny silver fish. It might have been a pleasant journey had it not been for Ben's threat to desert his bundle-collecting post and blame Jojo for it. Jojo had no time to stop and rest his foot even as it grew more painful.

The water darkened and slowed as he neared the Marshes, and tall grasses formed coarse clumps as the stones disappeared under a layer of mud. The Stream was full of a rot here but it smelled nothing like the rotten things on the beach and the grasses the rot fed were a deep emerald green, not the usual dull grey, and full of frog-song.

Jojo had never seen the frogs but their calls sounded normal so he hoped they were normal too, unlike the butterflies that were as big as his head. He hated their bat-like flap but they mainly kept their distance and disappeared altogether when birds squawked.

Jojo pushed himself on as fast as he could but the light seemed to be dimming. He had no idea what time it was and neither did anyone else. There were no watches or clocks in the Town which meant First Meal was at First Light and Last Meal at First Dark and *if* the sky were clear, which it mostly wasn't, Noon was when the sun hovered directly overhead.

He staggered to a stop at the first of the nut trees, relieved to see plenty of driftwood lying about and untied the bundle. There were ten pieces of rope and he hurried up and down the bank without pause collecting wood but it was still dusk before the last bundle bobbed out of sight.

There was nothing he could do about it, or about Ben missing Last Meal, *or* about walking back in the dark, *or* about missing out on Last Meal himself. At least with so many nuts scattered about under the trees he wasn't going to go hungry. Their papery husks crackled as he rubbed them off and he sat on a branch as he enjoyed the nuts' sweet crunchiness, then squatted by the water to drink. The Stream tasted of snow and Jojo screwed his eyes shut as memories flooded back of camping with his dad and Davy in the mountains.

Davy rushed out each morning, whooping as he discovered new tracks punched deep into the snow, and Jojo had loved the mountains ice-bright brilliance too, but mostly he'd loved Davy's excitement, unspoiled by the sneer of others.

Jojo took a shaky breath and sat back on his haunches. There was no snow visible on the Mountains which meant the Stream must come from *beyond* the Mountains, not that the Uncles cared. *God has granted us pure water and it would be ungrateful for us to question its source.* It was all but dark but the moon was up and he watched its reflection on the Stream's surface. Ripples made the golden fragments look like bobbing eyes and then he froze as he remembered that the sky was full of cloud!

CHAPTER 10

Jojo's brain went into overdrive. The owner of the eyes had to be in the branches behind him and while it could be Big Talons, since the world had flipped, it could be *anything* big enough to carry him off. Wild ideas of escape tumbled through his head. He could throw himself in the water and dive to the bottom, but he'd have to come up in the end, or he could swim like mad and use the current to get away, or he could flee into the trees and find a hole too deep for the creature to drag him out.

Jojo's breath heaved in and out but nothing happened and he slowly screwed his head around. He should be able to see whatever it was but the trees were empty and, heart pounding, he wedged himself upright. Now that he stood he saw it wasn't a reflection in the water after all but something *under* the water. It might still be dangerous but whatever it was gave off beautiful sparkling patterns and he was determined to add it to his treasures.

He found a long piece of driftwood, carefully slid it under, and gently raised the object from the water. Every nerve was primed to run but as he lay it on the bank he saw that it looked like a fern, even if its fronds were as smooth as wire, and with a central stem jagged where the top had snapped off.

He used the driftwood to gently turn it over and jumped back as sparks exploded. There was no smell of burning and he braced himself and turned it again with the same result. It might suddenly burst into flames as he carried it but there was no way he was leaving it behind even though it meant navigating the thorn trees *in the dark*, climbing down the shaft *in the dark*, and finding his cave *in the dark*, and then repeating it all *in the dark* to get back to the Town.

He could spend the night in his cave, he supposed, but he had no idea what lurked in the outer cavern's darkness and nor did he want to find out, and first he had to actually get there. He pulled his sleeve low to protect his hand and picked up the fern gingerly. Nothing happened and he wondered if it only fired up when shaken.

He carried it as gently as he could and while the fern's light stopped him tripping over bits of driftwood and rocks, it didn't show much of his surroundings and he found himself peering over his shoulder to check nothing followed. He'd spent two nights in the ocean surrounded by the grindings and smashings of things that threatened to grind and smash him, and the forest held terrifying noises as well. There were creaks and booms, and what sounded like church music, not singing exactly, but the high and low notes of an organ.

The Uncles had no need to warn people not to wander about at night. The earth was new and strange and no one knew what *unnatural* creatures roamed the darkness although there was plenty of speculation by the older boys in the Dorm at night. Jojo guessed a lot of it was intended to scare boys like him but his heart thudded as he followed the Stream. It was even scarier in the thorn trees. Eyes glinted down at him and wings *whap-whapped* as unseen creatures flew amongst the branches.

Jojo tried not to think about whether Big Talons hunted at night because whenever he did, he was sure he heard something following him. Even *if* Big Talons did hunt him, he reasoned, it wouldn't be on foot but sweat crawled down his back and to make things worse, it took him ages to find the shaft in the dark and then he only stumbled on it by accident.

He decided he'd mark the trees the next time he visited but at least the fern's light helped him climb down the shaft. The small space stank of sea water and Jojo wondered whether the waves had flooded his cave and washed his bottle and plate away.

Dread grew as he crawled out onto the cavern's damp stone and scrambled up the wet wall that led to his cave. The stench grew worse thanks to the wall's seaward side being full of trapped water. He just hoped the sea snakes and eels had escaped out the cavern's opening. They had no reason to stay, he told himself, as he crept along the wall.

Holding his fern aloft like a lamp he cautiously peered in and heaved a sigh of relief. It was dry inside and nothing slithered or wriggled about. Jojo lay the fern next to the bottle and plate, and settled with his back against the cave's pocked stone. He was so tired the morning seemed years ago. He rested his head back and had started to drift when something scraped outside and his eyes flew open. Every nerve tingled but all he heard was the crash of waves and their suck back down the beach. The outer cavern had always been too dark to explore and he had no idea how far it ran inland or what might lurk in its deeper corners.

He heard no more scraping but he was too wide awake to sleep and he picked up the bottle. The fern's light was dim but still enough to fill the bottle's clear glass and Jojo smiled in delight but then stones rattled down outside. His hands shook as he set the bottle down and got to his feet. The cave had only one exit, and even if he made it out, he had to beat whatever it was to the thorn trees or beach and then outrun it in the dark. Even with two good feet, he doubted he could do it.

The furtive *pad-pad* along the wall was unmistakable and Jojo frantically searched for a weapon. People scared off wild animals with loud noises and fire, or they did Before, and he grabbed the fern and crept to the opening. The creature was close now and then, as a shadow loomed in the cave's doorway, Jojo screamed and launched towards it with the fern.

CHAPTER 11

There was a second scream as sparks flew but no sound of anything fleeing and Jojo crouched, heart pounding, expecting attack. Nothing happened and the fern's dazzle subsided to reveal the intruder. 'Lee!'

'You scared the stuffing out of me,' she gasped, her hand clutching her chest.

'And you scared the *life* out of me,' retorted Jojo, his heart still trying to smash itself free. 'Why are you here?' he demanded, made angry by fear.

'Why are *you*?'

'It's *my* cave!'

'I doubt the Uncles would agree,' she muttered, 'but I meant why aren't you in the Boys' Dorm?'

'Why aren't you in the Girls'?' he shot back.

She made no reply, her gaze on the fern. 'What *is* that?'

'A fern.'

'A fern made of gold that shoots out fire? Now that *is* something.' Jojo resisted the urge to whip it out of sight. The fern was supposed to be *his* secret like *his* cave and *his* bottle and plates. 'It looks like the Uncles' cross,' said Lee thoughtfully.

'It's a *fern*,' snapped Jojo, going back into his cave and laying the fern next to the bottle. The two touched and he heard a faint chime which he ignored. He'd had enough strange things for one day. 'So why *are* you here?' he repeated more calmly.

'I found something and needed somewhere safe to keep it.' She paused. 'Like you keep your special stuff here.'

'What did you find?' Lee reached into her jacket pocket and Jojo leaned forward. It looked like some sort of baby bird, but it had four legs! 'That's *really* strange,' he muttered, as he tried to make sense of it.

'No stranger than the *Flotsams* who have the *nerve* to wash up at the Uncles' *God-given* Town!' she retorted.

'I guess you're right,' said Jojo, not meaning to have hurt her feelings. The creature's head might look like a bird's but now he saw the rest of it was more like a lizard with a bunch of odd bumps. 'Was it on the beach?' he asked carefully, thinking of the Uncles' warnings. They prohibited people keeping even the normal-looking animals that washed up, calling them *refuse from a time now ended*. Same with pets. *The food God has gifted us, is for His people, not for lesser creatures.*

'It was in a pocket,' said Lee.

'A pocket?'

'Yep. In a pocket of a jacket Finders brought from the beach with heaps of other clothes. It was my *chore* to sort them, remember, and there she was.' Lee's voice softened as she ran her fingers gently over the creature's stubbly head.

'It did well to survive in a jacket pocket in the ocean,' said Jojo, still trying to make amends.

'*She* did,' agreed Lee, her attention on the creature. 'A poor little mother and fatherless thing all alone in the sea.' Then her eyes flashed to his. 'She deserves a chance!'

'So you want to keep it here, in *my* cave, until it's big enough to fend for itself?' Lee should have asked him first but he guessed there hadn't been time. He doubted the creature would survive anyway. Davy had rescued lots of baby animals lost or kicked out of their nests but they always died, even with lots of help from their mum and dad. 'What are you going to feed it?'

'There's plenty of fish on the beach.'

'But it's poisoned!'

'According to the Uncles,' retorted Lee, still stroking the creature's head.

Jojo blinked. If the Uncles were wrong about the washed up fish, they might be wrong about other things and the Town might not be safe after all. Shadows thrown by the fern's glow made Lee look even more like his friend Chen from Before and like Chen, she said lots of uncomfortable things.

'The Uncles decide what they want in *their* world, and what they don't want, and they don't want stuff from Before,' continued Lee.

'But what if—'

'The trouble is, they still need lots of what washes up, so they've made up heaps of stupid rules. Why wouldn't you keep the chickens perched on wreckage? Or breed the sheep riding on bits of roof? And they don't want to know *anything* about the smoke from the Mountains. There could be a whole town there for all we know, with lots of stuff we need but will never have.'

'But the Uncles say the washed up animals are poisoned,' spluttered Jojo, struggling with Lee's shocking version of the Uncles' behaviour.

'No more than the rest us who washed up,' she retorted, 'although you could have a point. It might be why they don't like Flotsams as much as Boaters and Rafters.'

Jojo wished he didn't *have a point*, because it made him feel even worse about being a Flotsam. Axel and his Boater friends sneered at Flotsams like the rich kids at school sneered at the poor kids, and if the Uncles felt the same way . . .

'I'm calling her Griffy,' said Lee softly.

'How do you know it's a *she*?' demanded Jojo, rattled by his thoughts.

'How do you know *she* isn't?'

'I don't even know what it is,' said Jojo in exasperation. 'It looks like a couple of animals stuck together.'

'Which is why I'm calling her Griffy.' Jojo stared at Lee blankly and she sighed. 'Haven't you heard of griffins?'

'Are they the same as loongs?' he asked, which seemed a reasonable guess given Lee's obsession with myth.

Lee sighed again. 'Loongs are dragons, remember. Does Griffy look like a dragon?'

'Well, it's a bit scaly,' said Jojo, as gently as he could.

'That's because she's been in the water. I bet you were a bit scaly when you washed up. I certainly was.'

Jojo didn't want to talk about his first days in the Town. He'd expected his mum and dad and Davy to be there, but there'd been no one he knew.

'She'll grow fur or feathers when she's feeling better and then she *will* look like a griffin.'

Or like something poisoned by the sea's filth, thought Jojo, and the creature might even be dangerous when it was bigger. Jojo licked his dry lips and wished he'd drunk more at the Stream. 'We should be getting back,' he said.

'I'm staying with Griffy so she won't be lonely and as soon as it's light, I'm getting her some fish *and* something soft for a nest. She can't sleep on this hard floor.'

'You don't like climbing up the cliff,' Jojo reminded her.

'Griffy needs some fish,' she said determinedly.

'Well, make sure the Finders don't see you then,' said Jojo. 'I don't want them finding my things.'

'And *I* don't want them finding Griffy, so you be careful too.'

'I'm *always* careful,' he retorted, annoyed she'd forgotten whose cave it actually was.

Lee yawned and rested her head back against the stone. 'I'm so tired, I could sleep sitting up,' she said. Jojo felt the same way. It seemed an age since he'd found the plate and braved the blood crabs, and now there was the fern. It had dulled and Jojo wondered if it'd used up all its power.

Lee's eyes had closed and he closed his too but then a red light gleamed beyond his lids and they flew open again. He thought the fern had come alive again but it was still dull and then his blood ran cold. The light came from the creature's eyes!

CHAPTER 12

Lee seemed to sleep easily sitting up on cold, hard stone but Jojo barely slept at all. He kept waking to check on the creature but as the night wore on, the only light in the cave came from the fern. The creature probably slept too but its glowing red eyes confirmed it was anything but natural.

Jojo thought of the giant purple squid on the beach and of Big Talons perched in the thorn trees, but animals had changed well before the earth's upheavals had brought the ocean surging over the lands. He'd seen pictures of two-headed fish and of deer covered in knobby growths, and as sleep finally took him, he hoped there weren't even worse creatures he'd yet to meet.

Pale light had invaded the cave when Jojo woke and he painfully cranked himself upright and grimaced as he carefully sloshed his way across the flooded cavern floor to the opening. Cool, salty air wafted in, which was a relief after the cave's closed dankness, despite its taint of rot. The sky was its usual dismal grey and the sea its usual bleak vista of bobbing trash, but at least the tide was out which meant there'd be a beach to search for fish for Lee's little creature.

Jojo shivered as he recalled its gleaming red eyes and he again wondered what it was. To Lee it was just a lost little animal in need of care and he was reminded once more of Davy's hopeful face as his pudgy hands cradled some bedraggled, half-dead thing he'd found.

Lee sloshed across the cavern behind him and he coughed to clear his throat. 'Is the tide out?' she asked, peering over his shoulder.

She carried the creature in the crook of her arm like a baby and Jojo edged away. 'Yes, but who knows for how long,' he said. 'Let's get down there so we can feed the creature and head back to the Town before we miss First Meal. Mary won't save us food a second time.'

'Don't keep calling Griffy a *creature*,' said Lee sharply. 'She's got a name.'

'And glowing red eyes at night,' he retorted.

'Really?' Jojo thought Lee would be shocked or even frightened but she looked as proud as Jojo's mum when Davy managed to dress himself. 'What a clever little Griffy,' she crooned, and stroked the creature's skull.

'It'll be quicker if you leave her here,' said Jojo, looking away.

'But then I won't know what type of fish Griffy likes.'

'We'll bring back heaps of different ones and let her choose,' said Jojo hurriedly. If they didn't move soon, they'd not only miss out on First Meal but risk bumping into Finders too. He was relieved when Lee didn't argue and waited while she deposited the creature back in the cave, but the climb down was even harder than usual.

Yesterday's waves had washed away most of Jojo's perches, and to make things worse, he'd forgotten his stick in the cave. For once Lee was slower than him, and he called up directions and warnings about loose rocks until they reached the sand. It was piled high with wreckage, stinking dead things, and swarming with blood crabs. There were lots of birds too, screeching away in the distance, and Jojo wondered whether the giant waves had driven them

51

inland. He was too hungry to care. He just wanted to grab some fish and get to the Kitchens.

'A good day for crabs,' muttered Lee, peering about.

'And for Finders,' said Jojo. It would take them no time at all to collect as much wood, metal, poles, wire, plastic, rope, canvass, cloth and anything else the Uncles wanted. Jojo wondered whether the clear water near *the peak* had delivered any more treasure but he couldn't check, not with Lee around. The peak was one secret he was determined to keep.

He grabbed a sheet of plastic and tore some off for Lee. 'Bundle up the fish you want,' he instructed, then ducked as an immense, leather-winged bird flapped past his head. Others circled high above it too.

'Looks like it's a good day for the birds as well,' said Lee, following his gaze.

'*If* they are birds,' said Jojo shakily. They looked more like giant bats.

'Pterodactyls,' said Lee matter-of-factly. 'Probably blown in with yesterday's waves.'

Jojo expected her to grin but she looked serious. 'Pterodactyls died out millions of years ago,' he said, then faltered as he recalled Big Talons. But Big Talons' immense feet were probably due to the same poisons that produced two-headed fish. Whatever Big Talons was, it certainly wasn't some prehistoric ancestor bird come back to life.

'I'm starting to think that what *used to be* and what *is* have got mixed up,' said Lee. 'When the waters rose, everything changed.'

They couldn't have changed *that* much, thought Jojo, but he didn't want to waste time arguing. 'I don't care as long as they're after dead things and not us,' he said, but he cared very much. The idea of prehistoric creatures popping up around the Town was terrifying.

'Why bother attacking living things like us that'll fight back when there's heaps of dead things to eat?' asked Lee.

'Let's just get the fish,' said Jojo, not wanting to talk about pterodactyls anymore.

'Remember to get lots of different ones,' she called over her shoulder as she headed up the beach.

'I will,' said Jojo, although there was no way he'd fight blood crabs for fish they'd already claimed. He detoured around yellow-barred bodies tangled in seaweed, then a dead sheep with no sign of rot. Yesterday's waves had delivered lots of bottles too, as if a crate had washed from somewhere, but they were smashed which made his single, *intact* bottle all the more special.

He zigzagged up and down the sand collecting fish with the right number of eyes and no strange growths, bundled up his haul, and glanced up. Lee knelt on the sand further up the beach digging at something while three of the giant birds hovered directly above her!

'Lee!' he screamed. She glanced up and he frantically gestured skywards, but instead of fleeing, she kept digging, and Jojo clamped the fish-bundle under his arm and hobbled along the beach as fast as he could. He snatched up a plank but then one of the birds swooped. Jojo yelled and Lee ducked but stayed put, and he was horrified to see the birds regroup. They were working together! 'Run!' he shrieked, waving the plank, and this time she did, clutching her fish and whatever she'd dug up.

Jojo ran with her, snatching glances over his shoulder, but the birds had landed on the beach. He didn't pause to see what they did, just kept running until they reached the beach beneath the cavern, then he turned on Lee furiously. 'Why didn't you run?' he gasped. 'They could have *killed* you!'

'They weren't after me, they were after the dead sheep behind me,' she panted. 'I was simply in the way. Thanks for coming to help,' she added, when Jojo said nothing. 'I was digging something up for you.'

'What?' he demanded, then gasped as Lee slid something from beneath her bundle of fish and handed it to him. It was another plate.

CHAPTER 13

Jojo stared at in amazement. It was the same as the one Axel had smashed right down to having one rim snapped off. He marveled at how light and strong it felt and how it glimmered even in the dull light, but Lee had found it and that made it hers. 'It belongs to you,' he said reluctantly, trying to hand it back, but Lee would have none of it.

'I dug it up for *you* but if that's how you see it, I'll swap it for Griffy's fish.'

'I would've collected them anyway,' said Jojo indignantly.

'And I would've dug it up for you *anyway*,' said Lee in exasperation, 'and we're wasting time. Griffy's hungry and I want to get off the beach before Ben or Axel or some other idiot Finder turns up.' Lee started to climb and Jojo tucked the plate inside his shirt, wedged the bundle of fish under his arm, and followed. His foot was painful from his dash along the beach and Lee had already smashed up some fish and was feeding the creature by the time he arrived.

He plonked his fish next to hers and slid the plate from his shirt. It was astonishing to have a second plate and if there were two plates, there might be more. He shifted his treasures to the cave's furthest corner away from the little creature and wiped his fishy hands on his trousers. 'We need to get back or we'll miss First Meal,' he said after a while.

'Do you think Griffy will be okay on her own?'

'She's got plenty to eat,' said Jojo, and then Lee gasped and Jojo whirled. He feared sea snakes and eels had invaded the cave but they were alone.

'I forgot to find something for Griffy to sleep on!'

Jojo's breath hissed in relief but Lee looked ready to cry. 'Use your jacket and get another one from the Washroom,' he suggested.

'Good idea,' she said shakily. She made a nest of it on the floor and gently deposited the creature in the middle. 'You stay there, Griffy. I'll be back soon.'

Jojo suspected neither of them would be back *soon*, given they didn't know their Activities yet, but it was only as they neared the Town he realised the creature had nothing to drink. It would just have to wait until they came back *if* it lived that long.

Thankfully the ovens were still alight when they arrived at the Kitchens but only a few people remained, including a group of Uncles who sat in their usual place at the top table, speaking in low voices as they sipped their tea. 'The boss's here, I see,' muttered Lee, as they headed for the food.

She meant the Uncle called Markus but Jojo was surprised she'd spoken given they were back in the Town. It'd been Markus who'd explained how the Town worked when Jojo had first been well enough to leave the Infirmary.

'*All* members of the community contribute to the welfare of *all* the community,' Markus had said, 'and *all* voices in the community are equal.' But it hadn't taken Jojo very long to work out that Finders were *more* equal than boys like him, Boaters and Rafters were *more* equal than Flotsams, Uncles *more* equal than Aunts, and Markus *more* equal than the other Uncles.

Jojo avoided catching Markus's eye by staring at the younger Aunts at the Kitchens' far end. The building doubled as a school and they'd begun the day's lessons, using charcoal on plywood to help them and Jojo winced at the sound. The lessons were only ever English or arithmetic, and today it was arithmetic.

The Uncles said only younger children needed lessons in English and arithmetic and older children like Jojo, who could already read, write, add, subtract, multiply and divide, needed no lessons at all. There was little use even for these basic skills given the new world made it hard to *calculate* anything, and there were no pens or paper or things to read, but Jojo missed subjects like geography and art, and the books at home, and his comics.

He had a huge stash hidden away from Davy because Davy ripped out the pages of his favorite characters to cuddle them in bed at night. No comics every washed up and the few books that did were a mash of soggy pages, fit only for fire-starters, *once* they'd dried out.

Antonella was the Aunt who presided over the food today and her thin, heavily lined face was full of disapproval as she filled their bowls with soup and added thick slices of bread. Her hair was pulled back so tightly Jojo thought it should've smoothed out her wrinkles but the wrinkles had won. 'You two need to stop sleeping in,' she said, frowning at them.

'Thank you,' said Jojo, annoyed to sound like he thanked her for the reprimand, not the food. He had to be polite for Lee as well because she now stared at the floor. He followed her to a bench but she'd forgotten a spoon, and mugs for their tea. 'I'll get the rest of the things we need,' said Jojo grumpily.

The cutlery was stored in red, yellow, and blue plastic buckets next to the battered metal tea-tub which turned out to be almost empty. He had to scrape their mugs along the bottom and grimaced as he collected a swirling mess of tea bits. Jojo hated *bits* of anything floating in his drinks and even sieved his cordial, much to his mum's amusement.

He set the tea and spoons down on the bench and Lee nodded her thanks. It irritated him Lee refused to speak in the Town, because it left everything to him, but he tucked into his soup and bread, too hungry to complain.

Antonella had given him a nice white bowl rimmed with blue flowers but every bowl in the Kitchens was different because it depended on what washed up. Lee had a brown one with a rough finish but her spoon had fancy swirls, unlike Jojo's plain one, so he guessed it evened out.

He closed his eyes to savor every spoonful of soup and every bite of warm, nutty bread but then Lee's crockery clacked as she gathered it up and made her way out, and Jojo hurriedly gulped down his tea. The last thing he wanted was to be alone with Antonella and the Uncles.

'Joseph?' It was Markus's voice and Jojo froze. 'I think we need to speak. I will see you shortly in the Uncles' Dorm.'

CHAPTER 14

The air was mild outside but Jojo shivered. Lee was waiting for him on the step but neither spoke as Markus exited behind them, strolled along the street, and disappeared into the Uncles' Dorm.

'What does he have to say he can't say here?' muttered Lee. 'He's just being a bully, that's all.'

'I'd better go,' said Jojo, his throat almost too tight to speak.

'I'm coming with you,' said Lee. Jojo felt a surge of gratitude but they both knew girls weren't allowed in the Uncles' Dorm. 'I'll sit outside so he'll know someone's waiting for you.'

'What about your Activity? Maybe you should make a start.'

'How can I make a start when I don't know what it is?' she asked innocently.

'Maybe you should find Mary and ask,' persisted Jojo, not wanting Lee in trouble on his account.

Lee shrugged. 'Plenty of time for that.'

'You don't know that,' he said, and dropped his voice. 'You need to get back to Griffy as soon as possible. She doesn't have any water.'

Lee's hands flew to her mouth. 'Oh! How could I have been so stupid!'

'You're not stupid,' said Jojo hurriedly. 'You didn't get much sleep last night, remember, *and* had to collect fish, and got swooped by giant birds . . .' Lee's face was agonised and Jojo had a flash of inspiration. 'The fish were *really* fresh and juicy. Griffy will be fine until we get back.'

Lee looked about to dash back to the cave and there were lots of people around to witness her direction if she did but thankfully she stayed put. 'I said I'd wait and I will,' she said thickly. 'Just don't be long.'

It'd be up to Markus how long Jojo would be but he held his tongue. Lee's face was set as she settled on the step of the Uncles' Dorm and the wood creaked as Jojo forced himself to the door and knocked. Markus's voice told him to enter and his stomach did somersaults as if he'd been summoned to the school principal's office.

Jojo imagined the Uncles' Dorm would look the same as the Boys' Dorm, with beds set next to each other along the walls but each bed was partitioned off from its neighbor in its own little room. It meant the Uncles could be alone whereas Jojo never could.

The room also had a large open area at the front set with a long table and chairs. Jojo guessed it was where the Uncles decided things about the Town. Markus sat on the far side of the table and gestured Jojo to a seat opposite which increased the feeling of being in trouble.

He laid his stick across his knees, which at least gave him something to hang onto, and waited but Markus relaxed back in his chair and seemed content to simply look at him. The other Uncles mostly went to the trouble of shaving, using the blades that washed up, but Markus had grown a beard as silver as his hair and that, along with his height, dark brows and slate-grey eyes, made him even more imposing.

'I like to talk to all our young arrivals about how they are settling in,' he said finally, steepling his fingers. 'You have been here two months, Joseph, how well do *you* feel you are settling in?'

Jojo stared at Markus in bewilderment. The Uncles discouraged talk about time, even down to naming the day of the week, and no one had *Happy Birthday* sung to them to celebrate turning a year older. *God has given us a new place to begin again and we must live in the present by his Grace.* Jojo had soon lost track of time and was shocked two months had passed but it was made worse by knowing his family should have turned up by now. Markus's grey eyes bored into his and Jojo's knuckles whitened on his stick. 'I . . . I'm settling in okay,' he choked.

'*Okay*?' repeated Markus. '*Okay* is an in between sort of word, Joseph, that tells me very little. I would rather you told me you are settling in very well, that you understand your part in helping the community, and that you feel happy and safe here.'

Markus smiled but his eyes didn't change and Jojo's stomach tightened. 'Or you could tell me you do not feel very settled, that you do not understand your part in helping the community, and that you do not feel happy or safe. And given your recent *behaviour*, I rather think *that* is a more accurate answer than *okay*. Would you not agree with me, Joseph?' he added softly.

Jojo's thoughts tumbled about like the trash in the ocean. The idea of arguing with *any* Uncle, let alone Markus, was terrifying but Markus's description was not how he felt at all. And what did Markus mean about Jojo's *recent behaviour*?

'I don't feel unhappy,' he said, and felt his face warm.

'In that case, I am at a loss to know why you are letting our community down,' said Markus.

Jojo's face grew hotter and he had trouble meeting Markus's eyes, a sure sign, Jojo feared, that he lied. 'I don't know how I've let the community down,' he mumbled, his gaze on his stick.

'Everyone in the community has Activities, Joseph, as I am sure you know. Even the smallest Flotsams have Activities they complete, once they have finished their lessons, of course. It is the Activities that keep us *all* happy and safe. I explained when you joined us, Joseph, that God has granted us a place to start again and the tools to do so, but that we must *all* work not to waste God's gift.'

Jojo's head jerked up. 'I do my Activities!'

'Badly and late,' said Markus baldly, 'which is almost like not doing them at all.'

Ben had obviously complained about waiting for Jojo's driftwood bundles but Jojo *had* sent all ten, so it was unfair to say he hadn't completed his Activity. 'I'm sorry I was late yesterday,' he said stiffly. 'Lee and I almost drowned on the beach.'

Jojo had expected Markus's stern face to fill with sympathy or concern but it did neither. 'You and Lee should *not* have been on the beach,' he said. 'The beach is full of dirty broken things from a time now gone. The only people who should be on the beach are Finders, who are mature enough to judge whether whatever washes up is useful for God's purpose.'

'I like the beach, it's quiet,' said Jojo quickly, panicked Markus was about to forbid him from going there.

'A quiet place is good,' said Markus unexpectedly. 'It allows us the solitude we need to consider all we must be thankful for. It is why the Uncles labor to build the Sanctuary. Once it is complete, you will find it a more comforting place than the beach *and* many times safer.

'In the meantime, you would benefit from spending your free time with boys your own age. There are several in the Town and I have instructed the Finders to collect any balls that wash up or other pieces of games. There is land north of the Gardens where it is safe to play.'

Markus gave another bent-lipped smile. 'You can go now, Joseph, as I know your Activity is waiting and that you wish to complete it *properly* this time. We will speak again when you are more settled.'

CHAPTER 15

Jojo trudged along, barely aware of where he went. He felt ashamed as if he'd committed a terrible crime and he felt angry too at Markus's unfairness and at being too weak to stand up for himself. It took him a while to notice the patches of sunlight on the path which meant the sun had broken through for the first time in days, and that he wasn't alone.

'I'm sorry,' he muttered to Lee, wondering why she bothered to hang around with him.

'I'm guessing Markus said a whole lot of nasty things to you.'

'Some of them might be true,' said Jojo, wondering if he really were lazy and disorganised.

'*None* of them are true!' said Lee fiercely and gave him a quick hug. 'Markus makes people feel bad so he can boss them around more easily.' Jojo hadn't been hugged since a wall of water had washed everything away and he stared down at the ground. 'Our *Activities* are the same as yesterday's, by the way,' said Lee eventually. 'Mary came by while I was waiting for you.'

She picked up a stone and hurled it into the water, angry again. 'If the Aunts were all as nice as Mary, this place wouldn't be half so bad!'

'Markus doesn't like us being on the beach,' said Jojo, his gaze now on the Stream. 'He says I should be playing ball games with other boys my age.'

Lee snorted. 'With your dud foot?'

'He might not have noticed,' said Jojo.

'Oh, he noticed alright. Nothing escapes *that* man's flinty eyes.' Lee hurled another stone into the Stream, this time with greater force. 'He's even meaner than I thought!'

Jojo didn't want to think about Markus anymore let alone talk about him. 'I need to start my Activity,' he said. They turned back towards the Town but Jojo could tell Lee was still angry by the way she stomped along.

'As soon as I get the clothes sorted, I'm heading back to Griffy *along the beach*!' she exclaimed

'You have to take her water, remember.'

'I haven't forgotten.'

'*And* find something to carry it in,' added Jojo. Lee's face told him she *had* forgotten that bit. 'There's plenty of buckets on the beach,' he said quickly.

'But I'd have to come all the way back to the Stream to fill it,' said Lee. 'Unless …'

'Unless what?'

'I visit the waterfall.'

'It's too dangerous!' exclaimed Jojo. The Stream poured over the cliff with a power that had carved a giant horseshoe out of the stone and gouged a hole in the beach. Bits of cliff crashed down along with the water too which made it risky to be anywhere near it. 'There's lots of buckets in the Store,' he suggested. 'Grab one from there and fill it at the Stream after your Activity. It'll be quicker than backtracking.'

'And be hauled before Markus for stealing? No way.'

'No one would know you didn't find it on the beach,' said Jojo in surprise.

'*Everyone* would know,' said Lee, and fell silent as some Aunts approached, not speaking again until they were long past. '*Everyone* knows *everything* that happens around here and lots are happy to snitch to the Uncles and Aunts. Why do you think Markus dragged you in?'

'I don't know,' said Jojo uneasily.

'Because we were late to our chores yesterday. Who collected the wood bundles you sent down? Was it Axel?'

'No, Ben.'

'Same thing,' snorted Lee. 'Those idiots can't wait to be Uncles so they can boss *everyone* around and not just Flotsams. Another reason to leave,' she muttered.

Jojo's stomach gave an odd lurch. 'You're leaving?'

'Well, there's no way I'm hanging around here.'

'But . . . where would you go? Everything's been washed away.'

They were close enough to the Town now to hear sawing and Lee stopped. 'Do you really believe we're the only ones who washed up?'

'No,' said Jojo uncertainly, 'but the others might be miles away or on the other side of the sea even. How would we get to them?'

'The boaters came in boats, didn't they? Where are the boats now?' Jojo stared at her blankly. Not only didn't he know but he'd never even thought about it. 'I don't know either,' conceded Lee when Jojo said nothing. 'The Uncles and Aunts are pretty quiet on that score.'

She rubbed some grass-seeds off her trousers as more Aunts approached. 'I don't care about their stupid boats anyway,' she whispered, after the Aunts had passed. 'I'm never getting on *anything* that goes on water ever again,' she added shakily, and took a deep breath. 'Smoke's coming from the Mountains and the Mountains are high and dry.'

'They're a long way away,' pointed out Jojo. 'What will you do for food, and warmth, and—'

'I'm not leaving *now*,' said Lee impatiently. 'I need time to prepare and Griffy needs time to grow but there's no way I'm spending the rest of my life here.'

Jojo was still thinking about Lee's words when he reached the Store. He understood why she disliked the Town's ramshackle bleakness, but it had food, and warm beds, and other people to talk to. And there were Uncles and Aunts to sort things out, and make decisions, and plan things.

There were probably other places where people had ended up but they might be worse and the smoke from the Mountains might simply be burning trash as the Uncles claimed. And yet . . . Lee's determination to go raised uncomfortable questions about whether he wanted to stay or go too.

The Store was as uninviting as yesterday with its stink and gloom and tangled, spider-infested rope pile, and even worse, the bundle of rope he needed had disappeared. Ben should have returned it to the heap but he might have been annoyed enough to hide it or even throw it away to make things hard for Jojo. And cutting new lengths from the rope pile still meant finding something to cut it with.

There'd been nothing useful in the tool pile last time but he saw it had been added to. There were more saws, hammer heads, and screwdrivers, some still wrapped in fine strands of seaweed. They rattled as he poked about with his stick and then something flashed, beautifully clean of sea-rust, and he picked it up. It was a piece of curved metal with one end honed to a point and the other, thicker end, obviously designed to slot into a handle.

The handle was long gone but Jojo remembered pictures of old fashioned farming tools from his school history books. It was too small for a scythe and he decided it was a sickle, a tool once used to harvest grain. The blade was still sharp and he ran his fingers over the silken metal and then jumped as footsteps sounded. His brain yelled at him to toss the sickle back but as Axel's silhouette loomed in the doorway, he dropped it into his pocket instead.

CHAPTER 16

Axel paused to let his eyes adjust to the gloom and Jojo snatched a steadying breath. He was sure the bulge in his pocket was obvious and Lee's warning about *stealing* pounded through his head.

'The Uncles sent me to *encourage* you to complete your Activity on time today,' said Axel.

'I . . . I can't start my Activity until I find where Ben left the rope,' said Jojo, glad the dimness hid his burning face. 'It's not where it's supposed to be,' he managed to add.

Axel's hands came to his hips. 'And where's it supposed to be?'

'With the rest of the rope at the back.'

Axel made a show of scanning the Store, even though it was impossible to see the darkest corners from the doorway. 'Is that the rope you're talking about?' he asked, pointing to a bundle behind the door. Jojo nodded, mortified he'd gone straight to the rope pile without checking the Store front first.

'You obviously need help to look for things *properly* too,' sneered Axel.

Jojo set off but it was soon clear Axel intended to accompany him all the way to the nut trees and stand over him while he worked, which meant it was going to be a long, miserable day. There would be no chance to eat nuts or enjoy the unusually sunny sky, and more importantly, no chance to search for anything as lovely as the fern.

The sunshine made even the dull sea-rusted Town look cheerful but Axel strode along on his long legs and Jojo had no time to do anything but try to keep up. It would have been a struggle even had he not juggled the rope bundle, his stick, *and* the pain in his broken foot, and he soon fell behind, which he guessed was what Axel intended. It gave the *mighty* Boater-Finder yet another reason to despise him.

Axel was a long way ahead by the time Jojo reached the Marshes and he was hot for the first time since he'd washed up. The Marshes' lush grasses looked invitingly cool and there were birds there too of normal sizes with normal songs, even if their purples, yellows, and oranges were anything but normal.

Blackbirds, or what should be called purple birds, orange wrens that used to be brown, and thrushes, still speckled but in different shades of yellow, flitted amongst the grasses or perched on pieces of driftwood.

Jojo's foot throbbed so badly he shed his sandals and stepped into the cool, soothing water. Mud squished between his toes and the birds made pleasant music as the water swirled around his broken foot. He used to swim in lakes like this, where ducks and pelicans drifted on the surface, and fish and mud eyes made their homes on the bottom, and he yearned to swim in them again. There were no waves to threaten him and no trash to make him sick, just the sweet smell of fresh water like home. The only thing missing were Davy's excited squeals as Jojo spun his rubber ring around and around.

There was a great flapping and splashing as the birds launched into the air and Jojo whirled. He expected to see Axel's angry face loom above the grasses, but the grasses were empty. The hair shifted on Jojo's neck but before he could move, something rough lassoed his ankles and wrenched him under the water. Whatever had him stirred up so much mud the water was a brown fog but then a huge muscular coil emerged from the murk, flung itself over his torso, and tightened. It threatened to crack his ribs and rammed the sickle hard into his side, and Jojo's vision blotched, but then the coil suddenly released him and with a stinging flick of its tail, the creature was gone.

Jojo floundered back to the surface gasping for air then staggered to shore, grabbed his things, and fled up the bank. He didn't stop until he was high above the Stream and then he collapsed on his back, sobbing in relief. Nothing bled or felt broken but his side was bruised from the sickle and his ankles sand-papered from the creature's scales.

It was definitely some sort of giant serpent but he had no idea where it'd come from or why it'd let him go. Jojo had been to the Marshes dozens of times and the Aunts went there often to harvest the tall grasses for baskets and mats, which meant the serpent had to be a recent arrival. But had it swum up from the sea or down from the Mountains?

Jojo struggled to his feet and hurried on, keeping well clear of the water, but the more he thought about the serpent, the more puzzled he became. It couldn't have swum up from the beach because it would've had to scale the waterfall, so maybe it'd been lying low in the Marshes all along and Jojo had disturbed it, or maybe it lived in a nearby hole and being a nice warm day, had decided to cool off. But whatever the reason it was there, nothing explained why it'd released him.

Axel waited for him near the nut trees and made an exaggerated show of looking Jojo's sodden body up and down. 'Decided you had plenty of time for a swim, did you?' he asked sarcastically.

'I fell in,' said Jojo, which was half true. He *had* fallen in when the serpent had ripped his feet from under him.

'No wonder you never get anything done,' said Axel. 'You seem to be as clumsy as you are—'

'Do you want me to collect wood here or further up?' asked Jojo, still rattled by his encounter with the giant serpent.

Axel's face showed surprise at the interruption before it resumed its usual scowl. 'You can get it here and be quick about it. Yash wants all the bundles down before Noon. He's got other Activities to do apart from waiting for you, and so do I,' he added, and squared his shoulders. 'The Uncles have chosen a few of us to search the Stream all the way to the nut groves' far side, but don't think I can't still check up on you.'

'Search for what?' asked Jojo, not wanting to be anywhere near the Stream if the Uncles believed it swarmed with giant serpents.

Axel rolled his eyes. 'Didn't you listen to *anything* the Uncles said at First Meal yesterday? I knew Flotsams were too dumb to find boats, but I never thought they'd be too dumb to ignore their *leaders'* instructions too.'

'I missed yesterday's First Meal,' said Jojo hurriedly, desperate to discover more about any serpents.

'Well, you'd better not believe the Uncles will accept *that* as an excuse for ignoring their orders,' warned Axel. '*Everyone* is to *immediately* report *anything* strange they see in the Stream and no one's to touch it, *whatever* it is.'

'Strange things like giant serpents?' asked Jojo.

Axel stared at him in disgust. 'No! Strange things like the golden cross.'

CHAPTER 17

Jojo hurried up and down the bank collecting drift-wood, not because he was worried about Axel, but because it distracted him from his *crime*. The gold fern wasn't a cross, he told himself over and over again but, according to Axel, the Uncles had ordered that *anything* strange in the Stream be reported, and the fern was definitely strange and had definitely been in the Stream. At least only Lee knew about it and even *if* Jojo had to hand it over, he still had his bottle and plates, which hadn't been in the Stream. But that wasn't much comfort because the Uncles might take them anyway and then he'd have nothing.

He was barely aware of fastening each bundle and sending it off and was watching the last of them bob out of sight when the grass rustled behind him. His heart raced as he feared the serpent had returned but it was more likely to be Axel and he struggled to relax his face as he turned, convinced it had guilt written all over it.

It was Raj and Jojo's breath emptied in relief. 'You've done well,' said Raj, with a smile. 'I thought you'd only be about halfway through.' Axel had probably given the Finders a detailed description of how dumb, lazy, clumsy, and slow Jojo was and despite Raj having earlier called Axel an *arse*, Jojo knew there was no way a Finder would side with a Flotsam against another Finder. 'I thought your foot might slow you down a bit too,' continued Raj.

'It does but there's plenty of driftwood lying about so I didn't have to search far.'

'Yes,' said Raj and peered upstream. 'Plenty of driftwood coming down from the Mountains amongst *other things*.'

'Other things?' repeated Jojo, suddenly aware of the sickle in his pocket. Given his sodden jacket, its shape must be obvious.

Raj pointed upstream. 'See that?'

Jojo's heart missed as he half expected to see something shiny in the water but all he saw was driftwood. 'No,' he said in a small voice, fearing it confirmed his stupidity.

'That piece of wood there on the bank, with the black end.'

'Yes,' said Jojo, puzzled why Raj had bothered to point it out.

'It's been burned,' said Raj, going over and picking it up. Jojo followed curiously. 'And this end's been cut,' continued Raj, running his hand over the sharp edge.

'It's been used in a fire?' said Jojo uncertainly.

'Exactly,' said Raj. 'Someone's cut it to size and then burned it.'

'Then why's it in the Stream?'

'Good question,' said Raj, turning it over in his hands thoughtfully. 'Maybe it got washed in. The Stream isn't always this calm, Jojo, although the Uncles believe their god is done with storms. It's why they built the Town so close to its banks.'

Jojo's stomach tightened as it always did when things became less certain. He didn't know what Raj meant by *their god* but Raj was certainly worried about the Town's location. 'It's not *that* close,' said Jojo.

'Depends on the size of the storm,' said Raj matter-of-factly. 'A big storm mightn't affect the Town but I reckon there'd be enough of a flood for the Gardens to go.' He hurled the wood into the Stream with surprising ferocity and they watched it swirl away. 'Maybe that's what the people in the Mountains did,' said Raj softly. 'Threw a piece of cut, burned wood into the Stream to let us know they're there.'

'Couldn't they just come and tell us?' said Jojo, *and bring news of all the others there like his mum and dad and Davy*.

'Maybe *their* god won't let them or *their* Uncles won't,' added Raj harshly. Jojo looked at him startled. He'd never seen Raj angry before. 'I'm heading back,' said Raj briskly. 'We can walk together.'

'I'm pretty slow,' said Jojo, wanting to be alone to look at things and think.

'I'm not in a hurry,' said Raj.

They walked in silence, which seemed awkward at first, but after a while Jojo almost forgot Raj was there. The sun glinted off the water and pale clouds framed patches of sky that seemed impossibly blue after weeks of grey. It was the blue of Before, of hot summer days golden with light, and of cold winter days brilliant with frost, before the earth had shaken, the waters risen, and the old world been washed away.

'The Uncles believe their god will heal *everything*,' said Raj, speaking for the first time as they neared the Marshes. 'That everything will be as it was Before or even *better* but I don't think there's any way back, whatever gods are in charge.'

Jojo kept his eyes on the lush grasses. Raj spoke as if there were lots of gods whereas his mum and dad had only ever mentioned one. In a funny way, Raj reminded Jojo of Lee, because Raj questioned things like Lee did. 'Do you think things will always be like this?' he asked cautiously.

He wanted Raj to smile and say that everything would be just fine, but Raj's brows were low over his eyes. 'I think things will always be like this *here* or if they change, it will only be slowly, but here is only a small place, Jojo, and there are lots of places that might be better.'

'It sounds like you want to leave,' said Jojo, thinking of Lee again. He wondered how many other people in the Town wanted to leave too.

'Well, I don't want to stay here but that's not the same thing as wanting to leave.'

Jojo couldn't see any difference and he was still puzzling over it when shadows swept the ground and he ducked. Raj simply stared skywards and Jojo followed his gaze. Enormous birds circled high above and their size told Jojo they were the same as those that'd swooped Lee on the beach.

'There are so many strange things here,' murmured Raj. 'It's as if, when the lands broke and the seas rose, creatures from the old stories escaped back into the world.'

'That's not possible, is it?' asked Jojo, thinking uncomfortably of Lee's little creature. But Griffy was just some bird or lizard made strange by the sea's poisons.

'The Uncles think it is,' he said, making Jojo's stomach flip, but then Raj shrugged. 'They believe their god sent a flood to test them as Noah was tested. The story of Noah and his Ark is pretty old, Jojo, and lots of people call it a myth just as lots of people would call these birds a myth, yet here they are, with their pterodactyl heads, flapping about on their giant bat wings. Of course, it might be just that Time's been turned on its head along with the lands.'

Jojo licked his lips, not much comforted by the weird idea of Time being changed. 'Do you think the birds are just here, near the sea, or everywhere?'

Raj shrugged again. 'I have no idea but the sea's so dirty, you have to wonder whether things are more normal in cleaner places. There might even be places where everything's the same as Before but the Uncles are happy here. They think it's safe because their god sent them a sign.'

'But it isn't safe,' said Jojo quickly. 'There's an enormous serpent in the Marshes.'

Raj's head swiveled. 'A *serpent*?' he asked, and listened without interruption to Jojo's stumbling account. 'Why do you think it let you go?' he asked curiously.

'I don't know,' said Jojo. He was just grateful it had.

'Do you think there's something even bigger in the Stream that frightened it off?' asked Raj.

Jojo shivered; he hadn't thought of that! 'I didn't see anything but I didn't look either,' he admitted. 'I just wanted to get away from the water.'

Raj gave him a brief pat on the back. 'I can certainly understand why, but a serpent or snake of that size is dangerous even if it stays in the Marshes but it might slither down to the Town and attack people there. You need to tell Markus about it as soon as we get back.'

'Yes,' said Jojo, although the thought of speaking to Markus was almost as scary as the serpent.

CHAPTER 18

Raj stopped when they came level with the Gardens. The Aunts' voices drifted down from the higher ground and Jojo glanced up to where they worked. The day was still sunny and thankfully, there was no sign of the giant birds. He could almost imagine he was back in the time of Before. The high-pitched chatter of the younger Flotsams who helped the Aunts reminded him of Davy's excited babble as he rushed between the swings and see-saw at the park and Jojo wondered whether the Town could be a good place after all *if* there were more sunny days and more happy voices.

'I have to help with a stone wall around the Gardens,' said Raj, 'although I have no idea what it's supposed to keep out,' he added more softly. 'Anyway, remember to tell the Uncles about the serpent.' He gave a nod and turned up the path to the Gardens.

Raj's parting words suggested Jojo could tell *any* Uncle about the serpent, not just Markus, and he quickened his pace, keen to get the ordeal over with. But when he reached the Town, it was so quiet only the distant sound of hammering told him it hadn't been abandoned.

He poked his head into the Kitchens in the hope that Uncles might linger to discuss important matters but the building was empty of everything except the delicious smell of bread. His mouth watered but there was nothing to be had until Last Meal and he continued on to the Uncle's Dorm and knocked. It seemed deserted too but the door squeaked open as he was about to turn away.

The Uncle who regarded him was short and bent with eyebrows so tangled Jojo half-imagined birds lived in them.

'What do you want?' the Uncle demanded, his stare fixing Jojo like a bug on a pin.

Jojo licked his lips as he struggled to drag his thoughts from the brows' possible nesting sites. 'I need to tell an Uncle … *Raj* said I need to tell an Uncle about the big serpent I saw in the Marshes.'

'And Raj is?'

'One of the Finders,' said Jojo, taken a back by the Uncle not knowing Raj.

'And you are?'

'Jojo.' The Uncle glared at Jojo as if he lied and Jojo licked his lips again. 'One of the Flotsams,' he added, and wondered if he would forever be just *one of the Flotsams*.

'A serpent, you say?' Jojo nodded. 'In the Marshes?' Jojo nodded again. 'You need to speak to Markus about something like that. He'll be back before Last Meal.'

'Can't you tell him?' asked Jojo desperately, but the Uncle showed no signs of having heard him and Jojo was left staring at the sea-rusted door. He forced himself in the direction of the hammering, the sickle heavy in his pocket. All he wanted was to get the meeting with Markus over with and get back to his cave.

Because the Town's buildings were lined up along a single street, Jojo expected the new building to be next to the last in the row, the Infirmary, but it was off across the sweep of grasses nearer the cliff. Silhouettes worked on the roof and went to and fro carting wood and Jojo guessed all the Uncles were there except the one who hadn't known who Jojo was and was no friendlier once he did.

Jojo's foot ached and he stopped and leaned against the Infirmary wall. It seemed strange to set the new building so close to the ocean's stinking cargo but Markus had talked about a *sanctuary* that would be quiet, so maybe that explained his choice.

'Been for another swim, I see,' said a raspy voice behind him. It was Mary and Jojo was grateful for her smile after the bushy-browed Uncle's glower. 'A good day for it,' she went on, hair bouncing about as she gazed at the sky. 'You don't stink, so I'm guessing you swam in the Stream.' Jojo nodded. 'Probably best to undress next time,' she added.

Jojo wanted to tell her about the serpent but he had a feeling Markus would be angry if he didn't hear about it first. 'I fell in,' he said instead, and felt his face warm.

'Well, that can happen to the best of us,' she said, eyeing him. 'The good thing is that you managed to *fall out* again,' she added, and hobbled away up the street.

Jojo didn't think Mary believed him but she'd been nice about it and as he looked back to the Uncles, he doubted they'd be nice about anything, including being interrupted and certainly not about the sickle if they noticed it bulging in his pocket.

His mum's voice echoed in his head telling him to put it back but then other voices sounded. Axel's was clear and Ben's, and Jojo guessed the rest belonged to Finders too. He ducked behind the Infirmary and watched them pass and go on towards the Uncles, then limped in the opposite direction, keeping out of sight at the back of the buildings until he turned up the slope towards the thorn trees.

He checked behind him often as he dodged the trees' jagged branches but saw no one. People seemed to prefer the familiarity of the Town and Stream to the shade-shrouded forest full of weird sounds and odd bird calls, or the beach strewn with stinking dead and broken things. Jojo didn't blame them but he needed to escape those whose presence reminded him of those who were missing.

He limped along just inside the tree line, the forest's spicy smell a welcome change from the sea's stench, and didn't pause until he was opposite where the shaft opened deeper in the trees. It'd taken him ages to find this spot last night in the dark and he'd promised himself he'd mark the trees.

He had the sickle, which was handy, but he didn't want to make marks other people would notice and investigate. He eyed the roots of a thorn tree, all but hidden in the grass, but it would be pointless making marks he couldn't see either. Maybe he should mark a few branches instead. He glanced up and froze. Big Talons was perched just above his head!

Big Talons was usually content just to watch him but after Jojo's tangle with the serpent, he wanted the bird gone. He willed Big Talons to leave but the bird seemed happy with his branch, and after a while, Jojo returned to the problem of making marks. Gouging out some bark low on the trunk would probably go unnoticed unless people were searching for it and he slipped the sickle from his pocket.

But then, the whole forest erupted. Ear-splitting shrieks tore through the air and twigs rained down as branches fractured. Jojo crouched, searching the trees for some sort of monster then saw it was Big Talons. The bird was so desperate to fly away that it smashed back and forth between the branches. The ruckus continued until Big Talons finally broke free and then the *whump-whump-whump* of its wings faded into the distance.

Jojo still crouched, waiting for the *whump-whump* of his heart to quieten too. Something had scared Big Talons badly and earlier, something had scared the serpent, and whatever it was, had to be bigger and deadlier than both. Nothing moved or sang in the forest, not even the smaller, more normal birds, as if they hid in fear.

Jojo straightened and dropped the sickle back into his pocket. The trees were so riddled with broken branches that there was no need to mark them after all.

CHAPTER 19

Jojo was still jittery as he descended the shaft, and the cavern's stench did nothing to tame the hair on the back of his neck. At least his cave looked the same, except for a bowl of water which told him Lee had visited and probably wasn't far away.

He picked his way to the cavern's opening, thankful to feel nothing wriggle underfoot, and peered out. The sun made the ocean look startlingly different. It was still a huge raft of floating garbage but the sunshine brightened the yellow, white, and red paint on debris, and lit the green-blue-aquas of the water between. Waves even left a glittery film on the sand as they ran back down the beach.

He could see Lee in the distance and laboriously climbed down the cliff and headed in her direction, dodging rotting animals and grateful that the blood crabs scuttled out of his way again. Lee carried a yellow bucket as she trawled up and down collecting fish. 'Did Griffy eat all the last lot?' he asked in surprise. Lee nodded, busy scooping up something with bronze scales. 'But there were heaps and Griffy's only small!'

'But growing fast,' said Lee proudly. 'Which is why she needs more fish.'

Jojo wondered whether the eels and sea snakes had slithered into the cave for a free meal or some creature from deeper in the cavern had visited but he kept the possibility to himself. There was no point in Lee worrying too.

He grabbed a nearby length of plastic and scooped up a fish. 'No more Griffies in pockets today?' he asked lightly, as he worked.

'Nope. Any more golden ferns?'

'No, but there was a giant serpent.'

Lee's head swiveled. 'A giant serpent?' Jojo described the encounter which was easier this time given he'd already told Raj. 'It's *really* weird it let you go,' said Lee thoughtfully when he'd finished.

'Maybe it decided I'd make really bad eating,' joked Jojo.

'Or there was something even worse in the water that frightened it off,' said Lee, and Jojo nodded uneasily, having had the same thought. 'I supposed you'll have to tell the Uncles,' she said, as she dropped another fish in the bucket.

'Raj said to.'

'The Finders are such know-all's,' snorted Lee. 'What does Raj expect the Uncles to do? Hunt the serpent down and kill it?'

'Raj's alright but Axel and Ben are *arses*,' said Jojo, enjoying they way Raj's word rolled off his tongue.

'You realise the Uncles will think it's the devil.'

Jojo looked at her startled. 'Why?'

'They're really big on Bible stories like Noah and his Ark, remember, and they'll think it's like the story of Adam and Eve where the serpent was the devil in disguise. It got Adam and Eve chucked out of Eden and caused all sorts of troubles for all the humans since.' She grinned suddenly. 'Maybe they'll go after it with their gold cross.'

'How come you know so much about the Bible?' asked Jojo, poking at something pinkish with his stick. 'Did you go to church a lot?'

'We had heaps of books at home with all sorts of stories in them. Adam and Eve and the Garden of Eden, Noah and his Ark, Zeus and Apollo and Icarus, and heaps of Greek and Roman gods, and Irish myths about the Morrigan and . . .' She glanced down. 'What's that?'

'A piece of something,' said Jojo, rolling the pink blob onto the plastic. 'It looks okay.'

'It's a starfish arm.'

Now that Jojo looked at it closely, he saw that it had raised bumps all along its length. 'Won't Griffy eat it?'

'Griffy would probably eat anything at the moment but let's put the arm back in the water. It might grow back.'

'It's the starfish's body that grows a new arm, not the other way around.'

'Starfish can do both. It depends on the type of starfish.'

'So what type of starfish is it?' challenged Jojo.

Lee shrugged. 'I don't know but let's give it a chance anyway. There's plenty of *dead* fish for Griffy to eat. She doesn't need a live one.' Jojo thought the starfish was pretty dead too but Lee scooped it up and sent it spinning out over the waves. 'Good luck, little starfish,' she said softly.

Jojo had noticed how quickly Lee went from happy to sad and dredged around for something to say. 'I saw Griffy had fresh water. Did you use that bucket to collect it?'

'Yep, and it took me ages to find one that didn't leak. Plenty on the beach but most are broken.'

'So you backtracked to the Stream to fill it,' murmured Jojo, relieved she hadn't risked the waterfall.

'Why would I do that when there's fresh water on the beach? It's hard enough climbing up to the cave with a bucket of water, I can tell you, without carting one through the thorn trees, down the shaft, and through the narrow hole. What I really need is a bottle.'

Lee meant *his* bottle but Jojo didn't want to risk it. 'There's plenty of bottles on the beach,' he said, despite knowing they were broken.

'*Bits* of bottles. You were super lucky to find yours.'

There was a short silence and Jojo moved uncomfortably. 'I'll fetch another bucket of water for Griffy from the waterfall,' he said. 'Then she'll have plenty.'

'Okay,' said Lee, but Jojo could tell she wasn't happy. He avoided her eyes as he tipped his fish into her bucket and tossed the plastic away. 'I'll see you back at the cave,' he said, and set off along the beach.

There were plenty of buckets on the beach because they tended to float but they also tended to break more easily especially if they'd been in the water for a while. The first few Jojo dug up looked perfect from the top, but were missing sides or bottoms, or had cracks or broken handles, and he'd passed the path up to the Town before he found a whole one.

The blood crabs were busy with their usual feasting but Jojo was more worried about facing the waterfall. The crabs scuttled off anyway and Jojo wondered whether the Finders had started to beat them away from any finds and the crabs were learning to get out people's way.

The waterfall's roar grew and Jojo soon regretted his offer to brave the fall's tumbling rocks to collect water. Noise never hurt anyone but he was reminded of Davy who screamed every time a plane flew over no matter how many times Jojo's mum and dad told him he was perfectly safe.

The waterfall's bellow battered him like a giant hammer and every instinct screamed to get as far from it as possible but unless he wanted to lend Lee his bottle, he needed to get as *close* to it as possible instead.

CHAPTER 20

Jojo heard the waterfall's roar long before he reached it but nothing prepared him for the storm of water as he rounded the last jut of cliff. Sound couldn't hurt him, he told himself. Spray fell in a hard rain and the waterfall-gouged pool at the bottom was full of rocks smashed from the cliffs.

There was no way Jojo could hold a bucket under the fall without it being dashed from his hands and he wondered how Lee had collected water. Knowing her, she'd probably stood directly underneath and dared any rocks to hit her.

It would be easier to fill the bucket from the side but as he crept closer keeping hard up against the cliff, the spray was so thick he had to bury his face in his elbow to breathe. He was getting his second dunking for the day.

The waterfall had the same wet-stone smell as the mountain's mossy gorges at home and there were the same slides of water down the stone. He pressed the bucket hard up against one but only captured a dribble. A bigger trickle above looked more promising and he clambered up the stones to discover that it came from a narrow cleft.

The trickle proved easy to collect and Jojo peered into the cleft while he waited for the bucket to fill. It was like a magical, sparkling world inside. Shafts of light from cracks that must open to the ground above, mixed with bright curtains of water that fell from the roof. Jojo was so entranced the bucket overflowed down his trousers and his head was still full of the wondrous sight as he made his way back along the beach.

By the time Jojo reached his cave, he understood exactly why Lee had complained about hauling a bucket of water up the cliff. His arms and shoulders ached and he'd spilled half of it along the way.

'I've got the water,' he panted, but Lee barely nodded, her attention all on Griffy who gulped down bits of broken fish as fast as Lee could deliver them. A *thank you* would be nice, thought Jojo grumpily, as he put the bucket beside her and settled on the cave floor. The sickle jabbed into his bruised side and he pulled it from his pocket, surprised again by how shiny it was.

'What's that?' intruded Lee's voice.

'A sickle, though it's lost its handle,' said Jojo as he stroked its cool metal.

'Did you find it on the beach just now?'

'No. In the Store.'

He heard her sharp intake of breath and glanced up to see her astonished face. 'You *stole* something from the Store?'

'I didn't *steal* it, I just took it,' he muttered.

Lee hooted with laughter. 'You're amazing, Jojo! You seem so . . . *keen* to obey the Uncles' rules and then you *steal* something right from under their noses.'

'I'm not *keen* to obey their rules,' said Jojo indignantly. 'It's just that they're in charge and they've made the Town and they provide the food and—'

'The *Aunts* provide the food,' corrected Lee. 'You haven't told anyone about the sickle, have you?' she asked anxiously. Jojo shook his head. 'And no one saw you take it?'

'No,' he said, and licked his lips. 'I didn't mean to take it. I just had it in my hand when Axel turned up. I was looking for something sharp to—'

'You're *sure* Axel didn't see you take it because he'll go straight to the Uncles.'

'I'm pretty sure he didn't see me,' said Jojo, but he was no longer sure of anything. 'He didn't mention it.'

'Oh, he wouldn't, would he? He'd just save it up to use against you.' She lifted Griffy back into her jacket nest and scratched the little creature under the chin. 'You'll know pretty soon because Markus will haul you in again.'

Jojo's stomach did its usual tightening trick. 'I have to see him anyway to tell him about the serpent.'

Lee gave Griffy a final pat and settled on the floor beside him. 'Let me see,' she said, and Jojo reluctantly handed it over.

Lee's hair hid her face as she weighed it in her hand and then held it to the light. 'It doesn't look like a sickle,' she said eventually. 'Sickles have a straight bit on one end that slots into a handle. Sticking a handle on this would almost make a circle. Not much use for harvesting *anything*.'

'Well, what do *you* think it is?'

'It looks more like a claw.'

Jojo swallowed as his head filled with visions of Big Talons. He wanted to say it looked nothing like a claw but it did and *if* it were a claw, Big Talons was just a baby compared to its owner. Jojo half shook his head. The whole thing seemed impossible but yesterday a giant serpent had seemed impossible too.

'I think you're right,' he said reluctantly. 'How do you know all these things?'

'From books, like I told you. We had a whole house full of books but when books wash up here, the Uncles burn them,' she added angrily.

'Well, they *are* pretty soggy,' said Jojo, and paused. 'Is that why you don't speak in the Town? Because the Uncles burn books?'

Lee shrugged. 'The Uncles only want to hear what they have to say so there's no point in talking.'

'Mary's not like that.'

'Maybe not but it's the Uncles who run the show and they think they know *everything*. Well, they don't, and there're plenty of better places to live than here!'

Lee had no way of knowing that but her eyes glistened and Jojo didn't argue. 'We had lots of books at home too,' he said instead.

'And did you read them?' she asked thickly.

'Some of them but I mainly read my comics. I had a whole stack.' *Now under the water with everything else.*

'Comics tell good stories too,' said Lee, as if it were her turn to cheer him up. 'And they have lots of stuff about loongs, and unicorns, and pegasuses, and phoenixes.'

'And Godzillas,' said Jojo, fearing the claw belonged to something similar.

'Godzilla wasn't a real mythic animal like Griffy is,' said Lee, glancing fondly at the creature. 'I read somewhere it was made up by a film company.'

Jojo still struggled with Lee's belief that myth was real, especially given *myth* also meant a *lie*, but lots of things that were true of Before didn't seem to be true now. And he suddenly realised it didn't really matter whether Lee thought Griffy was a griffin because Griffy made Lee happy like the bottle, plates, and the golden fern made him happy.

The knot in his stomach eased but then tightened again as he remembered he still had to talk to Markus.

CHAPTER 21

Cloud had swamped the sun by the time they started back, to return the world to its usual gloom. Jojo was relieved to see no sign of Big Talons but there was no sign of any other birds either and he worried that whatever scared them away still lurked in the trees. He was glad when they came out into the open, despite there being nothing to stop a flip-wind from rolling them off the cliff, but they reached the Town without winds of any kind and stopped as they usually did on the slope above.

Lee never wanted to go back to the Town and neither did Jojo today. It had looked almost cheerful that morning but was back to its usual dreary colours. The dismal sight wasn't helped by not even a single building being straight, not that it was the Uncles' fault. They had to fit the warped wood together like a giant jig-saw puzzle.

No sounds of sawing or hammering came from the Sanctuary's direction which meant the Uncles had returned to get ready for Last Meal which meant Jojo had no reason to delay his visit to Markus.

Lee was obviously thinking the same. 'What will you tell Markus about the serpent?' she asked.

'Just what happened,' said Jojo in surprise. Lee stared away towards the Mountains and he leaned on his stick to ease his bad foot. 'Don't you think I should?' he asked uneasily.

'It's a shame you told Raj about it,' she muttered, her gaze still on the Mountains.

'Why?'

'Because otherwise, only we two would know.'

'But it's dangerous.'

93

'Maybe, but it doesn't fit Markus's story about Noah and his Ark, does it? The story he uses to prove we're all supposed to be *here*, in this *very* spot.'

Jojo shifted his weight back to his bad foot and off again. 'I still have to tell him in case it kills someone,' he said woodenly.

'I know,' said Lee, and sighed. 'I just don't think Markus will believe you, that's all.'

Lee's words repeated in Jojo's head as he made his way to the Uncles' Dorm. His mum would say telling Markus about the serpent was the right thing to do but what if Lee were right? It was still the right thing to do even if Markus ignored Jojo's warning and then, if the serpent attacked someone else, it would be Markus's fault. The understanding didn't make Jojo feel any better and he was actually relieved when Markus's voice told him to enter and not the grumpy bushy-browed Uncle's. He expected the Dorm to be crowded but only a couple of Uncles sat at the table with Markus which meant the others were at the Washrooms or in their own little cubicles.

Markus shifted to the end away from the others and gestured him to the seat opposite. The presence of the other Uncles made the situation less scary but Jojo still clutched his stick to still his shaking hands.

Markus stared at Jojo without speaking as he had last time, but the silence went on so long Jojo wondered if he were supposed to talk first. He cleared his throat but then Markus spoke. 'I am glad you *chose* to present yourself here, Joseph, rather than having to be summoned again.'

Jojo's stomach knotted and he tightened his grip on his stick. Markus obviously knew about the fern, or sickle, *or both*, and Jojo racked his brains for *any* excuse to lessen the seriousness of his crimes.

'The last time we spoke, I believed you had acquired an understanding of the importance of *not* letting our community down but it seems I was mistaken,' continued Markus. 'Even more troublingly, your present behaviour has forced others to let our community down too. I do not call that fair, do you, Joseph?'

'No,' said Jojo, so sick with dread he had no idea what he'd just agreed with.

'I believe Axel explained to you he had a *second* Activity to complete today in *addition* to helping you complete your *single* Activity. Is that correct, Joseph?'

'Yes,' said Jojo, although the exchange with Axel had been a lot less clear.

'Yet you delayed Axel by *deliberately* lagging behind on the trip to the nut groves, then exacerbated the delay by taking a *swim* near the Marshes. I presume it was a swim, Joseph, despite you telling Axel you had fallen in.'

'I … I was pulled in by a giant serpent,' said Jojo hoarsely, his throat so tight he could scarcely breathe.

Markus's slate grey eyes considered Jojo unblinkingly. 'Tell me about this giant serpent, Joseph.'

'I … my bad foot was sore so I dipped it in the water to cool it off and then a giant serpent grabbed my ankles and pulled me in and then it let me go.' The story sounded ridiculous even to his own ears but Markus's expression remained unchanged.

'You told *Axel* you *fell* into the water and now you tell *me* a giant serpent *pulled* you into the water and then it let you go.'

'It's why I came to see you,' said Jojo hurriedly. 'I … I'm worried about the serpent. The Aunts go to the Marshes and it might attack them too.'

Markus leaned forwards and steepled fingers. 'You have told me a story, Joseph, so allow me to tell you one in return. Do you know the story of *The Boy Who Cried Wolf?*'

It sounded familiar but Jojo was too busy grappling with Markus's suggestion that the giant serpent was just a story and he shook his head.

'The story is about a young shepherd boy who tricked his community by pretending his flock was being attacked by a wolf. The first few times he called *wolf,* the community ran to help him, but after a while they realised he was lying, so that when the flock really was attacked by a wolf, no one came to help, and the flock was lost.

'I would like you to think about that story, Joseph, and that lies not only hurt the liar by making him a lesser person, but hurt the liar's community too.'

'I'm not a liar,' choked Jojo.

Markus leaned back again but his eyes never left Jojo's. 'You told Axel you *fell* into the Stream, and now you tell me that a giant serpent *pulled* you in. Both stories cannot be true, Joseph.'

Jojo's face fired and he stared down at the table. Markus was right but things were a lot more complicated than Markus made out and Jojo raised his head again. 'I told Axel—' he began, but Markus raised his hand.

'We have established you have lied, Joseph, so there is no need for further discussion on that point. What you need to do now is to reflect on your behaviour. I am sure your parents raised you to value honesty but if they did not, God has granted you a new place to start again and live a good and honest life, and that is exactly what I, *and* the community, expects you to do.'

CHAPTER 22

Jojo stumbled away to the Stream. He felt as if he were at school again and had done something so terrible he was to be expelled and *everybody* in the school knew about it. A grey dusk had fallen and the Stream's clear water looked as grey as the ocean's waves and the sea-rusted debris tossed on the beach.

Jojo stared at it numbly. The broken things on the beach had all belonged to people who'd once lived somewhere else, just as he'd once lived somewhere else, and the Town was the same, built from the things washed up from somewhere else. The cups, mugs, plates, bowls, knives, forks, spoons and cooking pots they used in the Kitchens, the blankets that kept him warm at night, even the clothes he wore, had all belonged to people from somewhere else, people that common sense told him were dead.

His thoughts went to his mum and dad and Davy. His parents *had* brought him up to be honest which was why he *had* reported the serpent, and while it was true he *had* told Axel one thing and Markus another, it didn't mean he'd lied. And even *if* he'd told Axel about the serpent, Axel wouldn't have believed him because even Markus hadn't believed him and that meant the serpent was free to attack whoever it wanted.

He limped up and down the bank as he tussled with his thoughts. The only good thing about the interview was that Markus didn't know about the fern or sickle *unless* he did! Maybe he intended to make a public announcement at First or Last Meal and shame Jojo in front of the entire Town! Jojo took a shuddering breath. And maybe he deserved to be shamed because if he really were an honest person, he would have told Markus about the fern and sickle.

Jojo resumed his pacing. The truth was that everything in the Town had once belonged to someone else and that made him no more of a thief than the Uncles who *stole* things off the beach although he couldn't imagine arguing the point with Markus.

Food smells drifted down from the Kitchens but he didn't want to join those who seemed happy here. Markus called the Town a *community* but they were just a bunch of people who'd washed up at the same place and even that would've been okay had his mum, dad and Davy washed up too.

Hunger eventually drove his reluctant feet up to the Kitchens but most people had already eaten and gone, most likely including Lee, who was nowhere to be seen. At least Mary was in charge of the fish and greens, and there was still bread left, although no tea. He filled his mug with water and chose a seat away from some Aunts. Their conversation was too soft for Jojo to hear and feeling even more of an outsider, he crammed fish into his mouth, eager to be gone, but before he'd finished, Mary's cup chinked down beside him.

It took her longer to lift her crooked legs over the bench seat and even longer for her hair to stop its dance. 'I thought you were going to miss Last Meal,' she rasped.

Jojo coughed as the fish lumped in his throat. 'I had to see Markus,' he said, and coughed again.

'No one *has* to see an Uncle,' said Mary mildly. 'But the Uncles *and* Aunts need to know if something's wrong so we can keep the Town safe.'

Jojo sensed Mary's invitation to share what he'd told Markus but he'd already told her he'd *fallen* in the Stream and he didn't want her to think him a liar too. 'Do you believe there are people in the Mountains?' he asked instead.

'There could be.'

'So why don't the Uncles go and find out?'

'Because the Uncles *and* Aunts want to make sure the Town's safe first.'

'I think they should find out.'

Mary's bony hand closed over his, her palm roughened by work. 'I understand why you want us to, Jojo, but you've only seen what's here now, not what was here when we first washed up.'

'So, what *was* here?' challenged Jojo.

'Mainly lots of dead people and lots of dead animals. Our boats ran out of food and water two days before we arrived, and fuel the day before, so it was the waves that brought us here, as they brought you and others like you. There was a freshwater stream full of clean fish and groves full of berries and nuts. There was flat land to build shelters and enough washed up wood and tools to do it.

'But there were also terrible storms in those early days. To save ourselves and those who followed, we had to build shelters and find food, and we had to do it fast. Every waking moment was spent building and gathering. There wasn't even enough time to give the dead a decent burial so maybe it was a good thing that so many were taken back by the waves.'

Mary paused, as if she gave Jojo time to understand that his family might have been amongst those buried or taken back but Jojo could only bear to think about the table's rough wood. 'To make all the things you see, Jojo, we had to be organised,' she continued. 'The Uncles did the heavy work of building because *they* could, and the Aunts did the food-finding, the looking after of smaller wash-ups, and of the old, and of the sick and injured, because *we* could. Everyone had to do something, not just for themselves, but for everyone else.'

Mary had started to sound like Markus, with his accusations of Jojo's selfish laziness, and Jojo kept his eyes on the table.

'Imagine if the Uncles had only built houses for *themselves*,' continued Mary, 'and the Aunts had only found food for *ourselves*. The young and old and injured would have died by now.' Jojo heard her take a gurgling slurp of water and when she spoke again, her tone was lighter. 'Things are not nearly as desperate these days. For one thing, the weather's improved, although who knows how long that will last. Even so, to make sure no one goes to bed hungry *and* that they all have beds to go to, lots of Activities still need to be done.

'We have enough people for these Activities, Jojo, but we wouldn't if they went off to see what's in the Mountains or explored up the coast, so you can understand why the Uncles *and* the Aunts need people to stay here.'

Mary's hand gave Jojo's a final squeeze but Jojo could think of nothing to say. He longed to discover whether his family were in the Mountains and while he resented the way Markus made him feel, he understood why Mary sided with Markus. She continued to slurp her water and Jojo glanced up. The other Aunts laughed, as if they enjoyed a private joke, and his stomach tightened. It was Aunts like them and Mary who were most at risk from the serpent because it was they who collected grasses at the Marshes and regularly went past on their way to the nut groves.

Jojo licked his lips. 'I didn't fall into the Stream this morning,' he said softly. 'I was pulled in by a giant serpent. I thought ... I thought I was going to die but it let me go. I ... I told Markus, but because I lied about falling in, he thinks I'm lying about the serpent too.' Mary was so intent on him even her hair had stilled. 'I'm not lying,' he said desperately. 'I'm worried the serpent will attack other people too.'

Jojo feared Mary would tell him off like Markus had but her knobby hand closed over his again. 'That must have been terrifying, Jojo. Do you have any idea why the serpent let you go?' He shook his head and Mary sighed. 'There are so many strange things in the world since the waters rose or maybe they were always there and we just didn't see them. Thank you for trusting me, Jojo. I will warn the Aunts to be careful.'

CHAPTER 23

Jojo replayed his conversation with Mary in his head as he lay in bed that night. She'd been a lot nicer than Markus and Jojo clutched his blanket as he recalled how Markus had made him feel horrible and Mary had made him feel good again. Jojo's mum would be pleased that Jojo had persevered to warn Mary about the serpent too.

He turned to face the wall, punched the grass stalks in his pillow flat, and wished some feather pillows would wash up. He'd had a nice new one at home that Davy had kept *borrowing*. The Finders talked amongst themselves and, as usual, made no attempt to keep their voices down which meant Jojo heard most of what they said despite being at the Dorm's far end.

They usually talked about all the wonderful things they did and all the useless things Flotsams did but tonight they talked about their plans for tomorrow because the Uncles had cancelled everyone's Activities. Jojo's heart quickened and he strained his ears. Apparently the Uncles had made some sort of announcement at the start of Last Meal that since the Sanctuary was complete, the community should visit it to enjoy *a quiet time of contemplation and thanks*.

The Finders' voices were anything but quiet because once their visits were done, they were off to the nut groves. Axel had discovered some caves and the Finders sounded pretty excited about exploring them. Jojo was pretty excited too. It meant the Finders would be far from the beach and *that* meant he could check the clear water near the peak for new treasures.

He woke to the unfamiliar drip-drip of rain on the roof and the strange sight of the Town's buildings gleaming with water as he picked his way through the mud to the Kitchens. The low cloud and rain made it a good day for *quiet contemplation and thanks* inside the Sanctuary but not for trekking to the nut groves and Jojo hoped that the Finders still planned to go.

Antonella presided over First Meal, her face expressionless as her hand moved mechanically between the dinted soup pot and the motley collection of bowls. Jojo thanked her politely for his orange bowl of green soup, despite the colour clash, collected bread, a mug of tea, and a soup spoon, and slid onto the bench beside Lee.

It was crowded in the Kitchens but she ate with her head down as if alone and was already halfway through her soup. Jojo doubled the number of scoops to his mouth to catch up, drained his tea, and crammed the bread into his pocket so he could follow her out.

She had stopped under the Kitchens' eaves and Jojo stopped beside her and contemplated the gurgling rush of water down the gutters. 'Best get the Sanctuary visit over with,' muttered Lee and Jojo nodded. They set off, trying to dodge the worst of the slop until they reached the sprawl of tussocky grasses beyond the Infirmary. Low cloud hid their surroundings and Jojo hoped they headed in the right direction because even the waves' usual crash had quietened.

'What did Markus say?' asked Lee softly, as they walked.

'I'll tell you later,' he whispered, unsure who might be hiding in the murk.

The Sanctuary's faint outline emerged from the grey and Lee's hands came to her hips. 'It's supposed to be a *Sanctuary* not a church!'

'We're looking at the back,' pointed out Jojo, surprised it faced the sea.

'It's the same both ways,' she retorted, and as they made their way along the side, Jojo saw she was right. The simple rectangular building had pointed windows and a church's steeply pitched roof. 'The only thing missing is the cross on the top,' she muttered, as they reached the door. 'Raj will be furious.'

'Why?'

'Because he's Hindu, that's why! And he's not the only one here who isn't Christian. This was supposed to be a place for *everyone*!' Lee wrenched the door open and Jojo gestured frantically for quiet but they were alone. Rows of wooden bench seats sat either side of a central passageway and there was a raised platform at the end set with a table. Lee snorted behind him as he limped towards the table, but his attention was on the gold cross fixed on the wall above it.

Lee had called it a gold-painted tree branch when the Uncles had hauled it from the Stream, and its central part had definitely snapped off something bigger, but the cross-pieces weren't branches at all. They were wiry strands of growth crushed together. Jojo stared at it in shock but then the Sanctuary's door creaked open behind him and there was a rush of cold, moist air.

He nodded jerkily to the cross, as if he paid it his respects, slid onto the nearest bench seat, and dropped his head as if overcome by the Sanctuary's atmosphere. Lee did the same. The voices told him some Finders had turned up but the door soon banged shut again and Jojo snatched a glance over his shoulder. They were alone and he stared up at the cross. It was definitely part of his fern and the breaks told him there was a third piece still lying about somewhere.

Lee slid from the seat and made her way out and Jojo limped after her. It was even dimmer outside now and the rain heavier. 'Well, there's a thing,' she said, and laughed, but laughing was the last thing Jojo felt like doing. 'Maybe you should build your *own* church,' she chuckled, as they set off across the grass.

'The Uncles ordered that *anything* strange found in the Stream be handed into them,' he whispered, having to blink hard to clear his eyes.

Lee's head swiveled. 'What? When was that?'

'At the First Meal we missed.'

'So, you're going to be a *good* boy and give Markus your fern?' Her fringe was plastered to her forehead and water dripped from her chin.

'No, I'm going to stay a lazy, selfish, lying boy.'

'Is that what he called you?' she demanded indignantly.

'Sort of, and I *did* tell Axel I *fell* in the Stream when the serpent *pulled* me in.'

'Axel doesn't count,' she tossed off. 'So the stupid Uncles don't believe the serpent exists,' she muttered, as she stomped along. 'I just hope the next time it's hungry it has *Markus* for dinner.'

'That's not very nice,' said Jojo, as they cut behind the Town and headed towards the thorn trees. 'At least Mary believed me and she's going to warn the Aunts.'

'Well, that's *something*,' said Lee, sleeving the rain from her face. 'This weather's so miserable, it feels like night already.'

'And the waves are quiet,' said Jojo uneasily. 'I wonder what they're doing.'

'Well, there's one way to find out,' said Lee, and marched off towards the cliffs.

CHAPTER 24

The cliffs were dangerous, even in good light, and Lee was quickly just an outline in the murk. Jojo hurried after her but his stick slipped on the wet grass and he almost fell. 'Don't go too close,' he yelled.

'I'm not stupid,' she yelled back.

'There're cracks,' he yelled again, in desperation, and thankfully she stopped. He came level, his foot throbbing. 'I *know* the cliffs are crumbly,' she said, before he could speak.

'I said *cracks*, like the cracks behind the waterfall.' Lee looked at him blankly. 'Didn't you see them when you got Griffy's water?'

'Why would I go *behind* the waterfall to collect water? I just stuck my bucket on a stick and got it from the side.' Which is what Jojo should have done, he realised in annoyance.

'So tell me about these cracks,' she said, and Jojo did. 'Hardly a surprise,' she muttered when he'd finished. '*Everything's* rotten here.'

'The Uncles can only use what washes up and most of it's been in the water for a while,' said Jojo defensively.

'The sheep hadn't been,' said Lee, as they picked their way forward.

'What sheep?'

'The ones on the beach yesterday.'

'They were dead,' said Jojo.

Lee sighed. 'I *know* they were dead but not *rotten*, which means they can't have been in the water that long, which means they must have come from somewhere close.'

'And got washed away in the big waves,' said Jojo slowly. 'They might've been wild ones,' he suggested. 'It doesn't mean people had them.'

'No, but wherever they came from had grass, and water, and shelter or they'd have died ages ago. It means they came from somewhere *better* than here.'

But not necessarily better for *people*, thought Jojo, but said nothing. He knew why Lee yearned for *somewhere better* because he did too. 'Mary said the Uncles don't want people wandering off looking for other places because they need everyone here to keep the Town running.'

'They need everyone here to boss about *and* to build churches,' retorted Lee.

'You're probably right,' said Jojo, not wanting to argue. They stopped well short of the cliffs' edge but all they saw was a strip of rubbish-strewn ocean before a band of ragged cloud closed off the horizon. 'I've never seen it so calm,' he said uneasily.

'Neither have I,' said Lee.

Jojo hated how the waves pounded the beach to smash everything to pieces but the quiet seemed worse, as if the waves waited to pounce. 'Everything's so strange today,' he said. 'The rain, the low cloud, how dark it is. I want to see what's washed up but I'm not sure I want to go on the beach.'

'It reminds me of just before everything changed,' muttered Lee.

'Yes,' said Jojo, and wondered if it was why he felt so bleak. 'Let's get out of this rain at least. Griffy's waiting for you.' He turned but then Lee gasped, and he swung back. Her horrified gaze was on the horizon and while no gigantic waves hurtled towards, what he saw was just as terrifying.

Huge dark arms rose from the ocean like the grasping tentacles of a monstrous squid. 'Waterspouts,' he said wildly. 'Twisters that come down from the clouds and pull up water in narrow columns.'

'They're coming *out* of the sea,' she all but shrieked.

'It's hard to tell,' he said desperately, which was true given the rain and low cloud. He'd seen waterspouts on TV dance across lakes or oceans but these looped over to shoot up again. 'Or it could be a giant squid,' he suggested, recalling the tentacle on the beach.

'It's the Kraken,' said Lee hoarsely.

'You mean like an immense octopus?'

'No, I mean like *the* Kraken!'

Jojo watched the arms rise and fall in horrified silence. The Kraken of his comics had the strength and cunning of a very nasty god and the possibility that one lurked offshore was terrifying. The arms disappeared and Jojo feared it now swam landwards to pluck them from the cliffs.

'Let's get to the cave,' he said hurriedly and Lee nodded. The rain continued and he was glad to reach the thorn trees. They were still quiet and he wondered whether the birds knew about the Kraken and had gone somewhere safer. Jojo wished *he* could go somewhere safer too, preferably to Lee's lovely new land.

Jojo never entered his cave without worrying Finders had stumbled on it, smashed his bottle and plates, and reported the sickle and fern to the Uncles, but the cave was as he'd left it, right down to the stink of fish.

Lee scooped up Griffy as if she were a kitten and the dim light showed how much the creature had grown, which was no surprise given that all the fish were gone again. 'She eats an awful lot of fish,' he said.

'That's because she's a growing Griffy,' crooned Lee.

The bumps on Griffy's body were certainly bigger and the one on her rump now resembled a tail. Overall, she looked more lizard-like, despite her side-bumps, which were probably caused by the sea's poisons, but her head still looked like a bird's.

'You've done well to keep her alive,' he said, thinking of the little corpses he'd buried as Davy had sobbed beside him.

'Griffy's strong. She kept herself alive before I found her, like we had to.'

Jojo was glad the cave's dimness hid his face. His time alone in the ocean was part of a bigger pot of sadness he struggled to keep a lid on. 'We need to get her more fish *and* some more water,' he managed to say.

Lee nodded. 'Best get it over with before the waves turn nasty again.'

The rain made it a slow climb down the slippery cliffs, as did carrying their buckets, but Jojo was even slower because he kept searching the sea for giant tentacles. At least there was plenty of sand on the beach, which meant the tide was out, although Jojo worried it might return in a single violent sweep.

Lee already collected fish by the time he reached the sand and he volunteered to fetch water instead. He knew how to do it this time but as he headed off towards the waterfall, a mass of blood crabs blocked his way. Not only didn't they move, their black-stalked eyes watched him in a way that made his hair stand on end. He had to clamber over the rocks hard against the cliffs to get past them and they didn't feed again until he was well clear.

They were definitely upset about something. Maybe it was the unusually calm sea, or the arrival of the rain, or the appearance of a mythic monster called the Kraken. He gave each new crowd of crabs a wide berth and kept a careful eye on the waves until he reached the stepping-stones that led to the peak.

A shard of something shone in the foam and he slipped it into his pocket but he was mainly interested in any treasures at the peak. Leaving his bucket on the sand, he clambered onto the first of the stepping-stone rocks, across to the second, and onto the third then glanced back at the shore and froze. There were Finders on the beach!

CHAPTER 25

Jojo racked his brains for reasons he was on a rock, in the sea, in the rain. Pretending he played a childish game of explorer might work given Finders thought Flotsams were childish anyway, but he dreaded them joining in, discovering the peak's clear patch of water, and claiming anything that was there.

He turned back towards shore, waving his arms theatrically as he pretended to almost slip from a rock, and made sure he *did* slip from the last rock. The water was only knee deep but he made a show of floundering, knowing he looked stupid, and so hopefully wasn't worth bothering about.

For once Raj led the group and he was a fair way in front. 'Probably not a good idea to be in the sea on a day like this,' he said. 'In fact, probably not a good idea to be on the beach at all.'

'I like to see what's washed up,' said Jojo.

'So do the Uncles,' said Raj sourly.

'I didn't think there were any Activities today,' said Jojo as he reclaimed his bucket.

'There weren't until the rain showed up leaks in the Sanctuary roof that must be plugged *immediately*. We can't have the Uncles' god getting soggy now, can we?' He wiped the water from his eyes and squinted back at the distant forms of the other Finders. 'They're heading back. They reckon they've got enough bitumen for the job.'

'I didn't know they used bitumen on the roofs,' said Jojo, thinking of the sticky black lumps that littered the beach.

'They don't usually bother but apparently the Sanctuary's special.' Raj was angry about the *Sanctuary* as Lee had predicted. 'Did you tell Markus about the serpent?' Raj asked unexpectedly.

'Yes, but he didn't believe me because I told Axel I *fell* in the Stream, not that the serpent *pulled* me in, and Markus told me to go away and think about lying.'

Raj's hands came to his hips. 'Well, that's not going to keep people safe, is it?'

'I told Mary about the serpent and she said she'd tell the Aunts,' offered Jojo.

'That's something at least,' said Raj, scowling at the sea.

Jojo followed his gaze, relieved to see the waves empty of tentacles. 'Have you heard of a creature called the Kraken?' he asked hesitantly.

'Anyone who's read comics knows about the Kraken.'

'Do … do you think it really exists?' Jojo held his breath, not wanting Raj to think him stupid.

'Who knows?' said Raj, his dark eyes still on the sea. 'There're lots of old stories about giant octopuses or squid pulling sailing ships down into the deep, but there're also stories about dragons,' he said, and shrugged. 'It's understandable given the number of little wooden sailing ships that disappeared over the horizon and never came back. We know there are giant squid in the oceans because they wash up now and then. People probably saw them in the old days too and decided they were monsters.' He glanced back at Jojo. 'Why do you ask?'

'We saw something strange from the cliffs.'

'*We*?'

'Me and Lee,' said Jojo reluctantly, sorry he'd not pretended to be alone. Raj now peered in the cave's direction and Jojo crossed his fingers Lee wasn't halfway up the cliff.

'So, what *did* you see, Jojo? Not another enormous serpent?'

Raj's voice was lightly teasing and Jojo's face warmed. 'It looked like the legs of a giant octopus.'

'Close to shore?'

'Out near the horizon,' said Jojo sensed Raj relax.

'It was likely just cloud,' said Raj, making Jojo feel better. 'Or maybe bursts of rain, or maybe a giant squid, shaken from the deep by whatever washed away Before. Or maybe it *was* the Kraken. Hard to see *anything* in this weather,' he said matter-of-factly. 'So probably not worth telling the Uncles.'

'No,' agreed Jojo.

'But you can tell me what you see and maybe we can decide together what the Uncles need to know. After all, it's *their* job to keep us safe.' Raj's voice was angry again, but then he smiled. 'Be careful on the beach, Jojo. Nothing works like it used to and the sea's even weirder at the moment. We don't want it grabbing you back.'

Raj headed back up the beach and Jojo followed more slowly, not speeding up again until Raj disappeared up the path to the Town. Jojo didn't need Raj's warning to keep an eye on the sea but Raj's concern reassured Jojo he wasn't the terrible person that Markus claimed.

Trash rose and fell with deceptive gentleness on the waves but the waterfall's din more than made up for the sea's quiet. It roared over the cliff as it had last time, its fume adding to the rain, and it was a moment before he realised he wasn't alone.

Shapes perched on the stones around the pool and for a horrible moment he thought they were Finders but then he saw their long, curved beaks and great leathery wings. The birds' heads turned towards him as one and they shuffled as if about to take off, then settled again, and brought their attention back to the pool.

Jojo wondered whether they roosted here during the day, despite them not being here last time, or whether they were attracted by fish caught in the pool, but there were heaps of dead things on the beach and nothing explained why the birds just sat there.

Jojo found a long piece of driftwood and edged forwards, heart in mouth. He hoped Lee was right that the birds only swooped her because they wanted the dead sheep nearby. The birds shuffled again, making Jojo's heart rattle, but stayed put and he slid the bucket onto the driftwood and held it under the fall. There was a satisfying thrum as the bucket filled and Jojo braced as it grew heavier and glanced back at the pool. Rain sent ripples bulls-eyeing over its surface and he half expected to see the dark shadows of fish but something else glimmered in the depths instead.

His friend Chen kept big goldfish in an ornamental pond with scales that shone in the sunlight but there was no sunlight here and Jojo's breath caught. The Uncles' orders to hand over *anything* strange were clear in his head, as was his memory of the Sanctuary's gold cross, but what sent shivers down his back was knowing that the birds weren't here to roost, but to guard.

CHAPTER 26

Jojo's bucket was only half full but it was all he could manage if he were to get it *and* the new piece of fern back to his cave. He didn't know whether the birds would attack and what he'd do if they did, but there was no way he was leaving the fern behind.

The nearest birds shuffled away as he stepped into the pool's chill water but their reddish eyes glared at him Jojo wondered if it were a trap. The pool was full of rocks and he half expected the waterfall to rain more down on his head or the birds to mob him but nothing happened and he gently lifted the fern from the water and slid it dripping under his shirt.

He hoped the birds would lose interest once it was out of sight, like dogs sometimes did with toys, but their angry eyes followed Jojo's every move. He reclaimed his bucket and backed away but the birds turned as one and taking the fern suddenly seemed horrifyingly stupid. He had no idea whether this fern gave out sparks and hoped the birds didn't give him a reason to find out.

As soon as he reached the beach, a great *whump-whump-whump* erupted behind him and the birds were soon so close, their wingbeats lifted his hair. He was tempted to wave the fern but feared them seeing it might make things a hundred times worse. It might not work in the rain either.

He hurried along the sand as fast as he could, his stomach knotted with fear and telling himself that if the birds planned to attack, they would have done so by now. The blood crabs scuttled away at his approach as if they were terrified of the birds too.

He reached the spot below the cave and started to climb but the birds came at him from all directions as if they intended to wrench him off the cliff and drop him. His bad foot was on fire, the rain made the stone slippery, and the cavern opening seemed to get no closer but then it was suddenly there and he hurled himself inside. The birds shrieked in frustration and Jojo feared they'd force their way in after him but their *whumps* slowly receded into the distance.

'What on earth was that?' demanded Lee, appearing in the cave's doorway.

'Those big . . . leather-winged . . . birds,' gasped Jojo as he staggered across the cavern. 'They chased me . . . all along . . . the beach.'

'Why on earth would they do that?'

'Because I've found some more fern,' he panted, and slid it from his shirt. It glowed so beautifully in the cave's dimness that every moment of terror suddenly seemed worth it.

'I don't think it's a fern,' said Lee slowly.

'It *is*,' snapped Jojo. He picked up the first part and lined it up on the floor with the second part leaving a gap where the Uncle's piece fitted. But now he had time to looked at the new piece properly, he saw that its fronds formed a wide, rounded tip.

'I think it's a feather,' said Lee over his shoulder.

Jojo shrugged. 'Fern, feather, what difference does it make?'

'Quite a lot,' said Lee, picking up the bucket and filling Griffy's bowl. 'A fern grows in the ground and stays in one place while a feather belongs to something that flies about.'

'*Flew* about,' corrected Jojo. He closed the gap between the two pieces but it was all out of proportion. He needed the Uncles' piece for it to be whole.

Thuds sounded as Lee mashed the fish, followed by the little creature's wet gulps. These went on for some time until Lee finally washed her hands in the bucket and settled beside him. 'It's a pretty big feather even with a bit missing,' she said thoughtfully. 'Its owner must be enormous.'

'*Was* enormous.'

'It might still be around,' persisted Lee. 'The pterodactyls that chased you are certainly still around.'

'They're not pterodactyls,' said Jojo stubbornly.

'What are they then? Big birds with long beaks, humps on their heads, and enormous bat wings? Don't look like ravens to me.'

Lee was probably right but it was bad enough being in a grey miserable place without that grey miserable place having a giant serpent, an enormous Kraken, *and* a flock of pterodactyls.

Lee sighed. 'Whatever owns that feather has to be beautiful and it's so ugly here,' she said. 'Just imagine how it would shine as it flew across the sky. I bet its song would be nothing like the pterodactyls' screeches.'

Jojo didn't want to imagine *anything* because it led him to imagine what had happened to his mum and dad and Davy. 'Its song might be even worse,' he muttered. 'Have you ever heard a peacock sing?'

'It would be good to find the feather's owner,' persisted Lee. 'Where did you get this bit?'

'In the pool at the bottom of the waterfall.'

'And you found the other bit in the Stream beyond the Marshes, and the Uncles found *their* bit in the Stream near the Town. They've obviously washed down from the Mountains which is all the more reason to go see what's there.'

Jojo said nothing and the only sound the sluice of rain down the cliff-face. 'This is the first time it's rained since I've been here,' said Lee.

'Me too,' said Jojo. 'But Raj said they had terrible storms when he first arrived.'

'How long ago was that?'

Jojo shrugged. 'I don't know. I don't even know for sure how long I've been here.'

'Well, it's longer than thirty-five days, because that's how long *I've* been here.'

'You're keeping track?' asked Jojo in surprise.

'Of course. Father said …' Lee dropped her head so her fringe hid her face.

'It's a good idea to keep track,' said Jojo quickly. 'I wish I had but I didn't think I'd be here this long. I thought a big boat would turn up and take us all back to where we came from.' *And to the way everything was Before*. He realised now how childish the idea had been. The ocean delivered dead and broken things, not rescue boats.

'I thought that at first too,' said Lee thickly, 'but now I think that if there *is* somewhere else, it's in the Mountains. After all, that's where the smoke comes from.'

'You're still planning to leave?'

'Of course, and I want you to come with me.'

CHAPTER 27

Lee looked at him expectantly but Jojo's thoughts were as tangled as the Store's rope pile. He recalled Raj's words about not wanting to be in the Town not being the same as wanting to leave it, of how safe the Town felt, of how lonely Jojo had been in the ocean, *and* how hungry and thirsty, and he thought of his mum and dad and Davy, and of the smoke in the Mountains.

Lee waited and Jojo cleared his throat. 'I don't know *what* I want,' he admitted. 'The Uncles haven't been here *that* long. The Town might end up being a good place to live.'

'Not with *them* in charge. They want things to stay the same because it's *God's will*. They don't seem worried that it was *God's will* everything got swept away.'

'No one knows why that happened,' said Jojo uncomfortably.

Lee snorted. 'I bet the scientists do, but there's none here and probably just as well. Imagine Markus saying we're all like Noah and his Ark, chosen by God to wash up in this *fabulous* place, and the scientists saying the earth tilted here and sunk there, and the tides ran this way, and the waves that way, which meant things washed up on *this* beach or over there on *that* beach.'

'Is your dad a scientist?' asked Jojo curiously.

'You don't have to be a scientist to read books, Jojo, or to think about things. Nothing the Uncles say about Noah's Ark makes sense.'

'But neither do the pterodactyls *if* that's what they are, or the giant serpent, or the Kraken, although the giant serpent might be just a *really* big snake and the Kraken might be just a really big squid,' he added.

'And that feather might be from just a *really* big raven that just happens to have gold feathers that just happen to make sparks,' said Lee sarcastically.

Jojo sighed. It was hard to believe *anything* he'd seen lately was real. 'I found something on the beach too,' he said, to change the subject, and retrieved the fragment from his pocket. It seemed even smaller now and he wondered why he'd bothered picking it up.

'I think it's another bit of plate,' said Lee, peering at it. 'Let's see if it fits the pieces you have.' She went to where he stored his treasures but Jojo's foot was too sore to move. 'Well, that's weird,' she said, and Jojo reluctantly heaved himself up and hobbled over. It was even gloomier in the corner and he strained to see. 'What's weird?'

'You had one whole plate and a second, smashed up plate, right?'

'Yes,' said Jojo impatiently.

'Well, now you've got two whole plates.'

Jojo blinked. 'But—'

'The pieces have grown themselves back together,' she said excitedly.

'But that's impossible!'

Lee grinned. 'Tell that to a starfish arm that grows back its body.'

'It's not a starfish,' retorted Jojo.

'No,' agreed Lee. 'It's something else.' She laid the fragment on top of the plates. 'It'll be interesting to see if this new bit performs the same trick.'

'Where's the bottle?' asked Jojo suddenly. 'And the sickle?'

Lee lifted the plates but there was nothing underneath and she stared about. 'They must be here somewhere.'

The cave was small and didn't take long to search. 'Try under Griffy,' said Jojo, as a last resort.

'They won't be there,' said Lee, but she lifted Griffy in her jacket-nest anyway to reveal the empty stone beneath.

A horrible sick feeling had settled in Jojo's stomach. 'You didn't borrow the bottle to get Griffy water, did you?' he asked. *And broke it*. 'It doesn't matter if you did, I just need—'

'Of course not! You made it pretty clear you didn't want to share your precious bottle. And I didn't steal the sickle either if that's the next thing you're going to accuse me of!'

'I'm not accusing—'

'Yes you are! The bottle's gone so I must have taken it *and* the sickle!'

'I just asked—'

'You accused!'

'Maybe someone else's been here,' said Jojo desperately.

'Yep, sure. Taken your stupid bottle and broken sickle and left your golden fern behind. Your first theory that I'm a thief makes much more sense!'

'I didn't mean that,' said Jojo miserably. 'I just don't understand where they've gone.'

'Maybe Griffy stole them,' said Lee. 'I'm surprised you didn't think of that!'

'I'm sorry,' said Jojo thickly, wanting to fix things.

'So am I,' said Lee, still angry. 'Sorry I mistook you for a friend.'

She stomped out of the cave and Jojo heard scraping as she slid down the stone wall into the cavern. He should go back to the Town too because if somebody *had* been there, they might come back. It would be safer in the Town *unless* that somebody had already handed the sickle to the Uncles.

But Lee was right. It made no sense to leave the fern because it was the fern the Uncles really wanted. Jojo shivered. The cave had been his special place where he could escape those who thought him useless, or a liar, or lazy, and where he could hold the bottle that shone in a way nothing in the Town ever did. And he'd come to enjoy Lee being there too, who said things he barely even dared to think, and who didn't see him as useless, or a liar, or lazy.

But now she was gone along with his bottle and sickle *and* the cave's sense of safety. He sighed and glanced at Griffy. The little creature was certainly growing but into what? And more worryingly, what were his plates growing into?

He peered down at the finger-sized fragment, glad it looked the same, then picked up the newly mended plate and ran his fingers over its slippery surface. There weren't even any ridges or joins to tell where the breaks had been and he flipped it over and gasped. For a long moment he simply stared at it and then he took it to the cavern's entrance where the light was better. He had no idea how it'd happened or why, but the bottle and sickle had embedded themselves in the back of the plate.

CHAPTER 28

Jojo knew it was late when he climbed out of the shaft into the thorn trees but the gloom made it hard to tell just how late. The rain-soaked grass smelled faintly of the herb patch at home but the ground was so sodden water oozed out under his feet. He peered up at the dripping branches as he walked, relieved to see no sign of Big Talons, but there were no sign of other birds either and the trees' silence, along with the ocean's quiet, set his teeth on edge.

He found a new stick to help him along but the ground was slippery and it took an age to reach the Town. It looked even wetter than the forest. He picked his way down the street, the mud piles to each side telling him that the gutters had been deepened. He glumly wondered whether his absence had strengthened the impression he was lazy but even had he been here, the Uncles' strict work rules might have excluded him anyway.

Smoke from the Kitchens' chimney told him Last Meal was still in progress and he increased his pace to the Washrooms to clean up and find some dry clothes, then dodged the rain and puddles back. The smell of roast fish and baked bread drifted from the door along with the rumble of voices and Jojo scraped the mud from his sandals and went in.

It seemed everyone in the Town was there and already seated with only a few Aunts ahead of him in the food queue. Jojo collected his bowl of fish and bread, filled his mug, and looked for somewhere to sit. Uncles tended to sit with Uncles, Finders with Finders, and Flotsams with Flotsams, but the Aunts sat wherever they could because

125

they arrived later after cooking, or serving, or looking after the smaller children.

He spied the top of Lee's head bent over her food but she was wedged between Aunts on an already crowded bench. There was a space next to the bushy-browed Uncle but Jojo guessed it was because nobody else wanted to sit there either.

'Sit here,' rasped a voice and he glanced around to see Mary pat a narrow spot on the end of a crowded bench beside her. Everyone shuffled along and he mumbled his thanks, put his head down, and began to eat.

'Well, Jojo, what have you been up to today? Seen anything unusual?'

Mary was smiling but Jojo concentrated on tearing his bread in half. 'I've been to the Sanctuary,' he said.

'And what did you think of it?'

Jojo took a bite of bread and chewed slowly, as if he only considered the Sanctuary's good and bad points, but he actually searched for something useful to say. Time stretched and he glanced sideways, hoping Mary had given up, but even her hair tendrilled towards him.

'I don't understand why the Uncles built it so close to the sea,' he said, which was true, but he mainly didn't understand why they'd built a *church* and then pretended it was for everybody.

'The Uncles want it to work a bit like a lighthouse,' said Mary.

Jojo blinked. 'But it's got no light.'

'Well, that's true,' said Mary mildly. 'Lighthouses shine lights to warn ships not to run into reefs or rocks, but in this case, the Uncles want to warn the sea not to run into *us*.'

Jojo stared at her in confusion. Nothing stopped waves smashing onto beaches or cliffs, or the tides rolling in. 'They're telling the sea this is *our* place and for the sea to leave it alone,' explained Mary. Jojo nodded. It fitted the Uncles' belief God had given them the land.

Mary slurped her tea and wiped her mouth with a gnarly hand. 'The Sanctuary's site might seem strange to you Jojo, but remember that everyone here washed up.' She shrugged. 'Oh, some of us got here in boats, and others on whatever they lashed together, and some like you because they were brave enough to keep on swimming.' She smiled and her tea-wet hand briefly touched his. 'But however we arrived, it's natural to try and make sense of everything that's happened.'

She glanced to where the Uncles sat and lowered her voice. 'Some of the Uncles like to think *their* God had a hand in bringing them here and others that *their* God did. We're a fair old mix, Jojo, so the Uncles built a *Sanctuary* everyone could use, or those who worry about gods can use,' she added.

She smiled again and tucked into her bread but Jojo's head was too full of questions to eat. Why did the Uncles with *other* gods put up with a church and given that Mary was smart, why did *she* put up with the Uncles running everything, but he didn't know how to ask either question.

Mary finished her meal and Jojo stood up to let her pass. It took her a long time to shuffle her bent legs off the bench and clutching her bowl, fork, and mug in her knobby hands didn't help. At least he only had a broken foot to put up with. 'I can wash those for you,' he said quickly.

'Well, thank you, Jojo. That would be nice.'

Jojo watched her hobble away and by the time he thought to search out Lee again, her space on the bench was empty too. He would see her tomorrow anyway, he comforted himself, as he rinsed his and Mary's bowls, forks and mugs and set them back on the rack.

Antonella stood sentry on the door as she allocated the day's Activities. The Finders ahead were to work on the Town's roofs which told Jojo the Sanctuary's roof was not the only one that leaked.

'You'll be taking on a Finder's responsibilities,' Antonella told him, in a tone that suggested she doubted he was up to it. 'You'll collect bitumen off the beach and deliver it to the cliff path where others will bring it to the Town.'

Jojo nodded, pleased with the Activity. Being on the beach meant being able to search for bottles and pieces of plate, and he'd be nice and close to his cave when he'd finished.

Jojo was right about the Town's roofs leaking. There were puddles in the Boys' Dorm and the beds had been pushed out of their neat lines to avoid the drips. He had to weave between other beds to reach his which was still wedged in the corner, but with another bed pushed hard up against it. Jojo guessed it belonged to a younger Flotsam's, but it turned out to be Raj's.

He appeared and threw himself on his bed while Jojo was busy toweling off his feet. There were no pajamas so everyone slept in their clothes *after* they'd cleaned their feet but Raj didn't even bother to do that and Jojo could see how angry he was.

'Looks like Markus and *his* friends were wrong,' he muttered. 'Some Uncles wanted to use bitumen on the roofs in the first place but Markus and *his* friends said it wasn't necessary. They probably thought *their* god would keep them dry.' Raj snorted. 'I've spent the whole day fixing the Sanctuary roof while the Dorms continue to leak like sieves. The Aunts' Dorm is worse than here and they've got children with them!'

'But … didn't you say there were terrible storms when you first arrived?' said Jojo in confusion.

Raj nodded. 'You'd have thought Markus would take the hint but he said the storms were just a left over from when the seas rose, and the weather *has* been fine since, but it isn't *now*. We don't even know which season we're in or even *if* there are seasons anymore.' There was a long pause. 'Everything's so strange now there's no way of telling *what's* coming.'

CHAPTER 29

Jojo could tell from Raj's breathing when he finally slept and the Finders were quiet too, probably exhausted from their day's work, but Jojo couldn't sleep at all. He heard the hiss of the waves, the gurgle of the water down the gutters, the pit-pit of rain on the roof, and the plop of it on the Dorm floor. He'd thought the Town was safe but now nothing felt safe. Lee still talked about going to the Mountains and had wanted him to go too, although she might have changed her mind since their argument.

Jojo rolled over on his lumpy mattress to face the wall. His mum had talked to him about the importance of sharing, usually after Davy had taken something and lost or broken it, and Jojo *had* tried. But his bottle had been special because there was nothing here clean and whole, and now it was gone, and perhaps Lee's friendship along with it. He wanted to tell Lee what he'd discovered and hear her ideas about what it meant because Lee had ideas about everything, but mostly he wanted to say sorry to her again.

The rain had dwindled to a mist by morning but cloud still covered everything in a grey murk. The street had grown even sloppier and Jojo picked his way to the Kitchens and added his sandals to the muddy pile outside. Antonella dolled out the food with her usual grim efficiency, and Jojo settled at a table that gave him a good view of the door. He ate slowly, but there was no sign of Lee by the time he'd finished, and he rinsed his bowl, spoon and mug and reclaimed his sandals. He wondered if she'd eaten earlier or had already gone off to the Mountains. It was unlikely she'd left, he reassured himself, because Griffy was still too small.

The beach looked the same as yesterday, which either meant the tide had come in and was going out again, or was coming in, or had stopped working altogether. Jojo knew how the tides worked because his dad had explained how the moon pulled at the oceans and he'd also explained why it was best just to look in rockpools and to not disturb the creatures who, like Jojo and Davy, were simply trying to live their lives. But what Jojo mostly thought about was what Raj had said about *everything* being strange.

Flotsams were already on the beach and Jojo guessed the one in the distance was Lee. He knew Greg and Aram, though they hadn't spoken much, and Margy was there too, and another girl whose name he didn't know. It seemed they'd all been temporarily promoted to Finders and the Finders to Uncles.

Jojo dug up a couple of buckets to collect the bitumen but they turned out to be broken and in the end he tore up a sheet of plastic instead. The other Flotsams collected near the Town because there were plenty of sand-covered lumps of bitumen there but Jojo set off towards the figure he hoped was Lee.

There was no sign of the big, leather-winged birds but they might hover just above the clouds waiting to avenge the theft of their golden treasure. The sea's quiet added to Jojo's tension. He'd grown used to its pound, to the heave and fall of its cargo of trash, to the sudden changes in its reach, and its present calm felt like a trap ready to spring.

It *was* Lee in the distance but she ignored him, even when he stopped right in front of her. She carried a blue bucket already half full. 'You've done well to find a bucket

131

that wasn't broken,' he said, but the only sound remained the thump of the bitumen lumps she dropped in. Jojo licked his lips. 'I found out what happened to my bottle and sickle.'

'*I* took them, remember,' she said, not pausing in her collecting.

'I've already said sorry for thinking that,' said Jojo, and took a deep breath. 'I found out what happened to the bottle and sickle but I've no idea *how* it happened.'

Lee actually looked at him now. 'What do you mean?'

'You know the broken plate that joined itself together?' Lee nodded. 'The sickle and bottle are stuck in its back.'

'You mean like glued on?'

'No, I mean like melted *in*.'

'Well, that *is* interesting,' said Lee thoughtfully. 'The sickle looks like a claw but I don't know what a loong would want with a bottle.'

'A *loong*?'

'A dragon,' said Lee impatiently. '*If* the plates are dragon scales then the dragon's rebuilding itself like a starfish. It obviously needs a claw but why a bottle?' The whole starfish-dragon idea was so bizarre Jojo half expected Lee to grin and boast she'd tricked him as payback but she looked perfectly serious. 'I spent last night thinking about why a plate would mend itself,' she said, as if that explained everything.

'But dragons are mythical,' spluttered Jojo.

'So what? Pterodactyls went extinct millions of years ago and no bird has golden feathers like the bits you and the uncles have found, although …' She paused, brows kinked.

'Although what?' asked Jojo, already dreading her next wild claim.

'Think about it, Jojo. What bird's got gold feathers that give off sparks?' Jojo stared at her blankly, and Lee grunted. 'What *mythical* bird has something to do with fire?'

'You're the one who knows about myths,' said Jojo.

'And you're the one who reads comics and comics are *full* of myths,' she shot back.

'A phoenix,' said Jojo reluctantly.

'Exactly!' Lee grinned. 'This place is a whole lot more interesting than I thought.'

Lee might want things to be more *interesting* but all Jojo wanted was his old life back with its boring predictability of school, chores, and looking after Davy. Even the Town with its two meals of the same food every day and its repetitive Activities was preferable to prehistoric and mythic creatures springing back to life.

'Let's finish our Activity,' he said. 'Then we can get back to Griffy.'

'Yep,' said Lee, 'and see what your new piece of plate is doing.'

Jojo nodded, although finding out the piece was growing into a dragon was the last thing he wanted.

CHAPTER 30

Jojo guessed it was well past Noon before a younger Flotsam arrived to tell them the Uncles had enough bitumen. The other Flotsams wasted no time in following the messenger up the path, probably keen to get out of the rain, but Jojo and Lee headed in the opposite direction. The tide seemed the same and Jojo stared at the cloud-swathed horizon as he walked, fearful that a giant wave would appear or enormous tentacles, or both.

Lee followed his gaze. 'No Kraken today.'

'Or giant squid.'

Lee shot him an irritated look. 'You really are stubborn, aren't you? How do you explain the plate joining itself back together and taking the sickle *and* bottle along for the ride? Or maybe you think that Axel sneaked in to fix the plate he smashed. After all, I'm sure he feels *really* sorry for being such a bully.'

Jojo didn't want another argument but nor did he want to believe that the plates were making themselves into anything, let alone a dragon, or that the monstrous tentacles belonged to the Kraken, or that the poisoned little creature in the cave was a griffin. Then there was the giant serpent. It could just be a really big snake but there was no way to explain the fiery bits of fern.

'I can't explain the plate *or* the fern or why *I* ended up here or why *you* ended up here or why *everyone* ended up here. You've got lots of good ideas,' he challenged. 'Why don't *you* explain why the oceans washed everything away.'

'We don't know that they did.'

Jojo blinked. 'But—'

'We only know that they washed *us* away.'

'I … I didn't think of that,' admitted Jojo.

'Neither did I until last night,' she said thickly.

Lee seemed to have done a lot of thinking last night because maybe like him, she hadn't been able to sleep. She'd dropped her head and he gave her hand a quick squeeze. 'This weather's miserable,' he said, as if the rain were the only thing to be unhappy about.

'Maybe it's stupid to hope there's some place where nothing's changed,' muttered Lee. 'I haven't seen any planes go over or ships go by, have you?'

Jojo shook his head. 'But the world's a pretty big place. Some of it might be the same.'

'Yep, and in the meantime, we're stuck here.'

'We are until Griffy gets bigger which shouldn't be that long given the amount of fish she gobbles down,' he said lightly. Lee grinned and Jojo grinned too, relieved to be friends again.

The rain continued as they walked and Jojo swore under his breath as the crowd of blood crabs ahead showed no inclination to shift. It meant he and Lee had to squeeze past them on the softer sand near the cliffs. 'Sometimes they get out of the way and sometimes they don't,' he grumbled.

'They *never* get out of the way for me,' said Lee, eyeing them in disgust. 'They remind me of the Uncles.'

'That's not very nice,' said Jojo, as he pictured his mother's stern face.

'Oh, not in looks, except for Neville maybe. He's the one with the big eyebrows,' she added, in response to Jojo's blank look. 'Haven't you met him yet?'

'I've met him. He's a bit hard to talk to.'

'They all are,' said Lee, as they came down to the harder sand near the water again. 'They get an idea in their heads and they won't let go of it, like the blood crabs won't let go of whatever they're eating. I bet the crabs wouldn't even let go of their dinner if the pterodactyls attacked them.'

'Are you saying the Uncles are stubborn because they decided the roofs didn't need plugging with bitumen?' asked Jojo curiously.

'Well, that too but I was thinking of their belief that God meant them to be here because it was where their stupid boats washed up.'

'This place has lots of useful things like fresh water and fish,' pointed out Jojo.

'So have heaps of other places, I bet,' said Lee, and dropped her head again.

'We have to get Griffy some more fish,' he said, and forced a smile. 'At least your bucket will make it easier to get it up the cliff.'

The search for fresh fish took longer than usual because the gentler waves washed fewer onto the beach but there were plenty of rotting fish. For once Jojo wished the pterodactyls would appear to clean them up. Lee scowled and buried her nose in her elbow at the smell. 'If the tide ever decides to come in it would wash this muck away.'

'It's not washing *anything* away at the moment,' agreed Jojo, poking at a fish with his stick. It's bands of bright yellows and purples reminded him of sea snakes.

'That looks tropical,' said Lee, peering at it.

'No good for Griffy then?'

Lee shrugged. 'I don't know but I haven't seen tropical fish on the beach before.'

'Neither have I,' said Jojo, and felt uneasy without knowing why.

'And it's not like we've had a storm or big waves to wash them in from somewhere far away,' said Lee, sounding worried too.

'It's been still since the rain set in,' agreed Jojo.

'And we've had no tides,' added Lee.

'You have to have tides because of the moon,' said Jojo automatically, but the beach *did* look the same as earlier.

'Maybe the moon's decided to give up on us too,' said Lee grimly.

'Hard to tell with these clouds,' said Jojo, and paused. 'Maybe there's really strong winds out to sea pushing the water back. Dad says—' He stopped as Lee did whenever the topic of her family came up. 'Lots of things affect tides,' he finished lamely.

'And who knows what's happening out at sea?' said Lee. 'The Kraken could be lolling about sunbaking on its surface, for all we know.'

'Not in this weather,' said Jojo, wiping the rain from his eyes. It oozed down inside his clothes too. 'Do you think we have enough fish?'

'Yep. There's some left from yesterday but she'll need water.'

Jojo sighed. 'Plenty of it falling on our heads but I'm betting not enough to fill a bucket before Last Meal. Give it to me and I'll fill it at the waterfall.'

'I'll go, you went last time,' said Lee. She emptied the fish onto a scrap of plastic but Jojo shook his head. He knew she was keen to get back to Griffy, and he was keen to pay the peak a visit. He just hoped the leather-winged birds weren't at the waterfall to welcome him back.

He decided to visit the peak on the return trip because it would be silly to carry anything he found all the way to the waterfall and back again. The waterfall's roar grew and his stomach knotted as he neared it but there was no sign of the leather-winged birds.

Instead, there was something even more shocking. The Stream's shining fall was muddied by a great plume of dirty water that gushed from the cliff behind.

CHAPTER 31

Jojo knew water flowed under the ground because his parents had once taken him and Davy to see stalactites and stalagmites in caves carved out by hidden rivers and on a fishing trip, Jojo's dad had dug a hole to look for worms and showed Jojo and Davy how water seeped into it from the surrounding earth.

Jojo filled the bucket as fast as he could, keen to get away from what he guessed was an underground river. He didn't know if it were possible for one river to flow on top of another and the second river might not follow the Stream anyway but wander about *under* the Town instead. And even that wouldn't matter if it were deep underground but if it were close to the surface and it kept raining, it might carve out a bigger tunnel for itself and weaken the earth above and then the whole Town might be lost.

Jojo was so desperate to know Lee's thoughts he was tempted to go on past the peak but he didn't know when he'd have the chance to check there again. The beach was empty because anyone with any sense was holed up somewhere dry and he plonked the bucket down and set off across the stones, half hoping the patch of clear water would be empty so he could get back to his cave more quickly.

A blue disk shone against the creamy sand and his heart leapt but Jojo's delight was short-lived. The bottom of the blue bottle might be perfect, but the top had been snapped off. He was tempted to toss the bottle back but jammed it in his pocket instead and scrambled back to shore.

The blood crabs were in the mood to shift again, which quickened his journey, and Lee was still feeding Griffy when he arrived panting back in the cave. He set the bucket down, rubbed his aching arm, and pulled the bottle from his pocket. It looked like a wine bottle although he'd never seen a blue one before, nor one with such clear glass.

'You've found another bottle?' said Lee.

'Yes, but broken,' said Jojo, holding it up.

'It's a lovely colour,' she said and sighed. 'You're good at finding things on the beach.'

'It was you who found the second plate,' he pointed out, settling on the floor.

'Yes, but I was with you.'

It was a curious thing to say and Jojo licked his lips. 'The sickle wasn't on the beach and neither was the first bit of fern.'

'Well, as the *feather* belongs to a phoenix, it doesn't count.'

Jojo blinked in confusion. 'What—'

'A phoenix can fly in from *anywhere*,' she said impatiently and settled beside him, Griffy perched on her arm. 'She can grip on now,' she said proudly.

That was because she'd grown claws on her front feet, though her back feet remained malformed nubs, not that Jojo pointed it out. 'You've done well to raise her,' he said instead.

'Unlike your loong, she hasn't had to put herself back together,' said Lee, as she stroked Griffy's stubbly head.

'It's not *my* dragon *if* it is a dragon,' said Jojo.

'What else could it be?'

'At the moment, it's a couple of plates.'

'A couple of plates?' scoffed Lee. 'One whole plate plus a sliver of a plate, plus a broken plate that's stuck itself back together *and* absorbed a sickle, which I think's a claw, *and* a bottle, and now you've found a second bottle.'

'I almost threw it back.'

'But you didn't.' Lee's brows kinked. 'It'll be *interesting* to see what the loong does with it.'

Jojo thought *terrifying* was a better word. 'Have you heard of underground rivers?' he asked.

'Well there's the Styx. It's the river the dead have to cross in the Underworld. Why?'

Lee's answer was hardly comforting and Jojo was sorry he'd asked. 'I think there's one under the Stream,' he said, and described what he'd seen at the waterfall.

Lee stroked Griffy's chest as she listened and the creature's eyes closed. 'You think the Town's in danger?'

'I don't know,' he admitted. 'It depends on how deep the underground river is and where it goes. The cliffs are pretty crumbly there and anything close to them or the waterfall might be in danger.'

'Like the Sanctuary?'

'Yes.'

Lee smiled sourly. 'Imagine Markus's reaction if his precious Sanctuary fell in the sea.'

'It might have people in it.'

'That would be horrible,' said Lee, in a small voice.

'And that's not the only problem,' continued Jojo, his thoughts running ahead. 'If Markus and the other Uncles believe the Town's unsafe, they might shift it somewhere else and then *everything* would have to be rebuilt.'

'Markus won't shift the Town,' said Lee with such certainty Jojo stared. 'This place is *God-given* remember.'

'Do you think we should tell him about the second river?'

'It's only a guess and he's already accused you of lying.'

'Well, maybe *you* should tell him,' suggested Jojo.

Lee gave a snort. 'You think Markus would listen to me? You've seen the way he bosses the Aunts around and I'm only a *girl*. There's no way I'm wasting my breath on him.'

'So, what do we do?'

'Keep an eye on the Sanctuary, I suppose, until we come up with a better idea.'

CHAPTER 32

They didn't speak as they trudged through the sodden thorn trees back to the Town. The trees were still ominously quiet although their spicy scent was a nice change from the sea's stink. Lee's fringe formed a wet curtain across her face and water dripped from her chin. 'I'm sick of this rain,' she said, as they neared the Town.

'So am I,' said Jojo. 'I bet it's drier in the Mountains,' he added morosely.

'Yep. I bet the sun shines there everyday and they have chocolate for snacks because the Aunts are in charge and not the Uncles.'

'Chocolate for snacks and ice cream for dessert,' said Jojo, continuing the game.

'And lots of people we know,' said Lee, her voice full of longing.

'Yes,' said Jojo, thinking of his mum and dad's smiles and Davy's clumsy hugs, but he said nothing and Lee went quiet too. They stopped on the slope above the Town as they always did because Lee never wanted to go back and Jojo was beginning to feel the same. Maybe Lee's discontent had rubbed off on him or Raj's or maybe Jojo had simply been slower to see the Town for what it was: a ramshackle collection of buildings cobbled together by desperate survivors and ruled over by men with very definite views about everyone's futures.

But *if* there were an underground river, the Uncles were wrong about the Town being safe, and *if* people were in danger, keeping an eye on things was worse than useless.

'I think we should check on the Sanctuary,' he said suddenly. 'That was Plan A remember,' he added, in response to her blank look.

'Okay,' she muttered. 'I can't get any wetter.'

They headed off over the soggy ground towards the cliffs, Jojo using his stick to test whether the ground felt softer in places but it all felt the same. 'If there's Uncles there, you'll get some Brownie points for wanting *quiet time to think about things*,' whispered Lee, as they neared the small building.

'We need to look at the ground *outside* first,' said Jojo.

'And then I'm checking out the feather,' she replied.

They trudged around the building in ever-widening circles but saw nothing strange. 'No extra soggy patches and no cracks,' murmured Jojo, but he knew from TV that things like landslides could happen without warning.

'Let's take a look at the feather,' said Lee.

Jojo followed her back through the murk to the Sanctuary. It was dry inside but if the cliff *did* give way, the Sanctuary would fall in the ocean and take them with it. The creaking floor added to Jojo's tension but Lee seemed oblivious as she strode to the building's far end and stared up at the fern.

'It's definitely part of your phoenix feather,' said Lee.

'Or decoration off some building or other,' he countered.

'Which glows and gives off sparks.' She glanced sideways at him. 'Really Jojo, you seem to have awful trouble with mythic animals.'

'I don't want more strange things turning up in my life,' he admitted.

144

'Yet they keep coming,' said Lee softly. 'The loong, the giant serpent, and now a phoenix.'

'We don't even know the feather belongs to a phoenix.'

Lee grinned. 'At least you're admitting it's a feather now, but you're right. It could be a Roc's or Sirin's, or even a Griffin's, although Griffy doesn't look like she'll have golden feathers.' Lee paused. 'We won't know what the feather's from unless it gets to be whole again.'

Jojo shrugged. 'Not much we can do about that.'

'There's lots we can do about it,' said Lee and pushing the table against the wall, she clambered on top.

'Lee!' exclaimed Jojo in horror. 'Someone will come!'

'They're all eating or staying nice and dry,' she said, lifting the feather to peer underneath. 'It's only hooked on with a bit of wire. It'd be easy to remove.'

'*Steal*, you mean,' he hissed, staring over his shoulder to the door. 'Get down before someone comes!'

'*Everything* here's already been stolen,' she said, not moving. 'One more theft won't make any difference.'

But Jojo knew there'd be an uproar. The Uncles would interrogate everyone and being a *liar* would make him the prime suspect. Even the *thought* of Markus towering over him made his hands sweat. 'Get down,' he pleaded.

'No one would know,' she said softly, and then the door creaked open behind them.

CHAPTER 33

Jojo froze and Lee stayed where she was. It was pointless pretending she wasn't interfering with the cross and as footsteps creaked their way up the floor, Jojo forced himself to turn. It was Raj and Jojo all but collapsed in relief. They still had a lot of explaining to do, but of all the people who could have discovered them, Raj was the least likely to tell the Uncles.

He stopped, hands on hips but Lee had dropped her head and Jojo licked his lips. 'We were trying to work out what the cross really is,' he said.

'Why?'

'Because it doesn't look like a cross,' said Lee unexpectedly. She jumped down, landing with a thud, and pulled the table back into place.

'So what *does* it look like?' challenged Raj.

Lee had turned her back as if she contemplated the cross and Jojo licked his lips again. 'Like a bit of decoration off a building,' he said. 'Lots of pieces wash up.'

'This washed *down* in the Stream,' pointed out Raj.

'From the Mountains,' said Jojo, surer of himself now because he knew that Raj believed people lived there too.

'You've chosen an odd time to examine it,' said Raj suspiciously. 'You're missing Last Meal.'

Raj was missing Last Meal too, thought Jojo, unless he'd already eaten, and given Raj's annoyance with the Uncles' *church*, it was odd that Raj was there too.

'Being here alone was a good time to have a proper look,' admitted Jojo. 'But we mainly came to check the ground.'

Raj's eyebrows rose but he listened without interruption to Jojo's description of his discovery at the waterfall. Lee had settled on a seat but she kept her face towards the cross as if she were fascinated by it.

'It's probably just leakage from the Stream,' said Raj eventually.

'But the water's muddy.'

'It would be if it seeped through cracks in the Stream bed.'

Raj was right and Jojo felt silly but also very relieved. 'Is that what happened in the storms before I washed up?'

Raj shrugged. 'No one checked, as far as I know. The Uncles don't have the same interest in exploring as you and Lee.'

'Do you think the Uncles should be told?' asked Jojo, hoping Raj would volunteer.

'They should probably have a look,' said Raj, which wasn't really an answer. His gaze went to the cross. 'So, do you think the Uncles' god has sent them a sign?'

'I don't think it's a cross,' said Lee, again surprising Jojo she'd spoken. 'You can see where it's broken off something else.'

Raj shrugged again. 'People see what they want to see and believe what they want to believe,' said Raj and paused. 'You should get yourselves to the Kitchens before they close.' Jojo nodded. Raj obviously wanted time alone and he made his way out, Lee hard on his heels.

'It's strange that Raj turned up,' she whispered, as they set off across the soggy grass. 'You'd think the Uncles' *church* would be the last place he'd be interested in.'

'It's lucky it wasn't Markus,' said Jojo, with feeling.

'Or Axel or one of the other Finders.'

147

'I hope Raj tells the Uncles to about the waterfall and then they'll check it.'

'Why would they bother? A *God-given* land must be safe and even *if* they did check it, they'd decide it's just the Stream leaking, like Raj did.'

'Do *you* think it *is* just the Stream leaking?' asked Jojo.

'It might be or it might be an underground river hollowing out a bigger tunnel under the Town. Since the earth became the sea, it's hard to predict anything.' She paused. 'But I *do* think we should give the phoenix a chance to be whole.'

'You mean steal the Uncles' cross?'

'I mean bring the pieces back together.'

It was the same thing and Jojo's stomach knotted. 'Even *if* we did have all the pieces, they mightn't behave like the plates have.'

'You're right. A phoenix isn't a loong but if a loong can regrow itself like a starfish, maybe a phoenix can too. And why should it spend its life all spread out, not knowing where its other parts are or whether it will ever see them again? We should give it a chance,' she repeated thickly.

'Let's think about what we can do overnight,' he said.

'We already know what we can do,' retorted Lee. 'Leave it in pieces or help it become whole again.'

Lee said nothing more, even during Last Meal, which thankfully was presided over by Mary. They were almost the last to eat which meant there was no tea left but Mary filled their bowls to the brim and gave them double helpings of bread. Jojo half hoped she'd sit with them, but she was still cleaning up when he followed Lee out and only paused in her work to tell them their next day's Activities. Lee was to sort clothes again and Jojo was back to collecting driftwood.

'Looks like it's business as usual,' murmured Lee, as they paused under the Kitchens' eaves out of the rain.

'Maybe the Uncles expect the rain to go on for a while,' said Jojo. 'The Town still needs things done even though it's wet.'

'I'm sick of the rain,' said Lee. 'I wish it would stop.'

CHAPTER 34

Jojo had grown used to the pit-pit of rain on the Dorm's roof and the smell of wet wood, but the louder plops on the floor had ceased, thanks to the Finders' and Uncles' work on the roof. Raj's bed was empty and Jojo wondered if he were still at the Sanctuary.

He dried his feet and pulled the blanket up but his head was too full of Lee's words to sleep. His mum would say taking the cross was stealing but he already knew that, yet the idea of *any* creature being forever in pieces was horrible. He told himself the thing was simply a fancy gold feather and that lots of things glowed in the dark, even the numbers on old fashioned alarm clocks, and yet the truth was that no feather gave off sparks or was guarded by leather-winged birds.

He'd told Lee he'd think about what to do overnight but their choices were pretty clear: take the cross to see if it would join with its other pieces or leave it where it was. He supposed he could tell the Uncles that their cross was really a feather but he could imagine their reaction, especially when they discovered that he had the other pieces.

He punched his pillow flat, turned to face the wall and then turned back again as an even worse thought occurred to him. If the Uncles believed the cross were a sign from God and Jojo revealed it was simply a piece of broken feather, they'd look stupid, and Jojo knew who they'd blame.

He must have dozed off because when he woke, Raj was back in his bed and sound asleep. The Dorm's darkness told Jojo it was still night and for a moment he had no idea what had woken him and then he realised the pit-pit of rain had stopped. It looked like Lee had got her wish, he thought sleepily, and then there was an almighty roar.

The Dorm shuddered as if hit by a train and boys yelled out as they were jolted from their sleep. Some of the younger Flotsams cried and Jojo feared the Dorm's roof was about to blow off. Lightning yellowed the room as thunder cracked and then the rain started again, battering the Dorm's windward side like machinegun bullets. Some Finders got up and bolted the shutters and slowly the hubbub quietened.

Jojo guessed most of the boys had gone back to sleep but his thudding heart stopped him joining them. Waves crashed against the cliff which told him the tide had turned at last but there was another sound too, lower than the wind's roar, but just as powerful. Jojo slipped from his bed, grabbed his stick and sandals, and tip-toed out. It was a struggle to get the door open and even harder to stop it slamming shut. He had to sit to get his sandals on or be blown over and rain swept in under the eaves to pelt him like gravel.

The mystery sound was louder outside and he struggled his way through the wind and rain and peered down. The Stream roared along in flood, white-capped, the dark shapes of logs swirling on its surface. Jojo guessed the Gardens were gone and if the water continued to rise, that the Town would be gone too.

He had the wild idea of knocking on the Uncles' Dorm to warn them but Markus would probably say that the Stream behaved as all rivers did after rain, or that God was in charge, or even accuse Jojo of calling wolf again. The flooded Stream was scary enough but it was what might be happening *beneath* it that really frightened him. He shielded his eyes against the rain and stared away towards the cliffs but the darkness was even thicker in that direction.

He fought his way down the street and the gale doubled when he reached the cliffs because there was no shelter at all there. The wind fired saltwater bullets into his face and added its roar to the Stream's roar and the ocean's pound, so that he was deafened as well as blinded. The only good thing was that the lightning had gone and taken the risk of being struck with it.

Shadows zigzagged over the grasses and he glanced up. He expected to see the leather-winged birds riding the tempest but there was only the boil of clouds and he looked back to the ground and gasped. They weren't shadows at all but massive cracks as sharp-edged as the broken crockery on the beach. One crack zigzagged towards the cliffs while a second zigzagged away closer to the waterfall. His heart faltered. The Sanctuary sat on the wedge of land between them!

CHAPTER 35

Jojo braced himself against the wind as he tried to think. Should he dash back and tell the Uncles? And if he did, would they believe him? He didn't know how fast the cracks were opening either and the Sanctuary might be gone by the time he got back. He took a ragged breath. The cracks might be shallow, like the surface cracks on mud when ponds dried out but the land here wasn't drying out; it was drowning.

The earth shuddered and he scrabbled backwards and landed with a sodden thump on his backside as the nearest crack run on towards the Town. It looked like a fat black snake sliding away from him. The earth shuddered again and the second crack did the same thing. Jojo didn't know when or *if* the cracks would stop but he did know that if he were to rescue the feather, it had to be now.

He fought his way towards the cliffs even as his brain yelled at him to go in the opposite direction. Lee was right that the feather needed to be whole but Jojo didn't believe it belonged to anything as fantastical as a phoenix, weird though the feather was. In some barely acknowledged part of his brain, Jojo didn't want the feather condemned to being forever scattered, like he and his family were.

He heard a faint shout, just audible above the tumult, and turned. A dim figure near the Infirmary gestured him back and a second shout told him it was Raj. Jojo pointed towards the Sanctuary and Raj's gestures became more urgent, but Raj stayed where he was which told Jojo just how dangerous the cracks were.

He forced himself on, wrested open the Sanctuary door, and struggled inside. The door slammed shut on his back, throwing him forward onto his knees, but he scrabbled up and fled up the central passageway. The building shuddered with each new gust and Jojo dragged the table against the wall, scrambled on top, grabbed the feather, and pulled. Nothing happened and he desperately pulled again before he recalled it was *hooked* to the wall.

He jerked it upright and it came loose, but before he could move, there was an ear-splitting screech of splintering timber and his back was suddenly whipped by wind and rain. Jojo turned, the feather clamped to his chest, but at first, he had no idea what he looked at. He could see the ocean's storm-tossed horizon straight ahead, while below his feet the fractured ends of the Sanctuary's floor were clear. And beyond them, he could see the beach, piled high with mud and stone and the Sanctuary's shattered remains.

But as Jojo struggled to comprehend that the cliff had collapsed and taken half the Sanctuary with it, the rest of the Sanctuary began to slide. The table slid off into space first and the walls tilted as they followed. Jojo screwed his eyes shut waiting for the crushing pain of death but nothing happened and he opened them again.

The view below was the same except there was more wreckage on the beach and instead of standing on the table, he was hanging in the air. The feather glowed against his chest with a power that stopped him from falling *and* from being blown away. But even as he realised this astonishing fact, the feather's glow dimmed and he dipped lower and, hit by the wind, moved inland in a series of jerks. Land appeared below which was a relief but then his speed picked up until he feared he would be blown all the way to the Mountains.

The feather lost more of its light, as if a dimmer switch had been flicked, and he was suddenly falling. The thorn trees rushed up to meet him and he gave a strangled cry as he bounced off branches in a series of punishing whacks, until a final bang filled his head with stars. He was vaguely aware of lying on wet ground and of his head hurting, and then there was nothing.

Jojo was so cold his teeth chattered and he forced his gluey eyes open. He was surrounded by trunks silvered by dawn but it still rained and winds still stormed in the treetops to send leaves slapping down on him. Jojo's head thudded and he wiped the rain from his eyes only to discover it was blood.

He still held the feather which gave off a faint glow and he struggled to sit up. Getting to his feet was even harder and he clutched a tree until his vision cleared. There were big gaps in his memory too. He recalled being in the Sanctuary, then hanging above it, then being blown inland, but how far inland? The branches' bend told him the cliffs' direction and he turned that way, wanting to orientate himself, but the feather abruptly became a dead weight.

It was hard to think with a hammer pounding away inside his skull but Jojo turned the other way and the feather grew lighter again. He wondered if it wanted to get back to its other bits by the quickest possible route but the idea was so ridiculous he would've laughed had he not felt so awful.

He decided to let the feather guide him given he had no other plan and shivered as he stumbled through the trees, resting when he had to. His eyes were half closed because keeping them open was too much effort and only knew he'd reached the shaft when he almost fell in.

It took him an age to climb down and the feather was dull by the time he reached the cavern. Its seaward side was awash and more water gushed in with every wave but he was too cold to care. He staggered to his cave, deposited the feather with the plates, and fell to his knees. The cave was chill but Lee's jacket was dry and Griffy's little body warm, and he curled up around her and slept.

CHAPTER 36

A low hiss, came and went, came and went reminding Jojo of Davy's soft snore and of the rustle of leaves outside their bedroom window. The trees sent leaf-shadows dancing across their bedroom floor and sometimes bird-shadows, and then Jojo helped Davy guess the bird-types from their outlines. But there was none of his bed's coziness and Jojo opened his eyes.

It was dark, the stone cold under his back, the air full of salt. He was in his cave but had only scattered memories of how he'd got there. Something stirred in the darkness but it was only Griffy. Surprisingly, he was lying right next to her. He sat up and groaned as pain escalated in his head. Griffy's red eyes gleamed momentarily then disappeared as she settled again, and desperate for comfort, Jojo stroked her soft feathers.

He recalled the Sanctuary sliding into the ocean and the piece of feather keeping him aloft but not much more. He had obviously made it back to his cave because he was here but was it still the same night or the next night? He felt more sick than hungry so maybe it was the same night but he was super thirsty.

He eased away from Griffy so as not to disturb her, rolled onto his knees, and waited for the cave to stop spinning before he struggled to his feet. His head pounded sickeningly and a careful exploration with his fingers revealed dried blood. He just hoped the gash healed cleanly because there was nothing in the Town to help him if it didn't.

The cave continued to sway and he wanted to curl up around Griffy again but he also wanted to see what was happening outside. He tottered through the cavern's water, leaned against the stone, and peered out. The air was crisp and the ocean clad in a silvery sheen so beautiful that even its cargo of trash failed to spoil it. He expected to see a full moon but saw stars instead, so dense their light filled the darker patches of sky in between.

Jojo had seen brilliant stars when he'd camped in the mountains and his dad had explained how city lights dulled their shine, but these stars were so bright they were like firestorms. Their beauty should have thrilled him but he felt even bleaker. For the stars to be this bright, there must be no electric lights nearby or maybe none left anywhere in the world.

He licked his chapped lips, sorry the rain had gone, and heard a steady drip-drip from the cavern's side. Water seeped from above and he funneled it to his mouth and swallowed greedily. He needed to lie down again but he needed water too and staggered back to the corner where he kept his treasures. The feather was still in pieces but gave off enough light to see the plates.

Jojo blinked. The fragment had grown to the size and shape of Griffy's dish and he gingerly picked it up and set it under the drips. The dish chimed as it filled reminding Jojo of how the first plate had chimed when Axel smashed it.

Jojo gulped down the water and sagged against the stone as he waited for the dish to fill again. Then something caught his eye and he stiffened. The sea's debris came in all sizes, some as big as icebergs, but this was no iceberg. Starlight gilded its prow, silvered its thrusting masts, and lit its billowing sails. It was a ship, not like the cruise ships on TV, or the fishing boats of his beachside holidays, but like the pirate ships of his comics. Such ships had given way to steam, then to engines fueled by oil, but there it was, right in front of him, its sails glimmering in the starlight.

CHAPTER 37

Jojo had to clutch the stone to stay upright. He was terrified the ship would turn towards him and terrified it would sail right on past to some *better* place, leaving him and Lee and Raj and the rest of them marooned under the Uncles' stern gaze.

Jojo felt too ill to shout or wave but that wasn't all that held him still. It was probably the starlight that made the ship appear ghostly but Jojo feared it was crewed by skeletons clad in rotting pirate gear like the ships of his comics. The idea was ridiculous but he stayed motionless until the ship had disappeared into the darkness, then he stumbled back to his cave and curled up next to Griffy.

His headache showed no signs of quitting and after a while he decided that the pirate ship was simply an hallucination caused by the blow to his head. But just before sleep claimed him, the uncomfortable thought came to him that he had a habit of making up excuses for things he didn't want to face.

The cave was lighter the next time he woke and his headache at a more manageable throb.

'Thank heavens, you're alive,' came Lee's voice from the gloom. 'All hell's broken loose in the Town. The Uncles are arguing over whether the whole lot will drop in the ocean and everyone thinks you're a hero though probably a dead one.'

Jojo saw her lift Griffy onto her lap and give her chin a scratch. 'Well, maybe not *everyone* thinks you're a hero because I figured you'd gone to rescue the *feather* not the

Uncles' precious cross.' Lee grinned then sobered. 'But I *was* worried you'd ended up in the sea. Raj told everyone he'd seen you go into the Sanctuary but not come out. The Uncles spent a whole day searching the beach for your body.'

Jojo sat up carefully and took a sip of water from his dish. He'd managed to avoid thinking about all the complications of his Sanctuary visit but now they crashed back. Lee reached forward and touched his arm. 'By the way, I'm *really* glad you're not dead,' she said thickly, and took a steadying breath. 'And I guessed you'd come here but I couldn't check until today *or* feed Griffy because Markus banned everyone from *wandering about* until the Uncles decided what else might end up in the sea.'

'How …' croaked Jojo, and coughed to clear his throat. 'How many days has it been?'

'Two. Griffy's starving,' she said, and hugged the little creature close. 'Have you been asleep *all* that time?'

Jojo took another sip of water. 'I don't know. I hit my head on something.'

'You sure did. You look awful.'

'I wouldn't know without a mirror,' said Jojo grumpily. 'But I'm super hungry.'

'You're in luck on that score,' said Lee, and extricated two thick slices of bread from her pocket. 'Mary gave me extra at First Meal. She said you'd need to eat *if* you were still alive.' Jojo crammed the bread into his mouth, offering up silent thanks to Mary. 'She's pretty smart for an Aunt,' continued Lee. 'She mightn't be a fast mover but there's nothing wrong with her brain, unlike the Uncles'. They reckon the waves washed your body out to sea after your *brave* attempt to rescue the cross.' Jojo was too busy eating to say anything. 'You *did* rescue the feather, didn't you?' asked Lee worriedly.

'Yes,' mumbled Jojo, cheeks bulging.

Lee's breath huffed in relief. 'Well, that *was* pretty brave.'

'It was probably pretty stupid,' admitted Jojo. 'I thought I'd have time to get in *and* out but the whole lot went.'

Lee gasped. 'You went *down* with the Sanctuary?'

Jojo shook his head and instantly regretted it as pain thudded anew. 'I was holding the feather and it sort of floated and then the wind blew me inland. I must have fallen and hit my head because I don't remember much about getting here.'

'You were super lucky,' breathed Lee.

'It was the feather that saved me or maybe it saved itself.' Jojo's face warmed at his ridiculous suggestion that a lump of metal could think but Lee seemed to have no such reservations.

'Which makes it more likely to be a phoenix feather,' she said excitedly.

'Why?' demanded Jojo.

'Think about it, Jojo. It kept itself in the air rather than falling in the ocean with everything else.'

'The pieces I found were *under* the water, as was the Uncles' piece,' Jojo reminded her.

'You're right,' said Lee. 'Maybe it changes when it's taken *out* of water, in fact, it makes sense that it *would* change.'

'Nothing makes sense at the moment,' mumbled Jojo.

'If it's a *phoenix* feather, it's connected to fire not water,' explained Lee, and shuddered. 'It must have been awful for it to be trapped under water, kind of like Griffy being trapped in the pocket.' Lee's claims were bizarre but Jojo didn't have the energy to argue. He was still ravenous but all he had was water and he gulped some down.

'That dish isn't from the fragment you found, is it?' asked Lee. Jojo nodded and regretted that movement too. 'Wow! Have the other bits of feather changed too?'

'No,' said Jojo, remembering just in time not to shake his head. 'At least, not the last time I looked.'

Lee set Griffy down, retrieved the feather pieces, and arranged them end to end on the floor. It was so obviously a feather Jojo wondered why he'd ever argued it was a fern. The wiry strands had untangled themselves to form a smooth, shining outline but the broken shaft showed no signs of mending.

'It's so beautiful,' breathed Lee, and Jojo had to agree. The feather was as long as his arm and gleamed like liquid gold even in the cave's dimness. Its owner must have been magnificent *and* terrifying as it streaked across the sky.

'It needs fire,' said Lee abruptly.

Jojo blinked. 'Fire?'

'A phoenix comes from fire. It needs fire to be whole again.'

'We don't have fire,' said Jojo. Even the Kitchens' ovens were only lit for First and Last Meals.

'I know. We'll have to do what Prometheus did.'

'Prometheus?'

Lee suppressed a sigh. 'You know, Prometheus in the myth who stole fire from the gods. In our case, we're going to have to steal it from the Uncles.'

CHAPTER 38

Jojo's head thudded as he dredged up reasons why stealing fire from the Uncles was a *really* bad idea. He wanted to say the feather was just a bit of wreckage from the time of Before, that stealing was wrong, regardless of the reason, and that they'd never get away with it, not with Aunts, Uncles and Finders wandering about, but he felt too sick. Lee had gone quiet too probably because she was already concocting a fire-stealing plan. 'I need to get back to the Town,' he muttered.

'Yep,' agreed Lee. 'You need to get your head seen to. I'll grab some fish for Griffy while you work out a story for Markus about how you *heroically* escaped from the Sanctuary. Then we'll go.'

Lee disappeared with the bucket but Griffy hopped about so much that Jojo had to pick her up. 'Don't fret,' he said, and patted her awkwardly. 'She'll be back soon.' Griffy was surprisingly heavy and he picked his way to the cavern opening to see her better. Her bony side-lumps *could* be wings, he supposed, and her head *did* look like a bird's but her rear half was still bare of feathers and her hind legs still ended in nubs.

'You really are strange,' he muttered, 'but I guess we're all strange in one way or another.' The clear night had given way to a cloudy day and he contemplated the sea's usual cargo of splintered timber, torn plasterboard, broken trees, cans, roofing iron, and endless, endless plastic.

He didn't want to think about giant squids *or* giant snakes, or birds that looked like pterodactyls, or plates that changed of their own accord, or golden feathers that shot out sparks. At least there were no ghostly galleons this morning and nor had there been last night, he hastily corrected. The pain in his head had been awful and he'd been dizzy and sick too, reasons enough for his eyes to play tricks on him.

Screeches heralded the arrival of the leather-winged birds and Griffy's back legs suddenly jabbed him hard in the stomach as she launched from his arms. Jojo managed to grab her in mid air but her claws raked his arms and her head snaked back, beak snapping, as she tried to bite him.

'It's okay Griffy,' he said soothingly, but it wasn't okay. She'd never acted like this before and he had no idea whether she wanted to join the leather-winged birds or escape them. A chime sounded behind him and she quietened so abruptly Jojo might have imagined the whole episode except for his scratched arms. The hair on the back of his neck stirred and he tightened his grip as bird shadows swept the cliff-face but Griffy seemed to have lost interest.

He went back to his cave and set her in her nest, then watched her warily. She stayed put and it was only then he noticed that his drinking dish had flipped upside down. He tapped it experimentally on the floor but the dull chink sounded nothing like a chime. Other creatures probably lurked in the cavern's darker corners and visited for a free meal *or* a free drink, he told himself. It explained why something as small as Griffy seemed to eat so many fish although it didn't explain the chime.

He took the dish back to the cavern's opening but the dribble of fresh water had dried up, and then he all but dropped the dish. The ghost ship was back and the daylight meant he could no longer pretend it was an hallucination. But the ship wasn't normal either because he could see the ocean's trash through its silvery outline.

He willed it to disappear but it didn't fade until it neared the next headland and by then Jojo had collapsed against the stone. Comics were full of ghost ships but he wasn't in any comic and he didn't even know whether he believed in ghosts. He was still trying to come up with an explanation when Lee's glossy black hair appeared up the cliff. 'You've done well,' he said, eyeing the bucket of fish, but there was no answering smile.

'I've seen something awful on the beach,' she whispered.

Jojo licked his lips. 'Like an old fashioned sailing ship?'

'No, like skeletons.'

CHAPTER 39

Jojo led the way to the cave but Lee was too upset to feed Griffy and he smashed up the fish and fed Griffy himself. He was slow, thanks to his headache, and Griffy gobbled up the fish as fast as he could deliver it so it was a while before he asked Lee exactly what she'd seen.

'I looked up from collecting fish and the skeletons were just standing there,' she said, swallowing convulsively.

'How many?'

'You think I bothered to count them?' she demanded shrilly. 'There was just a bunch of them staring at me.' She gave a burst of hysterical laughter. 'Or they would've been staring if they'd had any eyeballs to stare with.'

'Were they wearing clothes?'

'Bits of rotten cloth,' she said with a shrug. 'Who cares? They were *walking* skeletons! Apparently there are worse things here than Markus,' she added with a ghastly smile.

'Do you think they were *really* there?'

'Of course not! I made the whole thing up!'

'I didn't mean that,' said Jojo and licked his lips. 'I saw a sailing ship last night, like the ones pirates use in comics. I saw it again this morning, while you were on the beach. But it wasn't real. I could see through it, like an outline someone's drawn and forgotten to colour in. Where abouts on the beach were you?'

Lee was staring at him open-mouthed. 'You saw a *ghost ship* and didn't bother to tell me?'

'You weren't here last night,' he snapped, and winced. 'Sorry,' he mumbled. 'I've got a *really* bad headache.'

She settled beside him and took his hand. 'I'm sorry too. I was *really* scared you'd been killed and I'd be stuck here on my own.' Jojo heard her swallow. 'And the skeletons just now were terrifying.'

Tears slid down her face and he gave her a quick hug like he hugged Davy when Davy was upset. 'I'd better finish feeding Griffy,' he said awkwardly.

'She's always hungry,' mumbled Lee, and for a while only Griffy's wet gulps broke the silence. '*If* the ship were some sort of ghost ship, the skeletons were probably ghosts too,' said Lee after a while, her voice steadier.

'Did they leave footprints?'

'I didn't check and there's no way I'm going back.' There was a short silence. 'We should get back to the Town anyway so they can look after you in the Infirmary.'

'There's nothing much in the Infirmary,' said Jojo shortly. 'I just need a good sleep *after* I've spoken to Markus.'

Griffy finally seemed full and Lee lifted her onto her lap and stroked her as she would a cat. 'Have you worked out what you're going to say?'

'No and I'm a hopeless liar.'

'You don't need to lie,' said Lee thoughtfully. 'Raj's probably told them you were worried about the underground river so just tell Markus you saw the cracks and went to the Sanctuary to make sure the *cross* was safe. You don't remember much about the cliff collapsing or anything since. You just woke up in the thorn trees and then I came along. It's mostly true and given the giant gash and bruise on your forehead, not even Markus is going to argue.'

'I hope you're right,' said Jojo feelingly.

'And if I'd bashed my head too, we could *both* pretend the pirate ship and its crew of jolly skeletons weren't real.'

'And that Griffy was just a strange bird, and the plate had joined back together because it's magnetic, and the feather was a bit of tin covered in luminous paint.'

'You've forgotten the pterodactyls,' said Lee thickly.

'Oh, they're just *really* big bats,' said Jojo. He forced a smile but felt sick again, his headache showing no signs of leaving.

Lee obviously noticed because she helped him up. 'We'll go slowly,' she said, which was just as well, as the top of the wall seemed narrower. He slid down into the dimness on his backside to where Lee waited, but something lurked in the gloom behind her. Jojo's face must have shown his shock because she turned and gasped.

A group of skeletons headed away down a tunnel usually hidden in the darkness, their bony forms enveloped in mist. Jojo prayed no skulls turned in their direction but it seemed an age before the last of them disappeared into murk, taking the mist with them.

'I guess that proves they exist,' whispered Lee shakily. 'I hoped I'd imagined them.'

'I didn't want the sailing ship to be real either,' admitted Jojo.

'Why are they are here?'

'To get their buried treasure?'

'Do you really think that?' Lee's eyes were wide in her pale face.

'It's as likely as anything else,' muttered Jojo.

'I wish father was here,' said Lee longingly.

'Is he a scientist?' asked Jojo, though he doubted even science could explain such weird happenings.

Lee felt her way along the cavern as if she hadn't heard him and Jojo wriggled after her through the hole to the shaft.

She waited for him on the other side, her face curiously blank. 'My father's a priest,' she said, and started to climb.

CHAPTER 40

Jojo's broken foot slowed his climb up the shaft at the best of times and these weren't the best of times. His vision blurred and his stomach threatened to vomit. He half-hoped Lee had gone back to the Town without him so he could flop down and rest but she grabbed his arm and hauled him out. 'You look even worse in daylight,' she said, keeping a grip on him as they set off.

'Thanks,' he muttered, having to concentrate to keep upright.

'Which is good because Markus won't give you such a hard time.'

'What did he say about the Sanctuary falling into the sea?'

'As I told you, they were still arguing about it when I left.' She smiled sourly. 'Markus will find it hard to explain why God destroyed the land He gave us as well as His gold cross He sent as a sign.'

'They'll work something out,' mumbled Jojo, pausing to claim a new walking stick. 'Dad says when people *really* want to believe something, they come up with reasons why it's true.'

'So, if we *really* want to believe we saw walking skeletons and you *really* want believe you saw a ghost ship, otherwise we are obviously going mad, what reasons do *we* come up with?'

'That when the world got shaken up, Time got shaken up too, and maybe even the gap between the living and dead,' muttered Jojo, and blinked. The explanation sounded both logical and ridiculous at the same time.

'Wow, that's really good, but isn't Time like some sort of line, with dinosaurs up one end and us up the other?'

'Dad says that's only the way *we* see it and that other people in other lands see it as a circle or even a spiral.'

Lee's brows creased. 'I don't really know what Time is,' she said in frustration. 'I know about it being one o'clock, or this week, or last year, but that's just the way we *measure* it.'

Jojo took several deep breaths to try and quell his roiling stomach. 'Dad explained it to me once … but I only pretended to understand …to not look dumb. It was Raj … who said Time might have changed.'

'Raj?'

'The leather-winged birds were flapping about and he said … something about Time having got … mixed up.'

'But that doesn't explain Griffy and the loong, and the Kraken and the phoenix, and the giant serpent that almost killed you. Myth must have got all mixed up as well,' said Lee.

'Raj kind of suggested that too … which proves what my dad says.' Lee looked at him blankly and Jojo took another deep breath. 'If we *believe* that things like pterodactyls, dragons, Krakens and ghosts exist, then … we have to believe that Time and myth and even life and death have changed as well and … I don't think that's possible.'

There was a long silence which Jojo was grateful for given that talking was an effort. 'Well, what other explanations are there?' asked Lee finally.

'We could be imagining everything.'

'So, at exactly the same moment, we *both* imagined the skeletons trooping down the tunnel? And you imagined being almost killed by a giant serpent? And we just fed fish to an imaginary griffin? Come on, Jojo, you can do better than that.'

Jojo came to a stop, his thoughts on the stories in his comics. 'Okay, how about we've washed up on some long lost island where things have always been different?'

'I once saw a movie about a forgotten land, full of prehistoric animals,' said Lee. 'It would explain the pterodactyls.'

'I hope not because it means there's probably meat-eating dinosaurs here too.'

'Now that would be interesting,' said Lee as they went on. Jojo made no reply because he remembered other stories about dead and half-dead people who wandered about but then an even worse idea occurred to him.

'What is it?' asked Lee, her eyes keen on his face.

'I'm probably thinking weird things because of my banged head.'

'Tell me,' she insisted, not put off.

'None of us might have survived being washed away,' said Jojo reluctantly.

Lee's brows kinked. 'What do you mean?'

'I mean we might all be dead and in a world where everything else is dead too.'

'You mean like heaven?'

The Town was nothing like the heaven Jojo had heard about. 'No, like a place where all dead things end up . . . no matter when or where they lived,' he added, as he tried to make sense of his thoughts. His dad had spoken of different worlds on camping trips, when they'd stared up at the stars, and his mum had too, in her quiet talks with him about what Davy's world might be like. Lots of religions had a world of the living and a world of the dead, and sometimes a world in between.

'That's a really *weird* thing to say,' said Lee after a while.

'Blame my bang on the head.'

'But *if* we are dead, wouldn't we know it?'

Jojo wished he'd kept his mouth shut because if they *were* dead, they might just have found out. 'It was a stupid thing to say. Forget it.'

'But we still don't have any explanation for all the weird things.'

'Let's leave that up to the Uncles,' mumbled Jojo. 'I just want to sleep.'

It took them a long time to reach the slope above the Town and then Jojo could scarcely bear to look down. Thankfully the Town looked the same *except* for the clots of foam tossed from the Stream's rushing water. 'The Gardens are gone?' he asked.

Lee nodded. 'It wasn't a great idea to build them so close to the Stream.'

Jojo stared away towards the cliffs. Even from his vantage point, he could see how horrifyingly close the cracks were to the Infirmary. 'They need to shift the Town,' he exclaimed in alarm. 'It isn't safe here!'

'They'll only shift it if the Uncles believe it's what God wants.'

Jojo took several shuddering breaths. 'Do you think they'll shift it?'

'No.'

CHAPTER 41

Lee took Jojo's arm to steady him down the slope which turned out to be useful, because it emphasized his injuries to Axel and Ben who were first to see them. The two Finders stopped dead in their tracks and then hastened off towards the Uncles' Dorm.

'Typical,' muttered Lee. 'More interested in reporting *the news* than in helping. At least they'll pass on what a mess you are.'

'I'm not a mess,' mumbled Jojo.

'You don't have a mirror,' Lee reminded him tartly. 'And here come the Uncles, right on cue,' she added under her breath.

They strode up the muddy path, Markus at their head, and Lee's grip tightened on Jojo's arm, more from fear, he guessed, than to steady him. He had the wild idea of pretending to faint to avoid the whole situation but then Mary darted from between the buildings and enclosed him in a bone-crushing hug.

Jojo was swamped with gratitude at how fast she'd moved *and* for her hug, despite its boniness. He longed to keep his face buried in Mary's wild hair forever but she released him and he forced himself to look up. He expected to be impaled by Markus's slate-grey eyes but he stared skywards like the other Uncles, and their arms were raised in the same direction.

'Praise the Lord for the safe delivery of our son,' boomed Markus. Jojo registered dislike of the description but then Markus's attention suddenly fixed on him. 'How did you survive?' he demanded.

It seemed everyone in the Town had gathered to hear the answer. They jostled in a suffocating ring around him and Jojo took several long blinks, as if about to faint. 'The storm was bad … and I … I went to check on the cross, but then … the Sanctuary started to slip.' He blinked again, keeping his eyes closed longer this time to hide the lie he feared was clear in them. 'I … I don't remember much after that …just waking up in the thorn trees.'

'Did you—' began Markus, but then astonishingly, Mary interrupted.

'The boy's fit to collapse,' she said, in her gravelly voice. 'The best place for him is in the Infirmary. He needs that gash seen to as well. Plenty of time for talk later.'

Mary's bony grip replaced Lee's and Jojo kept his head down, expecting Markus to set Mary back in her place, but he heard squelching instead as the crowd parted to let him and Mary through. He didn't raise his head again until they mounted the steps to the Infirmary and then only to prize off his muddy sandals. His head was down again as Mary guided him to a bed and helped him sit, but it was no longer a pretense. He was desperate for sleep.

'Stay put while I organise clothes and food,' ordered Mary. He heard her feet pad to the door and the surprising authority in her voice as she bawled something, then her footsteps padded back, but not to the bed. He peered sideways. She was at the fireplace, stirring up the coals, then she filled a bowl from a kettle, grabbed a cloth, and padded back.

'Let's see what you've done yourself,' she said, and eased him out of his jacket and shirt. Not much of him had escaped being cut, jabbed or scraped, and he already had the bruise from the sickle. 'Looks like you've been tossed about in the sea's rubbish,' she said grimly, 'except you don't stink of it.'

'I don't remember much after the Sanctuary slipped,' mumbled Jojo, wincing as she cleaned his wounds.

'Probably just as well,' said Mary, intent on a scrape. 'The Sanctuary was a strange place to go, Jojo, given your worries about the underground river and cracks.' It seemed Raj had told everyone *everything* Jojo had said. 'Markus thought it was strange too,' continued Mary, 'at least at first.' Jojo sensed her smile but kept his head down. 'Now he believes your first visit there let God into your life.'

'My first visit?' echoed Jojo thickly.

'When you and Lee met up with Raj. He said you were worried about an underground river and Markus concluded you'd sacrificed your life for the cross. I for one am certainly glad you didn't.'

Jojo's mum said letting someone believe an untruth was the same as lying and Jojo managed to raise his head. 'The cross is clean and shiny and everything else here is dull and broken.' It didn't make much sense but given his pounding head, it was the best he could do.

'Well, you're right about that. The cross *was* nice and shiny,' said Mary, as she rinsed her cloth. There was a knock and Jojo stared at the floor again as footsteps creaked closer bringing with them the delicious smell of warm bread and fishy soup. 'Leave it on the table, Ben,' instructed Mary. There was the chink of bowls and cutlery and the footsteps receded. 'Now let me see that gash,' she said, and Jojo obediently raised his head.

Mary's eyes narrowed. 'This one's a whole lot nastier and will probably scar. If only we had someone who could stitch, *and* sterile needles, *and* surgical thread!' she exclaimed angrily.

'It doesn't matter,' said Jojo uncomfortably. 'I already have a broken foot—'

'Exactly! No child should have to limp through life in pain,' she said, rinsing her cloth and wringing it out with surprising violence. 'I'm sorry things aren't better here, Jojo. If Markus hadn't insisted we scuttle the boats, we might have searched for a better place.'

'*Scuttle* the boats?'

'Sink them,' said Mary baldly. 'Why fight to store them on such a treacherous coast when God's gifted us such a wonderful home?' she asked sarcastically. 'Noah didn't sink *his* ark!' she added.

Jojo's head whirred. He knew he'd never risk the seas again but wrecking the boats meant nobody had that choice. And now the Sanctuary, the very thing supposed to prove God meant them to stay, had gone *and* the Gardens, and the cracks meant that the Town might follow.

'But we're not staying here now, are we? Not with the cracks so close.'

'Ah, yes the cracks,' she said grimly, tossing the cloth aside and drying her hands. 'Are they a warning to shift somewhere safer or a test of our courage and resolve to stay?'

'But … but the whole Town might fall in the sea!'

'Or God might keep us safe because we've proved our faith in His will,' said Mary acidly, throwing the water out the door. 'There's food on the table for you, Jojo,' she said more calmly, 'but get out of those wet clothes before you eat. Then get some sleep. I'll check on you later.'

CHAPTER 42

Jojo found it easy to follow Mary's instructions. Sleep came quickly, his belly full and the Infirmary made snug by the fire. It was dark again when he woke, and he hobbled to the latrines at the back, then slipped into sleep again, not waking until light stole around the shutters. There was more food on the table which had gone cold but Jojo wolfed it down anyway.

His headache had faded which meant he could think again and he knew he was lucky to be alive or more accurately, lucky the feather had decided to keep him alive. Jojo grunted. The idea that a piece of metal could decide *anything* was ridiculous and he stared at his surroundings to distract himself.

The Infirmary looked the same as when he'd first washed up. It had the same six beds, table and two chairs, stack of crockery and cutlery, dinted kettle, pile of clean rags, drying herbs hanging from string, fireplace, and wood stack. The fire had burned down to coals but they still pumped out heat and he luxuriated in the warmth. But then footsteps sounded and he tensed.

It was Lee not Markus and even better, she brought more food. 'You really are King of the Flotsams,' she said cheerfully, as she set the roofing-iron tray down on the table. 'Maybe I should bow,' she added with a grin, as she unloaded a bowl of fish and greens, mug of tea, and double ration of bread.

She propped the tray against the table and flopped onto a chair. 'Mary says you're to rest today and I'm to keep you company,' she said, 'unless you want to sleep then I'm to leave you in peace.' Her grin broadened. 'It's fun watching

Mary boss Markus about. He wanted to grill you about the Sanctuary but Mary's making him wait until tomorrow. He's probably too busy arguing with the Uncles anyway. Some of them actually think it's no longer safe to stay here.'

'But it isn't safe here,' muttered Jojo, as he started on the fish and greens.

'Apparently God's looking after us which is why the cracks stopped before the Town.'

'The Sanctuary fell in the ocean,' pointed out Jojo between mouthfuls.

'It's certainly true God tests our resolve,' mimicked Lee. 'But are we to falter at our very first test? Is our trust in God to be so easily destroyed?'

'If the Town goes, people will be killed!'

'No according to Markus.'

Jojo stopped eating, feeling more sick than hungry. 'How do you know all this? Has there been an announcement?'

'They're still *in discussions*.'

'Then how—'

'I've been late to First Meal the last couple of days and it's interesting what you hear when you circle the Kitchens looking for a seat. No one notices that you've gone past twice.'

'I don't understand how Markus can say it's okay to stay here,' muttered Jojo, continuing his meal, but the trouble was he could. It was exactly what his dad said people did when they *really* believed something. They always found reasons for their belief.

'If the Town *does* fall into the ocean, I'm guessing Markus will say it's another *test*,' said Lee.

'*If* he's alive to say anything!'

'Oh, he'll be alive alright. People like Markus have boats stowed somewhere to carry him and his friends away.'

'Mary said they sunk the boats,' said Jojo.

Lee stared at him open-mouthed. 'Of all the stupid …'

'I wouldn't get on one anyway,' said Jojo.

'That's not the point. It means *no one* can get on one now.' Lee was so upset that she paced. 'The Mountains are safer anyway,' she muttered after a while.

'We don't know that. They might be even worse.'

'They're not going to drown us or smash us to pieces,' said Lee, turning on him. 'And the smoke means there's people there already.'

'Who mightn't want us there for the same reason Markus doesn't want them here.'

'In which case we keep on moving until we find somewhere better!' exclaimed Lee in exasperation. 'And *any where's* better than here *and* safer!'

Which was true because if Markus got his way, the Town wouldn't be safe anymore, thought Jojo.

'There's a fire!' said Lee so suddenly that Jojo jumped.

'It's why it's warm in here,' said Jojo, puzzled by her excitement.

'Don't you see? We can fix the feather with it.'

'We don't know that fire will work,' said Jojo. In truth, he feared it might simply reduce his lovely shining feather pieces to blackened lumps

'Imagine how beautiful the pheonix will look as it streaks across the sky,' breathed Lee. Her eyes shone as if she already saw it but all Jojo could think of was Markus's reaction, and he was willing to bet it wouldn't be good.

CHAPTER 43

Jojo had all day to think about the Uncles' reaction to a phoenix streaking across the sky because Lee had quickly gone off to *organise things*, whatever that meant. He must have dozed only to jerk wake again at her return, laden with food 'Last meal for the King,' she said, as she set it down.

'I've done nothing but eat and sleep,' said Jojo, yawning as he came to the table.

'Well, enjoy it while it lasts. I'm guessing being special ends tomorrow, right before your little chat with Markus.'

'Don't remind me,' muttered Jojo, starting on the bread.

'Just stick to your story about not remembering anything,' said Lee. 'It's true, anyway.' She went to the fire and hefted on more wood. 'The last thing we need is this going out,' she murmured, then glanced over her shoulder. 'I bent a bit of tin into a bucket but I won't fetch it till after dark. I don't want anyone seeing me.'

Jojo took a long slurp of tea. 'Is that what you've been doing all day?'

'That and gathering a nice pile of wood for the tunnel.'

Jojo's heart missed. 'What about the skeletons?'

'Didn't see any and believe me, I looked *really* hard.'

'Why not set the fire in the cavern?'

Lee plonked herself down opposite. 'Because of the smoke. The Finders would be there in a flash or the Uncles. There's less chance of smoke escaping from the tunnel.'

'Unless it's got holes in the roof.'

'Well, have you got any better suggestions?'

How about *not* pretending the feather's a phoenix that we can bring back to life with fire, thought Jojo. Then again, given the Kraken and the giant serpent, he supposed anything was possible. 'What'll happen if the phoenix *does* come back to life? It could be dangerous.'

'No more than the loong.'

'Or griffin,' retorted Jojo.

'Griffy wouldn't hurt anyone,' said Lee indignantly.

'Not when she's little but what about when she's full grown? She's a wild creature, Lee, and she'll be big and strong.'

'Less so than your loong,' said Lee stubbornly.

'It's only plates at the moment and mightn't even be a dragon,' said Jojo, aware that he dodged the question.

'It can mend and grow itself so it's powerful, whatever it is. Maybe you should toss it back before it mends and grows itself even more.' Jojo grimaced as he imagined hurling the plates back into the trash-filled sea. 'Well?' she demanded.

'It was lost and alone,' said Jojo woodenly. 'I'm not throwing it back.'

Lee nodded. 'It deserves a chance like Griffy does *and* the phoenix but I'm guessing they won't hang around once they've grown up. Why would you? If *I* had wings, I'd have flown off ages ago.'

Lee was probably right but there was nothing to stop them destroying the Town *and* killing everyone in it before they left.

It was late before Lee retrieved her bucket which looked more like a scoop to Jojo, but they scraped coals into it and Lee knotted her jacket into a sling around the hot metal. She picked it up to test its weight and Jojo's stomach

183

tightened. 'Be careful,' he whispered, suddenly wishing he was going with her. Lee nodded and disappeared into the darkness but Jojo lingered near the door, too restless to sleep.

The night was full of its usual cloud and the ocean full of its usual sound of pounding waves. Everything seemed normal and yet *nothing* was normal. Living with a bunch of strangers wasn't normal; the Uncles refusal to look for somewhere safer wasn't normal; and Lee's little creature certainly wasn't normal. Nor was the Kraken or the giant serpent or the golden feather or Jojo's collection of plates that changed and grew.

He wandered around the Infirmary and back to the door. There were no sounds of voices which was unsurprising given people usually returned to their Dorms after Last Meal. Early nights were followed by early mornings and days filled with Activities. And nothing would change if Markus had his way unless the Town *did* follow the Sanctuary into the sea, but then Jojo supposed the Uncles would simply rebuild it, as they'd rebuild the Sanctuary, and things would roll on the same.

The only way to change *his* life was to leave but the prospect terrified him. Lee was a lot braver than him, he admitted, or maybe she'd given up hope that her family would appear while he still hoped his mum and dad and Davy would wash up.

His mum had talked about how important hope was when they'd finally discovered why Davy struggled to speak. Jojo even remembered the exact day. It had been summer and sweltering in the car as they'd driven home from the specialist.

'Too many chromosomes,' his dad had muttered and then his mum had spoken about hope. The rest of trip had been taken in silence *except* for Davy who'd laughed and clapped every time he'd spotted his favourite red cars. There'd been lots of specialist visits after that and lots of special activities that Davy enjoyed, as he enjoyed most things.

Jojo's mum had also said that maybe Davy had just the right number of chromosomes and the rest of them had too few. Davy certainly didn't seem to worry about things, whereas Jojo worried about everything, especially what might be happening to Lee. 'Stay safe,' he whispered because it was all that he could do.

CHAPTER 44

Jojo was still in bed when Mary appeared the next morning. 'How's the head?' she asked, as she perched on the end.

'Good,' he mumbled.

'Headache gone?' Jojo nodded. 'Time you were up and about then,' she said briskly. Jojo had been well enough yesterday to be *up and about* but glad to be out of sight. 'The Uncles want everyone at the Kitchens for First Meal, so get yourself organised,' she said, rising and smoothing down her clothes. 'There's to be an announcement.'

The day was its usual grey and he thwacked his sandals together to send dried mud flying then made his way to the Kitchens. Others headed in the same direction and he felt their stares. Even Axel and his friends seemed to find Jojo fascinating. Jojo searched the Kitchens for Lee as he queued for food but she wasn't there and his stomach clenched.

He collected his food and was considering how quickly he could get First Meal and his Activity over with so he could search for her when a hand descended on his shoulder. 'I think it is fitting you sit with Uncles this morning,' said Markus's voice behind him, and then his hand steered Jojo to where the Uncles sat. They'd left a gap in the middle of the bench and Jojo found himself wedged between Markus and the bushy-browed Uncle.

His tight throat made it hard to eat but Markus seemed utterly relaxed as he conversed with the Uncle opposite and he didn't turn to Jojo until near the end of the meal. 'I understand you have been to the Sanctuary three times and so great was your concern for the cross, your final visit was during the storms,' he said. Jojo nodded jerkily, his gaze on the table. 'I also understand you were attempting to save the cross when the ocean rose against the land.' Jojo nodded again. 'Stand, Joseph.'

There was no mistaking the order and Jojo stood awkwardly. Markus rose too, his hand heavy on Jojo's shoulder, and the room hushed. The silence stretched and Jojo flinched when Markus finally spoke. 'We have amongst us one who does not doubt the cross as a symbol of God's intentions,' he boomed. 'A boy who risked all to save it and who barely escaped with his life. A boy who the oceans delivered to us in the most humble of ways and who, like the cross, was broken by what he endured. And yet a boy who, when shown God's glory, had no doubt about what he must do. And yet there are so many you who *do* doubt, who would crumble at just a fraction of what this boy has endured.

'He has been tested by the oceans and by the death of his family, but found solace in the Sanctuary and in the cross. Are we to show less courage and faith than he? To scuttle away from this place of plenty, gifted by God, at our very first testing? Our boats brought us here, guided by His hand, and here we have found all that we need to sustain ourselves *physically*. We work hard but without work, muscle and bone weakens and fails, just as faith weakens and fails when left unused.'

People nodded but there were uneasy looks too and then the bench jolted as the bushy-browed Uncle heaved himself upright. 'That's all well and good, Markus, but what are you intending that we do about the cracks? They've already eaten the Sanctuary *and* the cross, despite the efforts of this Flotsam here, and I'm of a mind to think they'll eat the Town.'

'The cracks have ceased their movement,' said Markus, with utter conviction.

'For the time being,' grunted the bushy-browed Uncle.

'The Uncles have agreed, Neville, as I think you know, to remain steadfast in our faith in God's gift of these lands. However, we are a community, and if there are those here who would like to further contribute their thoughts, I will remain in my Dorm until Noon to receive them.'

Markus sat and the Kitchens' conversations slowly resumed but Jojo felt numb. He slumped back on the bench but then Markus spoke again. 'Now you have recovered, Joseph, you are to return to your Activities, and as you are slower than other boys, I suggest that you start now.'

Jojo's face burned as he gathered up his bowl, spoon and mug, and clumsily extricated himself from the bench. He gulped down the rest of his tea, washed his utensils and set them back on the shelf, then waited in line to be assigned his Activity. Markus had used Jojo to prove a point then tossed him aside, but it was grief not anger that sat like a stone in Jojo's stomach.

But how did Markus *know* Jojo's family were dead? Had his mum and dad and Davy been buried in the Town's cemetery or had their bodies been reclaimed by the waves? And how had Markus known who they were?

Antonella's hair was scraped back so tightly it looked painted on. 'You'll collect reeds from the Marshes until Noon,' she informed Jojo. 'Choose the least damaged ones, tie them into bundles, and stack them in the Store.'

Jojo nodded, his thoughts on Lee. She'd missed First Meal and would be hungry. 'May I have some more bread?'

The words were out of his mouth before he could call them back and Antonella looked at him as if he'd demanded the moon. 'You've had your share.'

'I still don't feel well,' said Jojo, astonished by his boldness. 'It'd help me collect reeds more quickly.'

Antonella's brown eyes bored into his but she handed him a couple of slices. 'Don't ask again,' she warned. Jojo nodded his thanks, his hands trembling as he folded the bread into his pocket. He could probably thank his gashed head for Antonella's *generosity*.

The muddy street held dozens of footprints but none continued beyond the Town and the water was too high for him to take his usual path beside the Stream. He had to struggle along on the higher ground which was soggy too and strewn with wood washed down in the flood. He searched for burned pieces that meant there might be people in the Mountains but saw none.

The Marshes had been beautiful but now their emerald grasses were flattened and mud-covered. There was no frog song either and the giant, rainbow-coloured butterflies had disappeared. Jojo wondered how he was supposed to harvest *anything* when only the occasional stalk had escaped the flood. He picked his way about, using his stick to steady him, the mud all but sucking his sandals off, and was deep in the grasses when he stopped.

He'd seen snake tracks at home, as narrow as bike tyres in the dust, but this snake track was as wide as a *truck* tyre. It came from further up the slope and even as Jojo stared, he heard a soft, squelching sound.

CHAPTER 45

Jojo scrambled up the bank, losing his stick in his hurry, and kept going till he reached the thorn trees. Then he crouched in their cover, heart pounding as he strained for sounds of a giant serpent on the move. He considered fleeing back to the Town but Markus wouldn't believe him and Antonella would simply send him back to complete his Activity.

Nothing happened and Jojo was horribly aware he'd yet to collect a single bundle of grass.

His legs started to cramp and he slowly straightened and smelled smoke. He'd never smelled smoke beyond the Town and the smoke from the Mountains was too distant to smell. He wondered whether Finders camped nearby but since things had unraveled, they had been too busy to do anything but help the Uncles repair the Town.

Jojo faltered. *If* Lee had set a fire in the tunnel, and the tunnel had holes in the roof, the smoke might've travelled all the way here, *the same direction the skeletons had gone.* Even worse, *if* the smoke did escape from holes in the roof, the skeletons could too!

Jojo's neck pricked and he stared about. He was sure the tyre track belonged to the giant serpent but what if the squelching sound belonged to the skeletons? There were lots of reasons the skeletons wouldn't be tramping about on the soggy ground but he had trouble breathing. Lee had seen the skeletons too but it didn't mean they were the actual bones of actual people, he argued, and then recalled their bony feet had been silent on the tunnel's stone.

His breath whooshed out in relief but then he heard the squelching sound again. His brain told him snakes slithered not squelched but he wished Lee was with him because she had lots of good ideas about things. The squelching came from deeper in the trees and he wondered whether he should grab the grasses and hightail it back to the Town but the Aunts harvested here and the *squelcher* mightn't stay in the trees.

Jojo crept in the sound's direction, using the trees as cover. The smell of smoke strengthened and every nerve tingled as he peered from behind a thorn tree. The ground in front was so muddy that nothing grew and he half-expected to see the serpent's massive coils sprawled around its margin.

There was nothing there and he glanced up in case the squelcher had taken to the air. He was taken aback to see that smoke actually hung in the branches but then something moved in the clearing and his gaze jerked back to its mud. It was just a branch settling in the slush and there were other branches there too, sitting at odd angles or lying flat. Their side growth had been stripped away to form crosses and Jojo's heart missed as he realised it was the Town's cemetery.

Mary had told him how desperate those early days were so it was no surprise the graves had only been marked with branches, but it was strange that Markus had chosen such boggy ground and that he hadn't set the graves in rows. They were all over the place.

Jojo could barely force himself forward. His mum, dad, and Davy were here but the crosses were unmarked even by scratches. Markus was sure to have a map of who was buried where, Jojo reassured himself, but how had Markus known who the dead were in the first place? And as far as Jojo knew, there were no pens or pencils or paper in the

Town to record *anything*. Nor did Markus want any. He said they were to forget their past lives and celebrate their God-gifted future lives.

Jojo didn't feel like celebrating *anything* because the flooded graves meant his drowned family and everyone else in the cemetery were still under water. And *if* the smoke *did* come from the tunnel, it meant the tunnel ran under a place crowded with the dead.

He heard the squelching sound again and turned in time to see a grave begin to sink. Jojo watched in horror as the mound disappeared under muddy water and bubbles rose and popped on its surface. Not only did the tunnel pass *under* the dead but it *swallowed* them too.

Jojo stumbled back to the Stream, grabbed as much grass as he could carry, and set off towards the Town. The grass was muddy, the land was muddy, and he was muddy but all he could think of were the mud-covered bodies of drowned people being drowned a second time.

It rained on the way back, a short burst of heavy drops that washed him and his bundle of grass clean. It would please Antonella but he no longer cared. He just wanted to get back to his cave's safety.

He spread the grasses out in the Store to dry and hurried back into the thorn trees. Smoke drifted from the shaft but there turned out to be far more in the cavern and Jojo gasped when he saw why. It came from his cave!

CHAPTER 46

Jo crept along the top of the wall, braced himself, and peered into his cave. He expected everything to be charred, including Lee, Griffy, and his treasures, but everything looked normal except for the pall of smoke.

'You missed the fireworks,' came Lee's voice from the murk.

'Are you alright?' asked Jojo, straining to see her.

'Yes, but the feather's burned up.'

'Maybe it was a bad idea to put it in the fire,' he said, trying to keep the resentment from his voice.

'I didn't *put* them in the fire,' said Lee, emerging from the gloom with Griffy perched on her shoulder. 'I didn't get the chance.'

'What do you mean?'

'As soon as I brought the coals in, there were sparks and booms and things whizzing past my head,' she said, and shuddered. 'By the time I could see again, the feather had gone.' She drew a shaky breath. 'At least Griffy enjoyed the show.'

'So, you didn't actually see the feather burn up?'

'There was fire in the air, Jojo!'

'It might have been the pheonix coming to life again,' said Jojo, desperate his golden feather wasn't simply a pile of ash. 'And then it might have flown away.'

'That's a pretty wild idea coming from someone who took ages to even admit it was a feather.'

'It's possible it flew away,' persisted Jojo. 'And you said Griffy enjoyed the show.'

'What's that got to do with it?'

'I don't know,' admitted Jojo.

Lee's brows kinked. 'It's a good point though.'

'Why?'

'A mythic creature like a griffin might be pleased to see another mythic creature like a phoenix.'

'Or pleased to see it burn up,' countered Jojo. 'They might be enemies.'

Lee flicked her fringe from her eyes. 'Are they?'

Jojo shrugged. 'I can't remember any comics that had both of them in stories.'

'Or myths either,' said Lee, putting Griffy back in her jacket-nest.

Griffy's breast was completely covered in reddish feathers now and her side bumps were definitely wings. 'It won't be long before Griffy flies away too,' he muttered, then regretted voicing his thoughts as Lee's eyes glistened.

'It's right she flies away,' said Lee thickly. 'Who'd want to live here?'

'She'll probably visit,' said Jojo, hating to see Lee upset. 'Wild creatures remember who's been kind to them.'

'She might fly alongside us when we go to the Mountains,' said Lee, brightening. 'Even act as a guard.'

'Or scout from the air,' said Jojo, although it would be safer if Griffy *did* fly away. The Uncles would see her as a dangerously poisoned animal and Jojo doubted her welcome would be any better in the Mountains. 'I've got some bread for you,' he said suddenly. 'Sorry it's a bit squashed. I— '

Lee snatched it from his hand and crammed it into her mouth. 'I'm starving,' she said apologetically. ' Did Mary give it to you?'

'Antonella. She took pity on my bleeding head.'

'Antonella *has* no pity.'

'She's not that bad,' said Jojo, despite knowing she was. He wandered over to his treasures and sat down. At least his blue bottle and plates were still there and he leaned his head back against the stone and shut his eyes.

'I bet Antonella noticed I missed today's chores and gives me double tomorrow,' mumbled Lee, cheeks bulging. 'What was your chore?'

'Collecting grasses from the Marshes.'

'I'm surprised there's any left.'

'There weren't many and they were pretty muddy,' murmured Jojo, as Lee settled beside him.

'Did you see the serpent again?'

'I saw a massive track in the mud.'

'At the Marshes?' asked Lee anxiously.

Jojo nodded. 'And at the cemetery.'

There was a long silence. 'I've never been to the cemetery,' she muttered.

'You're not missing anything. Everything's sinking.'

'Where is it?'

'In the thorn trees above the Marshes.'

'What were you doing up there?' asked Lee.

'I heard a noise I thought was the serpent.'

'And was it?'

'No.' There was another long silence. 'My family's buried there.'

Lee's warm hand gripped his. 'Are the graves marked?' Jojo shook his head. 'Then how do you know they're buried there?'

'Markus told me,' said Jojo and took a shuddering breath. 'It was part of his speech at First Meal about why we're all staying here; about how I kept my faith in God by rescuing the cross even though my family's dead.' Jojo screwed his eyes shut but tears escaped anyway.

'So you found their graves,' said Lee in a small voice.

Jojo shook his head. 'Nothing's labelled,' he croaked, and buried his face in his arms.

Lee pulled him close but she didn't speak until Jojo could breathe again. 'I think Markus lied,' she said steadily. 'If your family washed up dead, no one would know who they were, would they? And if they washed up alive, and then died, someone would have told you. Probably not Markus, because he uses *everything* and *everyone* to get his own way, but one of the Aunts would have told you. Mary certainly would have.'

Jojo sleeved his face. 'Maybe I was stupid to hope anyway,' he said thickly. 'No one's washed up for ages.'

'Hope is never stupid,' said Lee with such conviction that Jojo's own hope woke. 'And while no one's washed up for ages *here*, people probably washed up all along the coast and might still be washing up. But Markus won't let us find out. He's got it stuck in his brain that God gave us this place and not only won't *he* shift, but he won't let anyone else shift either. It's why he said what he said about your family.'

Lee's hand gave Jojo's shoulder a final pat and withdrew. 'I'm going to believe that my father's alive until I know for sure he isn't and you need to believe the same about your family.'

Jojo had no idea what to believe anymore and he took a steadying breath. 'There's smoke at the cemetery.'

'Smoke? But how—'

'It's traveled up the tunnel and come out of holes at the cemetery,' said Jojo and paused. 'And the skeletons went up the tunnel too.'

'Do … do you think the skeletons have something to do with the cemetery?'

'I don't know,' said Jojo, 'but the graves are sinking.'

'I want to see it,' said Lee suddenly.

'It's not very nice.'

'I'll go on my own,' said Lee. 'You don't have to come.'

'No! The serpent might be there.'

'And you're going to protect me?' asked Lee dryly.

'At least I know how it acted last time.'

'Which was to let you go, which was really weird.'

'Yes,' said Jojo uneasily, reminded that worst things than the serpent might be lurking.

'Let's go,' said Lee briskly. 'I'll starve to death if I miss Last Meal as well.'

Jojo's drinking dish lay where he'd left it and he put it with the plates. They looked the same and he didn't know whether to be relieved or disappointed.

Griffy hopped about and Lee picked her up. 'What is it, Griffy?' she crooned, and set her back in the jacket, but Griffy refused to stay there.

'Just bring her with us,' said Jojo, keen to make a start.

'But what if she flies off?'

'Then it'll be her time to go.'

CHAPTER 47

Jojo worried that Griffy would slow them down but she perched on Lee's shoulder like a pirate's parrot. Her eyes were really red in the daylight and darted everywhere as if excited to explore the outside world. They kept to the trees to avoid being seen by wandering Finders and only came down to the Stream as they neared the Marshes, but there was no sign of the serpent's muddy print. 'The track was here,' said Jojo, pointing with his stick.

'The rain probably washed it away,' said Lee, and Jojo nodded. He'd forgotten about the downpour that had rinsed him on the way back. 'Where's the cemetery?' asked Lee.

'Straight up the slope. I'll lead,' he said, wanting to check for the serpent's track. He expected Lee to argue but she followed in silence which helped Jojo listen for sounds of slithering or squelching. The cemetery was as grim as he recalled and Griffy fluttered her bony wings as if she disliked it too.

Lee simply stared and it was Jojo who spoke. 'Awful, isn't it?'

'You can hardly tell where one grave ends and another begins, and they're all over the place,' she muttered. 'They should face east *and* be labelled. *Markus* should have labelled them!'

Jojo poked at the mud with his stick. 'Mary said there were so many dead when they arrived they didn't have time to bury them all before some were washed back into the ocean.'

'I bet *their* friends didn't wash back,' said Lee bitterly. 'I bet Markus looked after *them*!'

'Not very well,' said Jojo, gazing about.

'No, it's a rotten place for a cemetery. Markus probably chose it because the ground was easy to dig, though I bet he didn't do any digging!'

Lee was angry but Jojo sensed it was her way of dealing with grief. He wished *he* got angry instead of having a black hole open up inside him. Lee was peering at the branch-crosses but Jojo stayed where he was. The graves were unmarked but he knew why she had to check them.

'Jojo? Look at this.' She was staring at a grave and Jojo's heart thudded as he picked his way over. He was relieved the cross was bare of writing but then he noticed a giant claw stuck in the mud. 'Do you think it's from a bird like the one near the shaft?'

'Big Talons?'

'Is that what you call it?'

'I've seen it a few times but not lately …' he paused, as he wondered whether the torn off claw was the reason Big Talons had disappeared. Lee suddenly gripped his arm. The undergrowth was moving except it wasn't undergrowth but a mighty sweep of grey-green scales.

'It's trapping us,' whispered Lee.

Lee was right! The serpent was encircling the cemetery! But before Jojo could move, Griffy launched from Lee's shoulder.

'Griffy!' screamed Lee.

Jojo thought Griffy had fled but she flew straight at the serpent's head. The serpent hissed like a stream train, trees splintered, and Griffy's squeals added to the ruckus. 'Quick, while we have a chance!'

Jojo scrambled away between the graves and Lee followed but she stopped at the edge of the trees. 'It'll hurt Griffy!' she gasped, and went to dash back.

Jojo grabbed her arm. 'Griffy's clever!' he gabbled. 'She'll fly away!' Lee stared at him wide-eyed and then there was the crack and flash of lightning. 'What—' began Jojo.

'It's the phoenix,' cried Lee. 'It's helping Griffy. We have to help her too!' But then Griffy's squeals fell silent and Lee tried to wrench herself free. 'It's killed her!' she sobbed.

'We need to get out of here,' said Jojo urgently. 'If it's killed Griffy it'll kill you too and then Griffy will have sacrificed her life for nothing.' Jojo was sure he'd read that somewhere but it was still true. Tears tracked down Lee's muddy face but she didn't argue. 'We'll go back to the cave,' said Jojo. 'If Griffy's injured, she'll go there too.'

Lee stumbled away and Jojo followed. Commonsense told him Griffy was dead and if his feather pieces *had* miraculously turned into a phoenix, he dreaded what might happen next. Jojo was still on the wall when Lee disappeared into the cave and he heard her shocked exclamation and quickened his pace. He half expected to see a horribly injured Griffy, or the phoenix in all its dangerous fiery glory, or both, but he saw Raj instead.

CHAPTER 48

Jojo had no idea how long Raj had been there but it would've taken him just a few minutes to find Jojo's treasures. Luckily Griffy and the feather pieces had gone because while keeping Griffy was clearly against the Uncles' rules, it was nothing compared to stealing the Uncles' cross.

Lee stood over Raj, hands on hips, but Raj seemed relaxed as he sat propped against the wall. 'So, the Uncles told you to spy on us,' accused Lee.

'No,' replied Raj calmly.

'Then why are you here?'

'I followed the smoke.'

Jojo's gaze jerked to the smouldering bucket of coals. The smoke that had invaded the tunnel now headed in the opposite direction out towards the cavern opening on the cliff-face and he hastily tossed some of Griffy's water on them. The coals hissed and the cave filled with smoke.

'That wasn't very smart,' coughed Lee.

'No,' agreed Jojo, but nor was it very *smart* to leave the coals burning in the first place.

'Most people are at Last Meal,' said Raj, getting to his feet and brushing himself down. 'But if you want this place to stay secret, it's best not to have a fire.'

'Are you going to tell people about it?' demanded Lee.

'I can understand why you want to get away from the Town but if you miss too many meals, Mary will ask people to keep an eye out for you, just like she asked me.'

Raj nodded and disappeared out the cave door but Jojo didn't speak until he heard the scrape of Raj's descent down the cliff. 'At least Raj doesn't know about the shaft,' he muttered. Lee's head was down and he sighed. 'We should get back before Mary sends someone else looking for us.' The cave seemed horribly empty without Griffy and her abandoned jacket-nest made it worse.

'Mary won't need to send anybody if Raj tells her about the cave,' she said dully. 'He didn't say he wouldn't, did he?'

'No.'

'And we need to wait for Griffy or at least I do. You go if you want.'

Jojo was annoyed at being made to sound like a deserter. 'We *both* need to eat,' he pointed out. 'You're not going to be much use to Griffy if you're too weak with hunger to do anything.' Lee said nothing and Jojo took a steadying breath. 'Let's go eat and then come straight back.'

'But what if Griffy comes back injured and we're not here?'

'We won't be gone long. She'll probably just snuggle down in her nest and sleep.'

Lee didn't speak again until they reached the slope above the Town and Jojo didn't feel like talking either. He'd never felt less like joining those in the Town below.

'If Griffy doesn't come back, I'm not staying any longer,' said Lee woodenly.

The question as to whether Jojo would go too hung in the air between them and he licked his lips. 'But if your family washes up they won't know where you are.'

'Nobody's washed up for ages.'

'How do you know? We don't spend a lot of time in the Town.'

Lee's head came up. 'Noticed any new boys in your Dorm?' she challenged. Jojo shook his head. 'Any new people eating in the Kitchens?' Jojo shook his head again. 'Let's face it, Jojo, anyone who's going to wash up already has. This is it,' she said, gesturing to the Town below. 'And unless we leave, this is all it will ever be.'

'If Griffy's hurt, she'll need time to heal,' persisted Jojo.

'And she'll get it but then I'm going.'

'I've still got the dragon to look after,' said Jojo wildly.

'So you're admitting the plates are a loong now? Better late than never, I suppose.'

'I don't know what the plates are but they're alive in some way and I can't just leave them behind for Axel to smash up.'

'Maybe this time the loong will smash up Axel,' said Lee grimly.

People were moving about in the Town which told Jojo Last Meal had finished. 'Best get down there before they close the Kitchens,' he said, glad to change the subject, but then something bright streaked across the clouds and shouts erupted below.

'It's the phoenix,' said Lee excitedly.

'Or a meteor,' suggested Jojo.

'Well let's hope the Uncles' think so too and not just stubborn people like you,' she muttered, and stomped off down the slope.

The Kitchens were all but empty and the tea-tub *was* empty so they had to settle for water. At least Mary was in charge. She filled their bowls to the brim and gave them extra helpings of bread, then served herself and settled beside them. 'And how are you feeling today, Jojo?' she rasped.

'Fine,' he said, hoping she wouldn't ask what he'd been doing as well.

'No more headaches or dizziness?'

'I feel normal.'

'Whatever normal means now a days,' said Mary cheerfully and took a slurp of water. Jojo glanced at Lee but she'd bent over her food which meant he'd have to deal with Mary's questioning alone. 'Your Activity was to fetch reeds from the Marshes,' continued Mary, taking another slurp. 'Any sign of that big serpent?'

Mary grinned as if they shared a joke and Jojo was tempted to pretend everything was fine but he'd be lying. 'It was up at the cemetery,' he said softly.

Mary's hair danced in surprise. 'Up at the cemetery? What were you doing up there?'

'I saw a track I thought was the serpent's and went to find out.'

'That was a risky thing to do given it's already attacked you,' said Mary, and paused. 'This isn't an easy place for any of us, especially without our families, but its safer than other places along the coast.' Her gnarly hand closed over his, roughened by work but warm. 'Don't go looking for danger, Jojo, when there's more than enough of it looking for you.'

CHAPTER 49

Lee had quit the Kitchens by the time Jojo finished, and he expected to make the trip back to his cave alone but she waited for him in the shadows. 'What did Mary say?' she asked, as they set off together.

'You should've hung around to find out,' said Jojo irritably.

'Oh, you're much better at answering questions than me.'

'I don't have much choice given you always dodge them.' His neck prickled and he stared around but saw nothing amiss.

'Well?' prompted Lee.

'She asked if I'd seen the serpent again and when I told her it was up at the cemetery she said not to go looking for danger.' Jojo peered about again and heard a faint wash of sound.

'What is it?' asked Lee, her gaze on his face.

'The birds are back.' Now he really listened, their muted calls were unmistakable.

'You're right but aren't birds supposed to roost at night?'

'Yes but the nights here have never been quiet.'

'Whatever scared them away must have gone,' said Lee.

'Who knows? We don't know what scared them away in the first place.'

'Well, there's the serpent, the Kraken, and the pterodactyls,' said Lee, listing them off on her fingers. 'And maybe the loong plates and bits of phoenix feather *if* the birds sensed them.'

'And don't forget Griffy' added Jojo.

'No,' said Lee, and quickened her pace.

The bird calls were louder in the thorn trees but so were the creaks and booms and deep, almost musical notes Jojo remembered from his early days in the Town. In places the ground seemed to vibrate as if someone played an immense organ. Lee said nothing about the sounds and Jojo wondered if she were too worried about Griffy to notice.

He followed her down the shaft and through into the cavern but her shadowy outline had stopped short of the cave and when he joined her, he saw why. An eerie glow flowed from its doorway.

'If it's the phoenix, we don't want to be trapped in the cave with it,' he whispered.

'But what if Griffy's in there too?'

For a moment they simply stared at each other and then Jojo crept forward and peered in. Something moved in the corner where he stored his treasures, its outline dark against the glow, but it wasn't some huge, fiery bird.

'Griffy's here—' he began, but Lee pushed past him and Jojo followed. Griffy had lost a lot of feathers and was gashed along her back but it was the plates Jojo stared at. They glowed with a bright blue light.

Griffy's eyes gleamed despite her injuries and she showed no sign of wanting to quit her bed of glowing plates, despite them being colder and harder than her jacket-nest. 'I think the loong's helping her heal,' said Lee softly.

The possibility was no more ridiculous than anything else that had happened, supposed Jojo, like his plates having changed *again*. Griffy blocked much of his view but the blue bottle had disappeared which probably explained the blue light.

'We need to get Griffy some fish,' said Lee, worried again. 'She must be starving.'

'We're not climbing down the cliff in the dark,' said Jojo, with a firmness that surprised even himself. 'We'll get some fish as soon as it's light.' Lee must have seen the sense of it because for once she didn't argue.

Jojo settled with his back against the wall and Lee joined him but neither spoke. Jojo was weary but too much had happened that day for him to sleep. Markus's claim that Jojo's family were dead, Lee's claim that Markus lied, discovering the cemetery with its sinking graves, then the serpent's attack, Griffy and probably the phoenix coming to their aid, and Raj turning up at the cave.

Jojo kept thinking about how people came up with reasons for something they really believed in and wondered if it were what he did. He wanted to believe his family were alive and so, because they weren't here, they must be somewhere else. It was probably why Lee wanted to go to the Mountains, Jojo suddenly realised. If her family weren't here, then they might be there.

Lee's breathing told him she was asleep and he crept out of the cave to the cavern's entrance. He hoped the stars were back, even if they brought the ghost ship and skeletons, but the night was full of cloud. He stared at the grey waves, heavy with trash, and struggled to remember an ocean that was clean, and bright with the blue of day, and moon-silvered at night.

He feared that one day he'd forget about the world of Before and be grateful for the dirty, broken future that stretched before him. He half shook his head. Things wouldn't seem so bleak after he'd slept. But as he turned back to the cavern's darkness there was a sharp crack followed by several more.

He instinctively crouched in the shadows and Lee was suddenly beside him. 'Jojo? What is it?'

'I don't know,' he said, but he did.

'It's gunfire,' she whispered. 'Maybe the Town's being attacked.'

'By whom?' He sensed Lee's shrug and then a brilliant light streaked across the sky followed by a barrage of cracks.

'It's the Uncles,' she hissed. 'They're shooting at the phoenix!'

'But where did they get the guns?'

'Who knows, but if they're using them against the phoenix, they'll use them against Griffy *and* against your loong. We need to leave, Jojo, and we need to leave soon before they kill them all.'

CHAPTER 50

Jojo didn't feel like he'd slept at all but it was light when Lee nudged him awake and he wearily followed her down the cliff. The beach was as grey as the sky and the air almost as clammy as the cave's as they wordlessly collected fish. Jojo guessed Lee was thinking about the *exciting* trek to the Mountains but all he could think of were the warm beds and food they'd leave behind.

The blood crabs were up early too and Jojo comforted himself there'd be no crabs in the Mountains but there might be no people either, just trash burning as the Uncles' claimed and then what would they do?

He found himself staring in the Town's direction, worried armed Uncles would appear around the headland and Lee stared that way too. 'I wonder where they keep the guns,' she muttered, as she dropped fish in the bucket. 'Obviously not in the Store. Were there cupboards in the Uncles' Dorm?'

'I didn't see any but they have their own little cubicles.'

'Lucky them,' she said sourly. 'I wonder what other secrets they hide in there.'

Jojo blinked. 'What do you mean?'

'If they had time to stash guns on their boats maybe they had time to stash medicines.'

Jojo stared at the trash-lines sightlessly. The possibility the Uncles kept medicines just for themselves was horrible but even *if* they *did* have something to fix his foot, there were no nurses or doctors to use it. Not that it made him feel any better because *if* the Uncles *did* have medicines, Aunts like Mary must know.

Jojo licked his lips. Mary had been genuinely upset about there being nothing to help people like Jojo, he reasoned, so it was unlikely there was a secret stash of medicines. But as a Boater, Mary had to know about the guns and yet after the serpent's first attack, she simply said she'd warn the Aunts, not send the Uncles after it with guns, so she hadn't been honest about the guns, unless … Jojo's mouth went dry.

'What is it?' demanded Lee.

'Nothing,' he muttered, and scooped up another fish.

'You look like you did after Markus bullied you. Tell me!'

'I was just thinking,' said Jojo reluctantly. 'What if the guns we heard last night didn't belong to the Uncles?'

Lee stared at him blankly. 'You mean the Town's been attacked?' she asked slowly. Jojo nodded. 'But … who'd attack it?'

'People who want what we've got, I suppose.'

Lee stared at the headland again. 'I think we should get off the beach.'

'So do I. Have you got enough fish?'

No. We need a bucketful in case we can't come back straight away.'

'Let's get them then,' said Jojo quickly, and they hurried up and down the sand, grabbing anything not obviously rotten, then climbed back up the cliff.

Griffy gobbled down the fish as fast as Lee mashed them and Jojo wondered how long even a bucketful would last her. The morning light showed a second gash on Griffy's side but it was already part healed like the one on her back. 'She's a quick healer,' said Jojo, and wished his foot was too.

'*And* a good killer of serpents.'

'We don't know it's dead but she's certainly brave. She protected you,' he added.

'She protected both of us, as did the phoenix, and don't say we *don't know that*.'

'I feel like I don't know *anything* anymore,' he admitted. 'Nothing makes sense.'

'That's because you keep comparing it to Before.' Jojo said nothing and Lee glanced sideways at him. 'Do you remember when you first started maths?'

'What's that got to do with anything?'

'Maths has its own rules, right?' Jojo nodded. 'Well, I'm guessing *here's* got its own rules too. The way the ocean works and the seasons *if there are any*, and the creatures that live here, all have their own rules. I'm guessing this place has *nothing* to do with where we came from or the time before the oceans swamped the lands.'

'Are you saying there's no way back?' asked Jojo thickly.

'I don't know. The old world might still be out there somewhere but it's not *here*, is it? The serpent, the loong, the Kraken, the phoenix, Griffy, birds like Big Talons, the ghost ship, the skeletons …'

'You're saying we're *here* and these things are *here* so we have to deal with them *here*, not try to explain them away as if we were in Before?'

'Yes.'

There was a long silence. 'When did you figure all this out?'

Lee gave a shaky smile. 'It wasn't straight away,' she admitted. 'I've been thinking about the Mountains and what we'll find there. I used to think they'd be like Before but why would they be any different to the coast?'

'Then why go? It's going to be a hard journey,' said Jojo, *and a dangerous one.*

'Because they *have* to be better than here.'

'They might be worse.'

'Then we'll keep on moving,' snapped Lee, and sighed. 'We already know what it's like *here*, Jojo, and *here* might've been bearable without the Uncles, but they're not going anywhere even if the Town falls in the sea. I'm not living my life the way they want me to even if you're happy to.'

'I've never said I'm happy to live like they want,' retorted Jojo. Lee said nothing and Jojo took a steadying breath. 'I just don't see things as clearly as you. I'm not that smart.'

'You're the one who got all the bits of phoenix feather back together *and* found the bits of loong *and* escaped the serpent *twice*,' said Lee.

'*And* I'm the one who keeps hoping the Uncles will change even though they won't and that my family will wash up, even though …' He stopped. Common sense told him his mum and dad and Davy were dead but saying it out loud ended even the slenderest of hopes.

'I've kind of given up on my father washing up,' admitted Lee. 'If he's alive, he's alive somewhere else which means I'm on my own here and have to make my own decisions.'

'You're not on your own,' said Jojo, and gave her hand a squeeze.

'Not while we have Griffy,' said Lee tremulously.

'And the phoenix,' said Jojo.

'And your loong,' added Lee.

'Which is still a pile of plates,' said Jojo lightly.

'But with a bottle eye and sickle claw.' Jojo opened his mouth to disagree and shut it again. This place *did* have its own rules so there was no point arguing. He just needed to sort out exactly what those rules were.

CHAPTER 51

Griffy ate quickly but as the light grew, so did Jojo's worry about missing First Meal. 'We need to get back,' he said finally, despite fearing what they headed back to. 'Leave the rest of the fish on the floor so she can help herself.'

'But I need to break them up.'

'She'll have to get her own food once we leave,' pointed out Jojo.

'I hadn't thought of that.'

'There's plenty of fish in the Stream and Griffy's clever,' said Jojo quickly.

'We might not follow the Stream,' said Lee, but she stood and wiped her fishy hands on her trousers.

'We have no way to carry water so we'll have to.'

'But—'

'Let's talk about it as we walk,' said Jojo impatiently. 'Along with everything else we have to sort out.'

The journey back gave Jojo time to think about what the *everything else* was. As well as having nothing to carry water *or* food in, they had no way of getting food once they passed the nut groves. The Mountains were probably colder too and they only had the light clothes that had washed up, not the heavy jackets and boots of his camping trips with his dad. To add to their problems, Lee would have to carry Griffy and he would have to carry the plates.

The thorn trees echoed reassuringly with bird calls but Jojo grew anxious again as they neared the Town and Lee dropped her voice as soon as they left the trees' shelter.

The Kitchens' smoke hung in the air as usual but the streets were deserted which was odd given that First Meal must be almost over.

'Where is everyone?' whispered Lee.

'Maybe they've gone off to their Activities', said Jojo, keeping his voice low too. But there were no sounds of hammering or of anything else.

'I don't like this,' whispered Lee. 'It's as if everyone's left or is dead.'

'There's smoke from the ovens,' pointed out Jojo, although people might've eaten before leaving *or* being killed. The idea was horrible and he shivered.

'Maybe the gunfire last night *was* attackers,' whispered Lee, making him feel even worse.

'But someone's lit the ovens.'

'Maybe it's *them* having First Meal.'

Jojo licked his lips and then there was movement near the Kitchens and Lee grabbed his arm and yanked him down. A group appeared in the street, disappeared behind the Washrooms, then emerged and marched off up stream. Markus led with Axel and Ben behind him followed by Uncles and Finders, and all of them carried what could only be rifles.

'Our brave boys going off to war,' said Lee sarcastically, but Jojo was too relieved to say anything. 'They'll bring back the serpent's head and claim *they* killed it, not Griffy and the phoenix.'

'They're hunting the phoenix, remember. Markus doesn't believe in the serpent.'

'Markus will kill *anything* he says isn't one of *God's creatures* and they're searching *outside* the Town, Jojo. It means they'll eventually find our cave, kill Griffy and the phoenix, *if* it goes back there, and smash up the plates. The loong will never have the chance to live again.'

Jojo's heart missed. It meant they mightn't have even a single day before they must leave. 'Let's get to the Kitchens and find out what's going on.'

'If Antoinette's in charge the only thing we'll find out is that we're lazy and don't do our chores properly, and we already know that.'

Jojo's heart sank as they entered the Kitchens because Antoinette *was* in charge. She glared at them with her scraped back face as she doled out the food but could hardly accuse them of being late given Aunts such as Mary still ate. Jojo settled beside her and Lee sat on Jojo's other side and put her head down but it was Mary who spoke first. 'I worry when you two spend your nights outside the Dorms,' she said, hair dancing as her gaze darted between them. 'You know how dangerous these lands are, Jojo, you better than most, and the safest place for you *both* at night is in the Dorms.'

Jojo's face warmed but then Lee unexpectedly spoke. 'The Dorms aren't safe,' she said baldly. 'There's nothing to stop them falling into the sea like the Sanctuary.'

'The Uncles are keeping a careful eye on the cracks,' said Mary.

'That's no use if they open up in the middle of the night like last time,' said Lee.

Jojo cringed but Mary didn't seem offended. 'That's true,' she said mildly. 'Which is why Markus has set watchers to report any movement at all.'

'They still wouldn't be fast enough to save the Town,' persisted Lee.

'The Uncles consider that the land around the Town is stable,' explained Mary. 'The Sanctuary was built near the cliffs, remember, and the heavy rains weakened the soil. It's been dry since.' Mary paused. 'Markus is more concerned with other threats now.'

'What other threats?' demanded Lee.

'If you'd been here last night, you would've seen strange things in the skies.'

'Like the leather-winged birds?' interjected Jojo. If the Uncles thought the phoenix was just a shiny variation they might return their guns to storage.

Mary shook her head. 'As long as they stay on the beach, the Uncles are content to let them clean up the rotting things there. No, what lit up the skies last night was something else entirely.' Mary paused. 'We think it was a phoenix.'

CHAPTER 52

Jojo managed not to look at Lee but he guessed she was staring open-mouthed at Mary too. 'A phoenix is a mythical bird that's reborn through fire,' explained Mary, mistaking their shock for confusion. 'Markus believes such things have no place here, and after being attacked by an enormous serpent, I think you'd agree, Jojo.'

'But Markus doesn't believe in the serpent,' said Jojo, and felt his face fire.

Mary gave a small smile. 'He saw the phoenix with his own eyes, as did most of the Town, so he certainly believes in it.'

'Markus hasn't gone after the pterodactyls on the beach and they don't belong here either,' challenged Lee.

'I wouldn't call them *pterodactyls*,' said Mary evenly. 'But whatever they are, they stay out of the Town.'

'The Bible compares the phoenix coming alive again with Christ coming alive again,' persisted Lee. 'Why would Markus want to kill it?'

Jojo's face grew hotter and he stared at the table but the only sound was the slurp of Mary's tea. 'That might be something you can talk to Markus about,' she said, gathering up her bowl and mug. 'In the meantime, the Uncles ask that everyone stays in the Town where it's safest. It's why there's no Activities today.' Mary shuffled off the bench but Jojo couldn't think of anything to say before she moved away.

'Markus picks and chooses what he believes from the Bible,' muttered Lee.

'Are there griffins in the Bible?' asked Jojo curiously.

Lee shrugged. 'It mentions the dragon *and* the serpent, even though they're basically the same thing which is the devil in disguise.

'What about loongs?'

'The Bible doesn't use the Chinese name and loongs are a bit different too.'

'How?'

'They don't have wings or breathe fire and they usually live in water not caves.' Lee took a swig of tea. ' They're more like gods too.'

'You think the plates belong to a loong because they *washed* up?' Lee nodded and Jojo forced a smile. 'And they're *good* gods, right?'

'That's like asking whether a tree is good, Jojo. Trees are just trees and loongs are just loongs.'

Trees don't try to kill you, thought Jojo uncomfortably. He knew mythic creatures weren't like cats or dogs but he was pretty sure Griffy and the phoenix had come to their rescue during the serpent attack *unless* they were simply natural enemies of the serpent. Jojo licked his lips. Whatever Griffy and the phoenix were, they didn't deserve to be killed by *anyone*, let alone Markus and his band of Finder bullies, and the plates deserved the right to mend themselves, grow into something strong, and find their own home somewhere better.

No Activities meant there were more people in the streets which made it harder to find somewhere quiet to plan their departure. No one followed when they set off towards the cliffs and not only because a chill breeze swept over the exposed land. The cracks looked even worse in daylight and there was no sign of the watchers Mary said Markus had set.

'How can Markus say the Town's safe,' said Lee in disgust.

'God's testing us, remember,' said Jojo, and shivered. The phoenix had saved him when the Sanctuary had crashed into the sea and now he needed to save *it*. 'I think we should go tonight,' he said abruptly.

Lee blinked in surprise. 'But Griffy needs time to heal.'

'The longer we wait, the more likely it is Markus will kill the phoenix and then he and the Finders will search the cliffs for any more *unnatural* creatures and find Griffy.' Lee stared at him in horror and he took a steadying breath. 'Markus mightn't work out the link between the gold cross and the phoenix, but he'll certainly see the plates as unnatural and when Axel tells him I had an identical plate, he'll see me as unnatural too.'

'Do … do you think Markus would hurt us?'

'If he thinks we're in league with *unnatural* creatures, he might just throw us out to protect the Town, but he might also do something worse.' Jojo made a poor attempt at a smile. 'I don't want to hang around to find out.'

'I think you're right,' muttered Lee. Her hand fumbled for his and for a long moment they stood in silence, staring out to where the grey sky met the grey ocean with its endless cargo of trash. Screeches heralded the leather-winged birds and they watched them rise above the cliff then disappear as they swooped over the beach.

'I wish …' murmured Lee, and stopped.

'I wish too,' said Jojo softly. 'But we're here and our choices are to stay or go. Staying means risking things we care about like Griffy but going risks our lives because we don't know if there's anyone or *anything* in the Mountains, or *anywhere*, for that matter.'

Lee dropped his hand and pushed the hair from her eyes. 'Raj said there's been smoke from the Mountains lots of times.' Not *lots* of times, thought Jojo, but held his silence. Lee wasn't the only one who needed hope.

CHAPTER 53

The cracks meant no one bothered them on the cliffs and Jojo had plenty of time to wonder whether Markus had found the serpent's body *if* it were dead, and if not, whether it still lurked in the Stream he and Lee must drink from on their trek to the Mountains.

The thought of leaving still made his stomach clench but now so did the thought of staying. 'We need to figure out what to take with us,' he said.

'Is there anything useful in the Store?' asked Lee.

'There's plenty of building stuff like wood and tin, and there's rope and wire and buckets.'

'Any bottles?'

'Not that I've seen.'

'Packs? Boots? Rain jackets? Tents? Sleeping bags?' asked Lee, with a lopsided grin.

'I think all the clothing's in the Washrooms.'

'And I'm guessing any blankets are already in the Dorms,' she muttered.

Jojo wondered whether it were possible to smuggle blankets past multiple sets of eyes but even if it were, blankets were heavy. 'We have to carry *everything* we take, remember,' he said, thinking of his hikes with his dad. It hadn't taken Jojo long to regret the extra jumpers and snacks he'd insisted on taking.

'No one's going to notice if we dress in layers in the Washrooms, especially if they've gone to bed,' said Lee. 'Layers will keep us warm at night and we can bundle up other stuff in spare shirts. You know, use the sleeves like pack-straps,' she added when Jojo looked at her blankly.

'That's a really good idea,' he said, although it didn't solve their water-carrying problem. 'It's a shame we don't have the bottles. Maybe I should ask the dragon for them back,' he added lightly.

'Not sure that would work,' said Lee, 'but we could look on the beach. We need to get Griffy some more fish anyway.'

'Mary says everyone's to stay in the Town,' Jojo reminded her.

'According to Markus,' scoffed Lee. 'He and his brave soldiers have probably gone all the way to the nut groves by now unless they stopped at the cemetery to kill the *nonexistent* serpent.'

Jojo licked his lips. Markus might be absent but there were plenty of people in the Town to report them and then Markus would question them about *everything*. 'You're really scared of him, aren't you?' said Lee softly.

'He's a bully,' muttered Jojo, his gaze on the horizon.

'I hate bullies,' said Lee, with surprising ferocity. 'They pick on my Asian eyes.'

'They pick on my brother too,' said Jojo, recalling how sweet, happy Davy was targeted. 'He's got Down Syndrome.'

'What's that?'

'It makes you look and act different.'

'It doesn't matter what you've got, bullies will find *something* to be nasty about.' She flicked back her hair. '*If* we're seen and *if* we're reported, Markus can only get us *if* we go back for Last Meal.' Which was true but Jojo didn't want to miss what was probably their last decent meal. 'I'm worried they'll find Griffy,' she added.

'We'll get the clothes now then,' said Jojo.

'Or we could sneak back after dark,' suggested Lee.

Jojo shook his head. 'If Markus *has* found the serpent, he'll hunt down everything else he decides is *unnatural*. Now might be our only chance to get Griffy away.'

Jojo strolled into the Washrooms as if his only concern were to wash his dirty face and hands but his heart banged like a drum. He was to meet Lee back at the cave with the clothes *if* everything went well and if not … Lee hadn't wanted to talk about what to do if things going went wrong but Jojo's dad had insisted they had a plan if they became separated on hikes, and in the end, they decided that if one of them hadn't reached the cave by dark, the other would grab Griffy and the plates, head to the nut groves, and wait there for three days before going on alone.

The thought of Markus interrogating him sent shivers down Jojo's back and his hands shook as he filled a bucket from the tub, as if about to wash, then sorted through the clothes pile. There were lots of things his size which meant lots of boys his age had probably drowned. The understanding added to his churn and his arms were full of clothing before he realised he needed bigger clothes if they were to fit over those underneath.

He was searching for larger ones when footsteps sounded and he fled with his haul into a cubicle and shut the door. The Washrooms filled up with Finders and he recognised Ben and Axel's voices amongst the excited babble. No one seemed to notice the closed cubicle and the sound of splashing told Jojo the Finders washed straight from the tub. He pressed his ear to the door and discovered they had fired on a giant snake near the Marshes before it'd disappeared into the Stream. Axel boasted he'd wounded it but Markus had ordered them back to the Town before he could investigate further. Apparently Markus now met with the rest of the Uncles to decide how to eliminate the *two* ungodly creatures that threatened the Town.

It seemed an age before the Washroom fell silent and Jojo eased the door open. He'd decided to wear the clothes rather than carry them, because carrying them was obvious even from a distance while looking like an overstuffed scarecrow was only noticeable up close, and he had no intention of being up close with anyone. But as he slipped around the side of the Washrooms, he collided with a Finder coming the other way.

CHAPTER 54

They both stumbled backwards and Jojo racked his brains for something to say as he raised his eyes. It was Raj, who seemed to wander about as much as Jojo but Jojo's relief was short-lived. Raj's hard gaze was fixed on the collars and cuffs that emerged from Jojo's shirt. 'Why on earth are you wearing so many clothes?' he demanded.

'I'm feeling feverish,' said Jojo, with a burst of inspiration. 'I can't seem to warm up.'

Raj's gaze flicked to Jojo's gashed forehead. 'Maybe you should rest more. There's plenty of time to do nothing in since we were banned from leaving.'

'Did … did you go on the hunting expedition?' asked Jojo.

'If that's what you call it.'

'And did you find anything?' pursued Jojo, desperate to know the serpent's exact whereabouts.

'Yes, but *what* depends on who you ask. Was the snake that attacked you just a supersized python or Satan in disguise? And are we having a perfectly normal meteor shower or being threatened by the phoenix of myth?'

'Axel said he shot the serpent.'

'Axel,' muttered Raj. 'Him and his hot head friends fired so many shots he might well have. It didn't exactly move quickly, in fact, it already looked injured to me, not that it'll stop Axel from boasting about his *heroism*.'

'What will happen now?'

'I'm guessing Markus will use the Bible to justify killing the snake *and* the phoenix, *if* there is such a thing.'

Jojo swallowed dryly. 'Is that what the Bible says we should do?'

Raj shrugged. 'It's just a guess, Jojo. I'm not Christian but Satan's often shown as a snake. Anyway, Markus wants us all at Last Meal so make sure to tell Lee. He'll probably reveal some *grand plan* for keeping us safe and he'll be angry if people miss out on hearing all about it.'

Jojo wandered off towards the thorn trees hoping he looked like an absent-minded Flotsam taking a stroll. He half expected shouts ordering him back and didn't speed up until he reached the trees, then he hurried on, scrambled down the shaft, and hastened to his cave. He hoped Lee was already there but the cave was empty.

At least Griffy seemed pleased to see him. She flapped around the walls before she settled back in her jacket nest and Jojo squatted beside her. 'Not long now,' he muttered, as he stroked her breast feathers. He didn't think Griffy would be sorry to leave the cave behind but he certainly would. It had been his special place where he could escape the older boys and enjoy the shining things he'd found in the clear water near the peak.

The plates looked the same, right down to their soft blue glow, and he cautiously lifted each in turn. He half expected to see the blue bottle embedded in them but there was no sign of it, nor the sickle, nor the first bottle. He was reminded of when he and Davy had found a cocoon and how their dad had explained the magic things going on inside. But a caterpillar had everything it needed to turn into something new and so did a starfish. Everything the dragon used had been in the sea and they were about to leave the sea far behind. It meant the dragon might never be whole.

Jojo wandered around the cave. Maybe he should put the plates back in the sea. At least it would give the dragon the chance to find what it needed, but even the thought of leaving the plates behind was unbearable. And he should be doing something more useful than fretting, he decided, like collecting fish for Griffy. Given Markus's prohibition, he was probably safe from watchers but not from any hunting party and his hands shook as he grabbed the bucket and scrambled down the cliff.

There were the usual mobs of blood crabs but no sign of the leather-winged birds and Jojo wondered if the weather were to blame. Clouds boiled high into the sky and grew blacker even as he watched. It meant rain was coming which would make tomorrow's journey miserable and if it continued, risk the Town again.

He scanned as he hurriedly collected fish but there was no sign of Finders *or* of Lee and he feared Markus had collared her and forced *everything* out of her. Common sense told him Lee would never reveal Griffy's existence and if the Uncles *did* stumble on the cave, Griffy could simply fly away, unlike the dragon, which lacked what it needed to grow itself. Jojo faltered and then setting the bucket against the cliff, hastened off up the beach.

The wind was full in Jojo's face and heavy with the sea's stench. To make matters worse, the blood crabs refused to shift and he had to struggle through the softer sand. The air took on a peppery scent and as thunder boomed, Jojo knew he should find cover, but he pushed on till he reached the stepping-stones.

They were slopped by wind-blown waves and Jojo still wore all the clothes intended to keep him warm on tomorrow's journey. He hesitated but now was his last chance to find something to help the dragon. He scrambled across them, waves soaking his trousers, but the clear patch of water at the peak had disappeared! Jojo was tempted to hightail it back shore but he plunged his hand into the water's murky depths and felt something small and rough. It was just a mussel shell, gnarly with age and shut tight and as thunder boomed again, he dropped it in his pocket and struggled back to shore.

He hurried along the beach, flinching with each new crack of thunder. Lightning doused the sky in oily light and lit something odd in the waves. For a moment he thought it was a weird piece of debris or even another ghost ship, but it was the Kraken!

CHAPTER 55

Jojo's instincts screamed at him to run but nothing would move. Enormous suckered-arms rose slowly from the sea followed by a giant hulking body, water-sleeked, and blacker than night. The monster towered over him and Jojo's head filled with visions of how it crushed ships and swallowed down their hapless crews. But then the arms faltered, swayed, and curled in upon themselves like dry leaves did in fire. And then, with a mighty surge of water, the Kraken was gone.

Jojo felt like a marionette with the strings cut. His legs gave way and he collapsed sideways into the water. It's coldness shocked him into action and he scrambled upright and ran. He later had no memory of his desperate sprint along the beach except for the blood crabs scattering and his foot roaring with pain, but pain was nothing compared to terror of the Kraken.

He reached the cliff, grabbed the bucket of fish, and climbed. Dirt drove deep under his nails as he searched for holds while the wind buffeted him and thunderclaps assaulted his ears. He finally hauled himself into the cavern, staggered to his cave, and collapsed against the wall.

'What's happened?' exclaimed Lee, but Jojo simply gasped for air. She unclenched his hand from the bucket and helped him sit. He'd been scared alone in the ocean but nothing compared to this. 'Did Markus drag you in?' she demanded, crouching beside him. Jojo shook his head. 'Then what?'

'The Kraken,' he gasped. 'It was . . . right … on … the beach.'

Even in the cave's dim light he saw her pale. 'Here?'

'Further … further along. Nearer … the Town.'

'You're soaking, Jojo. It didn't pull you in the water, did it?'

'I fell in . . . trying to get . . . away. I thought … I thought it'd … eat me.'

Jojo screwed his eyes shut, overcome with horror, and Lee's arm come around him in a fierce hug. 'You're brave, Jojo. You escaped the serpent and now you've escaped the Kraken.'

Jojo managed to raise his head. 'I didn't escape. It let me go.' They stared at each other. 'It let me go like the serpent let me go,' he said slowly, as the strangeness of it all sunk in.

'You're like a hero in a story,' said Lee, settling beside him. 'You know, like the ones who have a special sword, or magic ring, or something.'

'All I've got is a broken foot,' said Jojo hoarsely.

'And a loong,' said Lee with a shaky smile. 'Never underestimate the power of a loong.' She reached into her pocket and pulled out some bread.

'How did you get that?' Lee grinned. 'You didn't steal it, did you?' The last thing they needed was a posse of irate Aunts after them, probably led by Antonella.

'You can either eat in, at the Kitchens, or have takeaway,' said Lee nonchalantly. 'We're having takeaway.'

'But how …?

Lee took several big bites of her own bread. 'I was on my way here when someone in the Kitchens shouted about the phoenix being back and everyone rushed outside,' she said, through bulging cheeks. 'And while they were peering up at the sky, I grabbed some of the food we would've had if Markus and the idiot Finders hadn't started trying to kill things. It's just bad luck I couldn't carry any soup.'

'You did well,' said Jojo gratefully, taking another bite of bread. 'You're sure no one saw you?'

Lee shrugged. 'We'll be gone by tomorrow morning anyway, and then—' There was a flash of garish light, followed by a deafening thunderclap, and then the sound of rain, not gentle, but in a mighty pounding deluge.

Griffy hopped from her nest and Jojo thought the storm had disturbed her, but she perched on the bucket's rim and started to eat. The lightning illuminated how Griffy gripped the bucket with her back feet and used her beak and front claws to tear the fish apart. There was nothing awkward or misshapen about her now. 'She really *is* a griffin,' said Jojo in wonder.

'Yes,' said Lee proudly. 'Her front half's an eagle and her back half's a lion, and she's grown suddenly, as if she knows she has to be strong.'

'Maybe her fight with the serpent helped,' said Jojo.

'How?'

'Maybe … maybe she grew because she had to be bigger to protect us or at least to protect you.' Jojo's face warmed. 'I …I read a comic once where a griffin guarded its owner.'

'No one *owns* a griffin but I get what you mean. Loongs are guarders too but of the whole world.'

Jojo resisted pointing out they hadn't done a very good job so far but it was unfair to blame loongs for what humans had done. 'Dragons only guard their gold,' he quipped instead.

'They're really guarding the earth,' persisted Lee. 'Father said the change happened because people began to think of gold as precious rather than the earth as precious. It's why dragons live in caves,' she added, and Jojo looked at her blankly. 'Because caves are *in* the earth.'

'You know so much stuff,' muttered Jojo, feeling inadequate.

'Like I told you, father and I used to talk about the things that turn up in the Bible *and* in myths. Dragons were similar to loongs until the church made them evil so St George could kill one. It was to show that Christ was more powerful than the gods people worshipped before.'

'Wasn't the Kraken worshipped too?' asked Jojo, flinching as thunder cracked.

'Not that I know of. It's supposed to live in the deeps and eat ships and sailors.'

Jojo shuddered. 'It's not in the deeps anymore.'

'No,' agreed Lee. 'Nothing's where it's supposed to be. Maybe—' A rat-tat-tat joined the thunder outside and Griffy's tail lashed. 'Gunfire!' exclaimed Lee.

'Markus and his posse wouldn't hunt the phoenix in this weather,' said Jojo uncertainly.

'They would if they could see it,' said Lee, and hastened to the cavern's entrance. So much rain drove in they had to shield their eyes. It was the blackest night Jojo had ever seen but a slash of gold streaked across the sky to light the heaving waves below. 'The phoenix! And it's coming our way!'

Lee was right! 'It's coming to where it knows it's safe,' he choked out.

'But they'll follow it,' cried Lee. 'And then they'll find Griffy and kill her!'

CHAPTER 56

Jojo was surprised by how calm he suddenly felt. It were as if he'd finally accepted the inevitability of leaving. 'Markus and the Finders won't kill Griffy because Griffy won't be here, and neither will we.'

Lightning illuminated Lee's shocked face. 'We're leaving *now*? In this weather?'

'We have no choice.'

She gulped convulsively but nodded and they hastened back to the cave and shrugged off their outer shirts. Jojo was aware of Lee bundling up Griffy's fish as he collected the plates, knotted the shirt sleeves into loops, and threw on the make-shift pack.

The storm continued its rage but the gunfire was just as loud. 'What about the coals and buckets?' asked Lee urgently, as she scooped up Griffy and set her on her shoulder.

'We'll hide them in the darkest part of the tunnel,' said Jojo quickly, instinct keeping his voice low. They grabbed the buckets and crept onto the wall but then something roared past his head with such force the draught all but knocked him from the wall. The air filled with a hot, metallic smell but Jojo's sight had been obliterated by the creature's brilliance, and by the time his vision returned, gunfire was all around them.

They flung themselves down the wall and Jojo tossed the buckets into the shadows. The phoenix lit the tunnel ahead like a car's headlights but they stopped at the hole in the cavern's side. The sound of voices on the other side was clear.

'They're at the top of the shaft,' whispered Lee.

Jojo pressed his ear against the stone and heard enough to know the speakers guessed the shaft led to where the phoenix had gone and they could use it to beat the climbers on the cliff. The boast suggested Axel or Ben but what froze Jojo's blood was their intention to fire down the shaft first incase the phoenix lurked at the bottom.

'They're going to—' he began, but then a deafening explosion of gunfire erupted and Griffy launched from Lee's shoulder and disappeared down the tunnel.

'Griffy!' screamed Lee, and before Jojo could stop her, she sped off down the tunnel after her.

Jojo set off in pursuit but Lee was soon out of sight. He daren't slow, despite his throbbing foot, in case the Finders fired down the tunnel as well. A glow marked the phoenix's direction but he had no idea where Lee was thanks to the tunnel's twists and turns. He snatched a glanced over his shoulder as he ran, shocked by how dark it was behind. The glow in front faded too which meant the phoenix was either a long way ahead or had taken a hidden turn or even a hidden exit. The possibility he and Lee ran headlong into a maze, soon to be pitch black, was almost as scary as being shot.

He staggered to a stop and clutched his knees in an effort to breathe. He wanted to yell Lee's name but had no idea how far sound carried and didn't want any pursuers to hear him. Reason told him the Finders had stopped at the cavern because they had no lamps and he hoped Markus would be content to just drive the ungodly creature away, but he feared that Markus was too single-minded to let anyone or *anything* defeat him.

Jojo licked his dry lips. The Kitchen's tea might be full of bits but it was warm and wet, and came with new-baked bread, and fishy soup or stew. His breathing slowly eased along with the throb in his foot but he could barely see his hand in front of his face. 'Lee?' he called softly, then again more loudly but heard nothing.

The darkness was scary enough but being alone in it made it a thousand times worse. He yearned for Lee's voice or the sound of her footsteps heading his way but heard a faint scratching instead. Probably just a rats, he reassured himself, but wondered again whether something lurked in the tunnel that had shared Griffy's fish. Even if it were only rats, they might be super big and super aggressive. And then there were the pirate ghosts that had marched away down the tunnel and that now might be marching back.

Their feet had been silent but even as the thought crossed Jojo's mind, he became aware of faint glow behind him and spun. The glow disappeared and then his breath whooshed in relief as he realised it came from his makeshift pack.

He unwrapped the plates, intending to use one as a lamp, but they only glowed when kept together and so he wrapped them again and slipped the pack onto his front so that its glow was thrown forward. The light was only as bright as a very bad torch but a massive improvement on total darkness. The scratching continued as he went on, but got no closer and after while he almost forgot about it, too busy worrying about finding Lee and a way out.

The tunnel had been dry but now drips plopped from the ceiling to form dirty pools and Jojo saw strange shapes and pale blurs on the floor ahead. His stomach clenched as he guessed what they were and then two red gleams pierced the gloom. Griffy! Lee hurled herself from the shadows into his arms and he held her tight. 'It's … it's awful here,' she mumbled, her head buried in his shirt.

'Yes,' croaked Jojo. 'We're under the cemetery.'

CHAPTER 57

It was a long while before Lee could raise her head. 'I ... I guessed it was the cemetery. Griffy's eyes make enough light . . . to see a bit . . . but . . . I stopped.' She took a shuddering breath. 'I didn't want to . . . step on anything.'

Jojo didn't even want to *look* at *anything* let alone feel it underfoot. These were the remains of people who hadn't found boats or rafts or debris to cling to and who might include his mum and dad and Davy.

'At least we know where we are,' he managed to say. 'If we can climb out, we won't be far from the nut groves.'

'I'm not climbing out through a grave,' mumbled Lee.

Jojo's stomach heaved as he imagined clawing his way past a corpse but the graves were too high to reach anyway, and that wasn't their only problem. 'There mightn't be any other exits which means we might have to go back.'

'I'm not going back. They'll kill Griffy.'

'The tunnel mightn't go anywhere,' pointed out Jojo.

'The skeletons used it.'

'I'm not sure that ghosts count. They can walk through walls if they're lost.'

'So why bother using the tunnel?'

Jojo blinked. 'Good question. Maybe it leads to a ghost resort and the pirate ship was simply a cruise liner.'.

'That's not funny.'

'No,' agreed Jojo. 'But if we keep going, we need to think about what's at the other end.'

'We need to think about a *hole* to climb out of so we can get nuts *and* berries to eat *and* water to drink,' corrected Lee.

'There might actually be an opening near the nut groves,' said Jojo, and recounted Axel's boast about finding caves.

'For once, I hope that idiot's right. Let's get going.'

'Don't you want a rest?'

'Not *here*,' said Lee, with a shudder. 'We'll rest at the nut groves *if* there's a way out.' She lifted Griffy back onto her shoulder and they averted their eyes as they picked their way past the human remains.

'The only good thing about not knowing where our families are, is not knowing for sure they're dead,' she said hoarsely.

'Markus said—' began Jojo.

'Markus says whatever suits Markus,' said Lee fiercely. 'You *have* to believe your family's alive, Jojo! Until we've proof they're not, we both have to believe!' Common sense told Jojo his mum and dad and Davy were dead but not knowing let hope to live on, and he needed hope more than ever now. 'We were never going to find our families if we stayed in the Town,' continued Lee more calmly. 'At least we've got a chance now.'

They kept a steady pace but the darkness seemed never ending. Jojo's foot throbbed and his wet clothes chafed but at least he wasn't cold. Thankfully the tunnel held no more nasty surprises and the plates continued to glow which was just as well as Griffy had fallen asleep. 'The loong's being super helpful,' said Lee, after a while.

'They live in caves so it's probably feeling at home.'

'*Dragons* live in caves,' Lee reminded him. 'Loongs live in water.'

'We don't know which one it is yet,' countered Jojo.

'I'm betting on a loong given you found all its pieces near water.'

'Not the sickle,' said Jojo.

'The sickle was in the Store which means it washed up.'

'True,' said Jojo. The other mythic creatures like the giant serpent and the Kraken had been in water too and he wondered if it meant anything. 'And the phoenix started off in the water,' he said thoughtfully.

'Or *ended up* in the water or at least its feather did,' pointed out Lee. 'I wonder what happened to the rest of it.'

'Maybe it's still in the weird mythic place the Kraken came from, and the pterodactyls, and the serpent, and who knows what else.'

'So, you're admitting they're pterodactyls now?' teased Lee.

'Given the skeletons and ghost ship, pterodactyls seem reasonable,' said Jojo grimly.

'As much as anything does.'

'Do you want to rest?' he asked.

'Not as much as I want to get out of this stupid darkness,' said Lee, which was exactly how Jojo felt.

'If we don't find an exit soon, we *will* rest,' he said.

'How long is *soon*?'

'Ten minutes,' said Jojo, plucking a figure from the air.

'I'll just check my watch then.'

'Starting *now*,' said Jojo dryly, but they had scarcely gone a dozen paces when the gleam of Griffy's eyes reappeared. She flapped her wings, as if she stretched after a nap, but took off instead.

'Griffy!' cried Lee, but Griffy simply hovered in front of them, and then Jojo felt a draught.

'There's an opening here somewhere,' he said excitedly.

'Griffy thinks so too,' exclaimed Lee. 'Which way, Griffy?'

Jojo doubted Griffy understood but her gleaming eyes headed to the right and they followed. The plates' glow showed a second tunnel and the air grew cooler as they went. Then the smell of wet foliage intruded and the stone gave way to the dim silhouette of thorny bushes.

'Just our luck,' muttered Lee, as they fought their way through their jab.

'At least we're out the tunnel,' said Jojo as he sucked his scratched hand. There was enough light to see a sky full of cloud but the rain had stopped.

'You've been to the nut groves,' said Lee, gazing about. 'Do you know where we are?'

'No,' admitted Jojo.

'The Stream will be down slope so let's head that way. We need a drink anyway.'

Jojo was annoyed he hadn't thought of that but at least the windfall gave him plenty of walking sticks to choose from and he picked a nice straight one. The steep, wet slope was still hard going especially as he wanted to curl up somewhere dry and sleep.

The Stream turned out to be beyond a scrubby stand of bushes and he joined Lee as she greedily scooped water to her mouth. He was super thirsty too and Griffy guzzled it down as well. The growing light showed the bushes to be a murky green but the Stream shone despite the lack of sun.

'Dawn's close,' said Jojo, as he sat back on his haunches.

'I certainly feel like I've walked through the night, in fact, several nights *and* missed heaps of meals. I'm starving.'

'So am I,' said Jojo, thinking longingly of Kitchens' food again.

'At least Griffy's got breakfast,' said Lee. She unwrapped the fish bundle and Griffy needed no invitation to tuck in. 'Griffy will have to catch her own breakfast from now on,' she added worriedly.

'Save her some for later,' suggested Jojo.

'It'll only go off. It's best she eats it now.'

Which was true, thought Jojo, and considered how much food he and Lee could carry. Nuts lasted longer than berries but not being able to carry water was the real problem. His dad said people could last a long time without food but only a few days without water, especially if it were hot. Jojo stared up at the grey sky. At least they didn't have to worry about that, he concluded glumly.

CHAPTER 58

The only sound was the Stream's clear chime and Jojo wondered if the birds had fled again. Griffy was quiet too as she perched on the bank so he didn't think she was the cause, unless the birds had sensed her presence. When he'd camped in the mountains, it'd been his job to build the fire each morning. It'd been freezing but being up early meant hearing what his dad called the dawn chorus. Every bird seemed to wake at the same time to celebrate the new day in song, and there had been plenty to celebrate because everything had been fresh, and clean, and bright.

'The water here tastes a whole lot better than at the Town,' said Lee.

Her gaze was intent on him and he managed to relax his face. 'It tastes of snow, which is weird given the Mountains don't have any. It must flow from the other side.'

'Water can't flow *over* mountains, Jojo.'

'I know that, but it can flow *through* if it cuts a gorge and I've seen plenty of those on hikes. It's how you get waterfalls,' he added.

'It could flow *under* the Mountains like the underground river does near the Town,' suggested Lee.

'Who knows? We're only going as far as the Mountains anyway.'

'Not if there's no one there.'

Jojo blinked. 'You're the one who insisted there were.'

'I never *insisted* anything but it's obvious to anyone with half a brain that smoke's more likely caused by people than trash suddenly bursting into flame.'

Jojo thought it was also obvious to anyone *with half a brain* it was stupid to go off into the unknown without food or water, but he kept his mouth shut. He was tired, and hungry, and super worried, and being nasty to Lee wasn't going to help.

'Besides,' continued Lee. 'Wouldn't you rather find somewhere better to live than the *wonderful* Town run by the *wonderful* Markus?'

The honest answer was *no* because despite Markus's bullying, the ramshackle buildings had food and warmth and where they headed might have nothing. But once Markus had pulled out the guns, they'd had no choice about leaving. 'I just want to sleep,' he said, not wanting to argue.

'And I just want to eat,' retorted Lee.

'Well, let's get to the nut groves then,' said Jojo, and hauled himself up. 'We can grab some nuts *and* berries for breakfast and find somewhere to sleep, then pack up as much food as we can carry, and decide which way to go.'

'We'll have to follow the Stream given we've got no water,' said Lee, grimacing as she reclaimed her shirt. 'Ugh, it stinks of fish. I'll give it a quick wash.'

'Don't,' said Jojo, impatient to be gone. 'You don't want a wet shirt.'

'You're wet,' she pointed out.

'My point exactly,' he snapped, and limped off along the bank. He expected Lee to stride on past but she fell into step beside him while Griffy flapped in the air around them. The light showed how much bigger she seemed every time he looked at her. 'I'm either super tired or going mad,' he muttered.

'Why?'

'Griffy's growing before my eyes.'

'You're right,' gasped Lee.

'But it's impossible!'

'Nothing's impossible *here*. Besides, we know nothing about griffins. They might suddenly grow, not grow gradually like us.'

Jojo found it hard not to compare *here* to Before or to accept Before might be gone forever and all he might have left was Lee. 'I'm sorry I've been so grouchy,' he muttered.

'We've *both* been grouchy,' said Lee, and paused. 'I've wanted to get away from the Town from the moment I arrived but I never thought I'd have to run for my life down a tunnel, in the dark, with guns going off everywhere, or pass under the cemetery with . . .' Her voice cracked and she cleared her throat. 'The heroes in myths are a lot braver than me.'

'They don't limp or stink of the sea either.'

'Or stink of fish like me,' said Lee, with a grin and Jojo grinned too. 'Come on. We'll feel better once we've eaten and slept.'

'I hope so,' said Lee. 'I certainly don't want to feel any worse.'

Jojo guessed it was close to Noon when they reached the nut groves but it was impossible to say given the sky was its usual grey. The ground was littered with nuts which made harvesting easy, and Jojo hurriedly rubbed off the papery husks and crammed handfuls of sweet meat into his mouth. He hadn't been this hungry since he'd washed up.

There were plenty of the luscious purple, crimson, and bright red berries the Aunts sometimes provided at First Meal and Jojo added these to his feast. He guessed the Aunts discouraged people from harvesting them to stop them being used up but there'd be two fewer mouths to feed in the Town so he figured it evened out.

'These are *so* good,' said Lee, wiping the juice from her chin. 'Markus was stupid to build the Town so far away.'

'They had to haul stuff up from the beach, remember,' said Jojo, and for the first time, had an inkling of how terrible those early days had been. Markus and his ilk might have arrived in the safety of boats, but there'd been nothing here except bodies and piles of wreckage. Raj said there'd been violent storms as well. There hadn't been time for discussion or argument, and there still wasn't, not with the Town one violent storm away from sliding into the ocean.

'We need to find somewhere to sleep,' said Lee, yawning.

Jojo nodded. 'But let's pack up some nuts and berries first, *and* have a good drink.'

'I'd rather sleep first. Markus and his posse are probably still at First Meal and it's a fair walk to here even if they've already set out.'

'There might be shorter tunnels we missed and Axel said he found caves near the nut groves remember.'

'Yep, but Markus doesn't have any light.'

'He didn't last night but he knows the phoenix went up the tunnel and there's bitumen in the Store. He could probably make some sort of flaming torch with it,' said Jojo, although he wondered if that only happened in adventure films.

'Markus isn't that smart,' said Lee, but she started to gather nuts.

'We both know he is,' said Jojo, following suit. 'And if he believes he's protecting the Town, he'll do whatever's necessary to kill the phoenix.'

CHAPTER 59

Jojo used a second shirt to pack up the nuts and berries and Lee insisted on making a bundle too, and then they had a long drink from the Stream and set off. Jojo decided that Axel's caves would be a good place to sleep but apart from them being *near the nut groves* he had no idea where they were.

'I bet Axel made them up to big note himself,' muttered Lee, after a while. 'Let's just find somewhere dry to sleep.'

Jojo didn't like the idea of sleeping in the open despite his whole body aching and not just his foot. 'I don't think its safe here,' he said slowly.

'Probably safer than Axel's caves, *if* they exist,' said Lee. 'They're probably connected to the tunnel we used and super simple for the serpent to slither up.'

Jojo licked his lips. 'Or Markus and the Finders to pop out of.'

'Imagine Markus and the Finders meeting the serpent in the tunnel,' said Lee with a grin. 'Now that'd be fun, wouldn't it?'

'I don't want people getting hurt,' muttered Jojo.

'And I don't want Griffy and the phoenix getting hurt,' retorted Lee. 'I just want Markus and his posse to go back to that lovely piece of cracked cliff that *God* gave them.'

'Let's just head towards the Mountains,' said Jojo wearily. 'At least we'll be going in the right direction then.'

'We need to keep close to the Stream, remember.'

'Or find bottles to carry water in, which seems unlikely.'

Lee gave a crooked smile. 'Oh, I don't know, Jojo. Nothing seems unlikely here.'

They went in silence because Jojo guessed that, like him, Lee was too tired to talk. The ground grew steeper and rockier, and the nut trees gave way to trees like pines but with needles so dark they were almost black. The new trees were empty of birds too which at least meant there were no squawks or shrieks to disguise the sound of voices, or slithering, or of other new and terrible creatures.

Jojo was grateful to only hear the Stream's rush and the whip of Griffy's wings as she swooped around them. He was worried she'd be seen but there was nothing he could do about it. She wasn't a dog that came to a whistle and nor had they fish to tempt her back. She was too big to fit on Lee's shoulder anyway.

Jojo hoped Lee would ask for a rest but it was he who finally stopped, his foot full of jabs of pain. 'It's different here,' she said dully, looking around.

'And not in a good way.'

'Griffy feels it too,' said Lee, staring up to where Griffy had perched. She looked like the griffins in comics, concluded Jojo in shock, but no comic could convey the piercing gleam of her red eyes, the might of her tearing beak, the strength of her muscular body, and the power of her wings. And she wasn't happy, her tail lashing as she stared around.

'I hope she remembers we're friends,' said Jojo uneasily.

He expected Lee to reassure him they were in no danger of becoming lunch but she looked troubled too. 'Griffy hasn't attacked us or gone off on her own, so I'm guessing she knows who we are.'

'But why did she grow so quickly?'

'Why did the phoenix feather turn into a phoenix?'

'That's not an answer,' said Jojo irritably.

249

'It's no use comparing here to Before,' said Lee in exasperation. 'Griffy's not a kitten growing into a cat, Jojo, and the phoenix feather was never a chick growing into a bird. They're mythic and obey mythic rules.'

'Which are?' demanded Jojo.

'Not the same as the rules of Before!'

Jojo stifled a retort. He knew it was pointless comparing his present life to his old life with his mum and dad and Davy, and school, and summer holidays at the beach, and everyday things that had sometimes been boring and annoying but had turned out to be really precious. His eyes burned and he rubbed them as if he were merely tired.

'I'm sorry,' said Lee thickly.

'You don't need to be,' said Jojo, staring away through the trees. 'None of this is your fault. We're both tired, that's all. Let's go get a drink and then rest. We certainly need to.'

'The loong hasn't changed, has it?' asked Lee, as they turned towards the Stream.

'Not yet,' said Jojo, patting the bundle. 'The plates are still the same size, and weight, and have the same blue glow.'

'Maybe it needs something else to change, like the phoenix did.'

'Griffy didn't need anything to double her size,' pointed out Jojo, steadying himself with his stick as the slope steepened.

'We don't know that. She might have used something less obvious than fire.'

'Such as?'

'I don't know. Maybe these trees,' said Lee, gazing about. 'They're certainly weird enough, or maybe she found something while we weren't looking.' Jojo hoped whatever it was didn't affect the dragon. He didn't want a full grown dragon to add to his problems.

Lee's hand suddenly fastened on his arm and his heart jolted. 'Listen!' Jojo expected to hear gunfire, or the shouts of Markus and the Finders, or the shriek of some new monster but then his blood ran cold. It was the sound he'd heard the night the Sanctuary had been destroyed.

CHAPTER 60

Lee's puzzled expression flashed to fear which confirmed to Jojo how bad he was at hiding his feelings. 'Tell me,' she demanded.

Jojo licked his lips. 'The Stream's in flood.'

'But we haven't had enough rain.'

'Not *here* but the Stream tastes of snow, remember, which means it comes from somewhere else, which means they must've had heaps of rain there.'

Lee brought a shaking hand to her mouth. 'But … if the Stream's in flood, the cracks near the Town will spread …' Jojo nodded but there was no way they could beat the waters back to the Town to warn anyone, even if they sprouted wings.

'At least Markus will have to do something now,' muttered Lee.

'Only if he's there and he's probably creeping about the nut groves with the Finders.'

'Then Neville and the other Uncles will have to do something, or Mary even.'

'They haven't so far,' said Jojo, and took a deep breath. 'Come on. Let's see how bad it is.' They continued down the slope, the roar growing as they neared the Stream, the black-needled pines blocking their view. Lee drew ahead as Jojo struggled with his stick and he saw her stop on the edge of the trees. She was motionless and he sucked in his breath as he came to her side.

'It's so beautiful,' she whispered, and all Jojo could do was nod.

The valley ended in a steep rocky cliff covered in lime-green ferns and lush emerald moss, and if that wasn't a strange enough sight, set in the very centre of the cliff was a perfectly circular cavern which the Stream roared out of to fall in a shining waterfall. The waterfall was wreathed in dazzling rainbows, and puzzled, Jojo glanced up to see a disk of sunny blue sky directly above. The disk reminded Jojo of the clear patch of water at the peak and he filled with wonder but then something thwacked past his head so close he ducked.

'Griffy!' cried Lee in alarm.

It was dangerous for Griffy to fly in the open when Markus might be about but the day was quiet and Jojo watched entranced as Griffy swooped amongst the rainbows. Her red plumage gleamed in the sun and her lion-tail streamed behind her like a flag and as Jojo watched, it seemed to him that this was where she was meant to be.

Shouts shattered the silence and then gunfire exploded all around them. He yanked Lee down behind a tree and crouched beside her. Lee had curled into a ball, hands clamped over her ears, shoulders shaking as she sobbed but Jojo cautiously peered out. He could see Markus now, standing sternly upright on the bank below while Finders crouched around him firing. Either they were really bad shots or Griffy was super lucky but there was no way her luck could last. And then, as he desperately wondered how to save her, he was blinded by a sheet of brilliant light.

He felt scorching heat and then as the firing stopped and his vision returned, he glimpsed the phoenix's fiery shape disappear into the cavern followed by Griffy's smaller silhouette. The bushes below were charred and the Finders nowhere to be seen but Markus still stood proudly erect despite the loss of most of his flowing beard. 'Is Griffy dead?' asked Lee thickly, and Jojo raised a warning finger to his lips.

'She followed the phoenix into the cavern,' he whispered.

'But she must be hurt. All those bullets … What about Markus and the Finders? Have they gone?'

'The Finders have gone but Markus's still there.' Jojo grinned. 'Most of his beard's burned off.'

'Shame the phoenix didn't get the rest of him,' she muttered, getting to her knees and peering around the tree. 'What on earth's he doing?'

Markus strode up and down the bank, obviously looking for something, and Jojo saw him select some driftwood and bend over it. His back was turned, blocking Jojo's view, but Jojo heard material tear.

'He's made a cross,' hissed Lee.

Lee was right. Markus had used material torn from his shirt to bind two pieces of wood together and Jojo watched him gouge a hole in the ground and jam the cross upright. 'It's like the Sanctuary,' whispered Jojo, as understanding dawned. 'Mary said Markus built the Sanctuary close to the cliff to show the ocean the land belongs to us and now he's showing the phoenix, *and* Griffy, and any other *ungodly* creatures that the land *here* belongs to us as well.'

'Not sure Griffy and the phoenix believe in crosses,' muttered Lee.

'It's what *Markus* believes in that counts,' said Jojo. 'If *he* believes the cross will stop ungodly creatures from coming any closer to the Town, he'll leave them in peace and then—' Jojo stopped as Markus's voice rang out. He faced the waterfall, his arms raised like an Old Testament figure from a film, and while Jojo caught only a few words like *evil, death and God's will*, Markus's meaning was clear.

Markus lowered his arms but still glared at the cavern as if he could destroy the phoenix and Griffy by sheer strength of will, then he abruptly turned on his heel and strode away. Jojo and Lee didn't move. 'Do you think he's really gone?' whispered Lee eventually.

'Let's wait a bit longer.'

'But what if Griffy's lying injured in the cavern or deeper in the tunnel?'

Jojo didn't want to enter another dark tunnel especially one full of water. 'She didn't look injured when she flew in,' he said. 'And we need to eat before we leave.'

'Down by the Stream. We need to drink too.'

Jojo would have preferred to eat in the trees in case Markus or the Finders returned but he followed Lee down the slope, his gaze on the Stream's clear, chiming water and the fall's rainbow spangles. The whole scene was like a little patch of the world before the oceans had risen and turned everything grey.

Jojo stared up at the patch of blue sky above the waterfall, as strange as the patch of clear water at the peak, and then movement caught his eye and he spun as a Finder stepped from the trees, rifle raised, ready to fire.

CHAPTER 61

Lee had frozen too and Jojo offered up silent thanks it was Raj and not Markus or Axel or Ben. 'I had a feeling you two might be here,' said Raj, as he lowered the rifle.

'Why?' demanded Jojo, desperately trying to concoct reasons for his and Lee's presence.

'You seem to be around when strange things happen. The serpent, the Kraken, the cracks …'

'And why are *you* here?' challenged Lee, recovering more quickly than Jojo. 'You should be on your way back to the Town's safety with your Finder friends.'

'They're not my friends and the Town's not safe,' said Raj evenly. 'But it isn't safe here either.'

'It's safer than the Town,' retorted Lee.

'The Town has food and shelter unlike where you're going, which I presume is the Mountains,' he said, as he eyed their bundles. 'At least you've got nuts and berries.' There was a short silence, and Raj glanced at the waterfall. 'This is a beautiful place to eat. I'll share First Meal with you.'

'We weren't planning on stopping here,' said Lee and flushed.

The lie was probably obvious to Raj too but he propped the rifle on the bank and pulled a cloth-wrapped wad from his pocket. 'Grab a seat,' he said to Lee, and settled on a stone. Lee stayed where she was and Raj sighed. 'We need to have a talk.'

'Or else you'll tell Markus where we've going?'

'No, in case your families turn up. I want to be able to tell them where you went and that I warned you of the dangers, and that you had food, and didn't leave just to spite Markus.'

Lee opened her mouth but Jojo managed to get in first. 'That's a good idea,' he said hurriedly, trying to ignore Lee's glare. 'If we just disappear, Mary will worry we've had an accident or something.'

He chose a stone next to Raj and dumped his bundles on the ground, and Lee had no choice but to do the same, then Raj handed them each a thick slice of bread . Jojo thanked him, relieved when Lee muttered her thanks as well.

'I guessed you were heading to the Mountains back at your cave,' said Raj. 'You did a good job cleaning it up, by the way. No one would ever guess you'd been there. And then, of course, you didn't show for Last Meal, and you're right, Jojo, Mary did ask me to keep an eye out for you.'

'If you tell her you've seen us, she'll have to tell Markus,' said Lee.

'Markus doesn't have as much power as you think,' said Raj.

'Really?' scoffed Lee. 'He flicks his fingers and you all grab guns to kill innocent creatures that never harmed anyone.' Her voice cracked and she strode back to the Stream and turned her back.

'It's understandable that Markus wants the Town safe,' said Raj softly, his gaze on Lee.

'So why doesn't he shift it? It's pretty obvious the cracks are dangerous.'

'He will in the end,' said Raj. 'He's not stupid, Jojo, and nor are the other Uncles *or* the Aunts. They work so hard to make something out of nothing that they need to believe that God's on their side.'

'Markus's god or your god?' asked Jojo, then wished he'd kept his mouth shut because he sounded petty.

'I was annoyed Markus built a church and pretended it was a sanctuary for everyone,' admitted Raj. 'But in the end, God is God.'

'Is that what Hindu's believe?'

'Sort of, but like most religions, Hinduism is more complicated than that.'

'Does your *Hindu* God say to kill a phoenix?' pursued Jojo.

'As God created everything, it includes everything we saw today, *and* the serpent, *and* the Kraken, *and* the pterodactyls, *and* people, of course, but I don't think God meant us to be mixed up. Mythic creatures aren't like dogs or cats or sheep or cattle.'

'But we *are* all mixed up!' exclaimed Jojo.

'Yes,' said Raj. 'We kept hurting the planet and in the end it hurt us back.'

Jojo swallowed dryly. He'd never thought of it like that. 'Do you … do you think things will ever go back to the way they were?' he asked.

'They'll probably go back to *something* but not to the way they were. That time has passed.' Raj looked sad but then he straightened. 'Not much we can do about it now,' he said briskly, 'except not give up. That's why Markus loves his crosses,' he added and smiled. 'You never gave up when you were adrift in the ocean, did you, Jojo? And you're not giving up now and nor is Lee. Have you worked out how long it will take you to get to the Mountains?'

'Not exactly.'

'You're not taking much food,' said Raj, his gaze on the bundles again.

'We'll gather more nuts and berries along the way,' said Jojo.

'*If* they grow along the way. What about water?'

'We've got nothing to carry it in so we're staying near the Stream.'

'You should've brought the blue bottle from the cave,' said Raj. 'It would've been better than nothing, even with a broken top.'

'Not with bits of glass falling in,' said Lee, coming back. 'I don't suppose you have a spare one on you?'

'They don't survive the beach, which is odd, given how much crockery does,' said Raj. 'Even those strange plates of yours survived, Jojo, and they're thinner than glass.'

'We need to get going,' said Lee, slinging on her bundles. Jojo donned his too, relieved that the daylight disguised the plates' glow.

'One last thing,' said Raj. 'If the smoke in the Mountains turns out to be burning trash, come back to the Town.'

'Why?' asked Jojo in surprise.

'Because, despite what you both seem to believe, there are people there who'll miss you.'

'And if there *are* people in the Mountains?' asked Jojo thickly.

'You still mightn't want to stay.' There was a long pause while Jojo digested the fact that any people there might be worse than the Uncles. 'And if you do stay,' continued Raj, 'send a message that you're okay.'

'But how?'

'Remember that piece of burned wood we saw?' Jojo nodded. 'Send more pieces down. You both survived the oceans, but everywhere has its dangers so don't do anything stupid.' He reclaimed his rifle, nodded in farewell, and set off along the bank.

CHAPTER 62

Jojo's stomach clenched as he watched Raj disappear around the Stream's bend. He feared he'd just missed his last chance to avoid the dangers Raj warned of. '*Don't do anything stupid*,' mimicked Lee, as she scooped water to her mouth. 'As if staying in place about to fall in the sea were *sensible*! Grab a drink, we need to move.'

Jojo drank but the water's strange snowy taste added to his churn. 'Which way do you want to go?'

'Through the tunnel. We have to follow the Stream, remember.'

'That doesn't mean using the tunnel,' said Jojo, dreading the water-filled blackness. 'The Stream probably comes back to the surface further on.'

'If Griffy's hurt, she'll be in the tunnel somewhere,' said Lee determinedly. Lee set off and Jojo followed but she didn't go far before she stopped at the cross. 'I've got a good mind to chuck it in the Stream,' she said in disgust.

'Not a good idea,' said Jojo. 'If it washes down to the Town, Markus will see it as a challenge by *ungodly creatures* and come back to finish them off.'

'You're right,' said Lee grudgingly. 'I don't want bullets flying about again.' She stared up at fern-covered stone that surrounded the waterfall. 'The climb's not going to be much fun either.'

'No,' agreed Jojo. The cliff was no higher than the one to his cave but the ferns hid foot or hand holds and the wet stone doubled their chances of slipping. 'We'll go slowly,' he said, despite not wanting to go at all.

They picked their way forward over the water-smoothed stones but even that was difficult with Jojo's broken foot. 'It

261

looks easier to the left,' said Lee and headed that way, but the pack suddenly jagged down on Jojo's shoulders.

'Wait,' he gasped and took a careful step to the right and then back to the left.

'What on earth are you doing?'

'Finding the best route or at least the dragon is,' said Jojo, and described how the phoenix feather had changed its weight to guide him.

'I suppose it's no weirder than anything else around here,' muttered Lee. 'And if you're right, the loong will take us where we want to go.'

'Or where *it* wants to go which might not be the same thing.'

'No,' said Lee uncertainly.

'I'm hoping it *is* where we want to go,' said Jojo, but Lee's face told him she shared his fears.

'The loong's never hurt us and neither have Griffy or the phoenix.'

'The dragon's still a pile of plates,' pointed out Jojo.

'*Griffy* would never hurt us,' persisted Lee.

'Griffy might not *mean* to hurt us but she might be like those lion and tiger cubs you see on TV. They're cute when they're kittens but eat you when they grow up.'

'I'm going by the tunnel,' said Lee abruptly. 'I can't leave Griffy there if she's hurt.'

'I have to go where the plates decide unless I dump them here.'

They stared at each other in silence. 'We should stay together,' said Lee eventually, although Jojo saw how unhappy she was. 'The plates might take us to the tunnel anyway and at least they'll protect us in the meantime.'

'Why?'

'The loong needs us to carry it wherever it wants to go.'

'A bunch of plates aren't going to be much use against something really big.'

'It'll probably just eat *me*,' tossed Lee over her shoulder, as she headed to the right. 'The serpent let you go remember, *and* the Kraken, and the blood crabs got out of your way, at least most of the time. You're obviously the *hero*, Jojo, like in myths.'

'Sure, a hero with a dud foot,' retorted Jojo.

'Achilles had a dud foot.'

'That was his *heel*,' snapped Jojo, and stopped. 'Of all the stupid …'

'What is it?'

'I've just realised something I was too dumb to realise earlier.'

'You're not dumb,' said Lee quickly.

'The blood crabs got out of my way whenever I carried bits of plate *or* the blue bottle, and I had the sickle in my pocket when the serpent let me go.' Jojo's breath whistled through his teeth. 'I think they're scared of the dragon.'

'Which means we'll have a safe journey,' said Lee.

'Unless we meet something even more powerful.'

'Nothing's more powerful than a loong,' said Lee with utter certainty.

Which might be true of a *fully grown* dragon, thought Jojo. 'We have to make it up the cliff first,' he said.

'You lead, given the loong seems to know where it's going.'

Jojo nodded but they hadn't gone far before he decided the loong had no idea where it was going *unless* it wanted to take them there by the longest, most roundabout route. To make matters worse, every time he saw a handhold or somewhere to wedge his stick, the plates sent him in the opposite direction. The sodden moss and ferns added to his struggles and he was soon covered in slime.

He stopped to ease his foot and grimaced as he wiped water from his eyes and guessed he'd slimed his face. Lee's face was grimy too. 'Where on earth is it taking us?' she demanded. 'Are you sure you're following where its weight goes?'

'Feel free to carry it.'

'I'm sure you're doing the best you can.'

Which was hardly a vote of confidence, thought Jojo. 'Unless the dragon's going to zigzag back, it's not taking us to the tunnel.'

'But it's where Griffy might be!'

'She could be anywhere,' said Jojo baldly. 'There's more than one tunnel. Maybe the dragon's taking us to a different one and they all connect up.'

'Yeah, and maybe there's a pile of treasure at the end, and maybe it's the pirates' treasure, and maybe the loong will fight the pirates for it.' Jojo said nothing and Lee took a shuddering breath. 'Sorry,' she said thickly. 'I don't know why I'm being so mean.'

'You're worried about Griffy, that's all,' said Jojo, and licked his lips. 'We could leave the plates here and go search for her.'

'But the loong needs to be whole!' exclaimed Lee, and took another shuddering breath. 'We'll take the loong where it wants to go and then come back and look for Griffy.' Jojo nodded but he knew their chances of finding an injured griffin in utter darkness were practically zero.

CHAPTER 63

The climb seemed to get easier after that and Jojo guessed it was because he'd given up worrying about the dragon and concentrated on finding a way up. Lee seemed happier too given that they hadn't argued again. He stopped when he came level with the waterfall cavern. The bottom half was full of water which left nowhere for him and Lee to walk anyway.

'Useless to anything without wings,' muttered Lee. 'I guess we can thank the loong after all.' She blew the fringe from her eyes and adjusted her bundles. 'Let's get this climbing over with.'

Jojo forced himself on but felt a draught on his face and saw a narrow crevice all but hidden by ferns. It looked like the perfect hidey hole for all sorts of crawly things and he took an experimental step to either side and scowled as the plates' jagged down on his shoulders. 'The dragon wants to go in there,' he said, pointing at it.

'Well, I guess it beats climbing up this slimy cliff but not by much.'

'It probably joins the Stream tunnel,' said Jojo hopefully.

'What makes you think that?'

'Nothing,' he admitted. 'I was just trying to be positive.'

'Being positive is overrated,' she retorted. 'Best get it over with.' Jojo pushed through the ferns, surprised the crevice wasn't full of cobwebs. 'At least there's nothing nasty in here,' said Lee, as she followed him in. 'And the loong likes it.' Jojo started. The plates' glow was as bright as a light globe, which was handy, given the crevice was dark. 'Come on,' said Lee, taking the lead. 'The sooner the loong gets to where it wants to go, the sooner we get to search for Griffy.'

The tunnel showed no signs of anything having been there but for all Jojo knew, the dragon might be leading them to their deaths. The plates' blue light showed how the tunnel floor steepened as they went on and swung to the right, and when it didn't swing back again, Jojo feared they walked in a circle.

'It'd be super useful if this was a short cut to the top of the Mountains, like the shaft is to the top of the cliffs,' said Lee.

'It looks more like a loop which means we're probably wasting our time,' said Jojo.

'We're only wasting our time if it goes downhill or turns left, otherwise it's acting like a spiral staircase or at least, a spiral ramp.'

Lee was right! 'I didn't expect the Mountains to be even weirder than the coast,' he muttered.

'They're not,' said Lee defensively. 'The sea sends super high tides one day and not the next, and sometimes they stop working altogether as if resting up to send something even worse.'

'I said the *coast*, not the seas,' said Jojo irritably. 'I already know the seas destroy everything.'

'Oh, you mean the lovely *coast* that has underground streams that eat buildings and that has tunnels full of ghosts. *That* lovely coast.' Jojo stifled a retort and they walked for a while in silence. 'Let's eat,' said Lee finally.

'I'm not hungry.'

'But you must be thirsty, because I sure am, and it's important to drink.'

'Drink what?' demanded Jojo.

'Berry juice,' said Lee, and slipped off her bundles. Jojo was tempted to keep walking but he did the same and they settled on the floor. She passed him a handful of berries and crammed some into her mouth. 'They're *so* good,' she mumbled, as juice dribbled down her chin.

Jojo closed his eyes as the sweet juice flooded his mouth. They brought back memories of sunny summer days, of the smell of dry grass, of Davy's excited babbles. It was a life Jojo knew had gone forever.

'What's worrying you?' asked Lee.

'Everything,' mumbled Jojo.

'Apart from that.' Jojo opened his eyes to see Lee's mouth kinked in a smile. She was all he had and he suddenly feared he'd lose her as well. 'Tell me,' she said softly.

That we're stupid for pretending our families are still alive, for believing there's something better in the world than the Uncles crooked houses, that one day, the world will be the same as it was before. 'What happens if we find a place in the Mountains but it *is* worse than what we've left behind?'

'I've wondered that too,' said Lee, and handed him more berries.

'And?'

'Father says people should look at things logically and so logically, I reckon we have three choices. We can stay in the horrible new place, *if* they let us, or we go back to the Town, or we keep on looking.'

'Isn't your dad a priest?'

'Yes, and now you're going to say he's not logical because he believes in God.' Jojo wasn't going to say it because he didn't want to upset Lee, but he was certainly thinking it. 'Father says faith and hope are important too, even if they're not logical.'

'The Uncles certainly have faith,' said Jojo sourly. 'And so does Raj, although his faith's different to theirs.'

'Father says faith does the same thing as hope.'

'Which is?'

'Stops you giving up.'

Jojo's breath emptied in a long sigh. 'Do you think the world will go back to the way it was?'

Lee shrugged. 'I've seen TV programs where cities abandoned because of war or nuclear accidents are taken over by trees. They grow all along the streets and even up through the walls of apartment blocks. It takes years but the whole place goes back to what it was before the cities were made, but the actual cities can't grow back, can they?'

'No. I don't suppose those TV programs showed pterodactyls flying about? Or griffins, or phoenixes, or dragons?'

Lee's warm hand touched his. 'There's no point in worrying, Jojo. We don't even know what happened to the world, let alone how to fix it.'

'I guess that just leaves hope then,' muttered Jojo, 'and I doubt—'

Lee gestured for silence. 'Did you hear that?'

There was a rustling like autumn leaves in wind. 'Could be bats,' he whispered, despite having seen no bats since he'd washed up. He strained his ears but the tunnel threw the sound around all over the place. One minute the sound seemed closer, the next further away.

'Look!' gasped Lee, and pointed. The plates pulsed with a blue fire so intense Jojo feared they would ignite and then the tunnel filled with an ear-splitting cacophony. Jojo threw himself flat to the floor, aware Lee did the same as a hoard of creatures swept past overhead. The noise seemed to go on forever before it receded up the tunnel. 'A great mob of pterodactyls,' gasped Lee.

Jojo nodded shakily. 'And headed the same way as us.'

CHAPTER 64

Lee quickly wrapped up the berries and they set off again. The plates had dimmed but Jojo glanced at them nervously as he walked. 'At least we were right about the loong being linked to the other creatures,' said Lee, after a while.

'Why do you say that?'

'Apart from the blood crabs getting out of your way and the serpent letting you go, the loong turned super bright when the pterodactyls appeared.'

'But it didn't stop them, did it? If the dragon were boss, they'd have U-turned, but they kept on going.'

'They only would've U-turned if the loong didn't want them there,' pointed out Lee.

'*If* the dragon really were boss, it wouldn't have let Griffy sleep on top of it or shared the cave with the phoenix,' persisted Jojo.

'The phoenix left as soon as it became a phoenix and Griffy only slept on the loong when she was hurt,' countered Lee. 'And that kind of proves it's a loong because loongs heal things and Griffy healed pretty quickly.'

'Griffins might heal quickly anyway,' argued Jojo, aware his weariness and the pain in his foot made him irritable. The tunnel seemed to be getting even steeper too.

'You really are in a bad mood, aren't you? What are you worrying about now?'

'Have you thought about what happens when we get to where the dragon wants to go? I'm betting it's not going to say thanks and wave goodbye.'

'You think it's going to eat us?'

'It's what dragons do.'

'Only after Christians got hold of them. Before then, they protected the Earth. It's a *loong* anyway, not a dragon.'

'You said loongs like water and dragons like caves, and we're so deep in a cave now the dragon's actually glowing with happiness.'

'If you're so scared of it why not leave it here,' said Lee in exasperation. 'We don't owe it anything.'

'We need its light *unless* you want to spend the rest of your life in this black hole!'

Lee glared at him and Jojo saw her take a deep breath. 'We need to sleep. It must be at least halfway through the night outside.'

'I don't see any beds,' said Jojo sarcastically.

'They're just around the next bend, right next to the café with the hot chips and chocolate!'

Jojo knew his grumpiness only made things worse but he could no longer pretend they'd find a lovely little town in the Mountains. Any survivors there would've clawed together whatever they could just like the Uncles had. The world of Before had gone and taken his mum and dad and Davy along with it, but he could say none of these things because it meant Lee's family had gone too. He mightn't have any hope left, but he didn't have the right to destroy Lee's hope as well.

Jojo had no idea how long he'd slept before he woke with a start. Lee still slept, sitting with her head on her knees, but the plates were back to their fiery best. He had the wild idea of shaking Lee awake and fleeing but stayed put, terrified of being pursued through darkened tunnels by pterodactyls or something even worse.

He gripped his hands to stop their shaking as apparitions loomed into sight, their fleshless feet rising and falling silently, their eyeless sockets fixed on him. Jojo buried his head in his arms, expecting their bony fingers on his throat but nothing happened and he forced his eyes open again. The tunnel was empty and only the plates' slow dim told him something had been there.

Lee roused and stopped in mid yawn. 'You look like you've seen a ghost.'

'Several in fact,' said Jojo hoarsely.

'The same ones as before?'

'Close enough and going the same way as the pterodactyls.'

'That's interesting,' she muttered, but Jojo thought *dangerous* and *deadly* were better words. 'Either the tunnel's super popular or everything's headed where the loong's headed.' She brightened. 'Griffy might already be there.'

'And the phoenix *and* the serpent.'

'And the Kraken I suppose, but it needs water. At least it'd mean Griffy's not lying hurt somewhere.'

Although she might still be terribly wounded, thought Jojo. 'Why would everything be going to the same place?'

'I have no idea but the phoenix needed all of its feather *and* fire to be whole again so maybe the loong still needs something.'

'And that *something's* where it's taking us or *making* us take it?'

'It's not *making* us do *anything* and it's only a guess,' said Lee.

'But a good one although it doesn't explain why the ghosts and pterodactyls are headed there too, *if* they are. The tunnel might split further on.'

'Let's think about it logically,' said Lee. 'It might be a coincidence, or this tunnel might split and they're going somewhere else, or they all want whatever the loong wants and we're in a race and there'll be a really big fight at the end.'

'There won't be a fight,' said Jojo, with such certainty Lee stared. 'The blood crabs and serpent already know the dragon's boss, remember, so if everything ends up in the same place, it's because the dragon wants them there.'

'That's a super weird idea but I think you're right.'

'This tunnel's super weird too,' continued Jojo. 'Shells have spirals but tunnels don't and tunnels aren't usually this steep.'

'It's like climbing a hill,' agreed Lee.

'Exactly, which means we can't be far from the surface then we can finish the journey above ground.'

CHAPTER 65

They ate nuts as they walked, too keen to get the journey over with to stop. Jojo longed to be free of the dragon's demands, or at least, those of the plates and for the first time he wondered how something as powerful as a dragon came to be broken. Maybe it'd been smashed by the same forces that had smashed the barrier between myth and his world, the living and the dead, and even Time. Logic could explain none of it which left him with faith and hope, he supposed, which weren't that useful either.

'What are you thinking about?' asked Lee after a while.

'The mythic creatures, the pterodactyls, the ghosts.' Jojo shrugged. 'I'm still trying to make sense of them.'

'No wonder you look so grim,' said Lee, and took his hand. 'Best not to think about it.'

'That won't fix anything.'

'Some things can't be fixed. Sometimes you just have to let them be, like when my mother died.'

Jojo looked at her in surprise. 'I'm sorry,' he said awkwardly.

'So was everyone else, especially my father. He had some very long conversations with God.' Lee sighed. 'Even *if* you did come up with reasons, Jojo, they wouldn't undo the mess. My mother didn't come alive again when we discovered the reason she'd died.'

Naming Davy's condition hadn't changed anything either, recalled Jojo. Davy's smiles and wet kisses had been the same *and* the bullies' nasty words but Jojo sense things *would* change when the dragon became whole again.

Lee's hand tightened on his. 'What's scaring you?'

Jojo licked his lips. 'What will happen when the dragon comes alive again?'

'I don't know,' said Lee slowly. 'The phoenix tried to avoid people, even when it was attacked and so did Griffy, but the serpent and Kraken went after you. All the stories talk about knights attacking dragons rather than the other way round.'

'What about loongs?'

'They're gods.'

'With the same ideas about right and wrong as trees,' said Jojo dourly.

'There are good gods in myths too.'

'But more bad ones,' said Jojo, and sighed. 'Sorry, I'm not trying to argue again.'

'I know, but we decided to give the loong the chance to be whole again so we'll just have to take what comes.' Jojo said nothing and Lee gave his hand another squeeze. 'The loong can't make a worse mess of the world than we did.'

'*We* didn't do it.'

'Well, people in general, although gods don't seem to care about individuals. The Uncles believe God saved Noah and his family because they were good but they can't have been the only good people in the world.'

Jojo nodded. 'And if God meant only good people to survive the latest flood, Markus and his friends wouldn't be around.'

Lee actually laughed and Jojo couldn't remember the last time he'd heard *anyone* laugh. 'Father says lots of Bible stories are to teach us things, not describe what really happened,' she said.

'So what's Noah and his Ark supposed to teach us?'

'Not to give up, I guess, although father says big floods are mentioned all through history, so maybe Noah's flood really did happen.'

'Perhaps—' began Jojo and stopped. The plates grew no brighter but he'd definitely heard a strange noise.

'Sounds like branches creaking in the wind,' whispered Lee.

'Yes,' said Jojo, but the tunnel's air was still. The sound of a flute joined the creaking and then the deeper notes of an organ. Odd groanings intruded too. 'I've heard these sounds before in the thorn trees.'

'So have I,' whispered Lee. 'It's like an orchestra warming up. You know, when everyone tests their instruments to make sure they're in tune so they can make beautiful music later.'

'Well, it can't be an orchestra,' said Jojo worriedly. 'Maybe there's even stranger creatures in the tunnel.'

'It doesn't sound like animal noises, even mythic ones, although we've only heard Griffy and the phoenix so far, and only when they were attacked not when they were happy. If there are lots of tunnels, it might be the wind blowing through them like giant flutes.'

'I can't feel any wind,' said Jojo, 'but it's a lot colder.'

'It could be far away or it could be the *Music of the Tunnels*, like the *Music of the Spheres*,' said Lee and grinned. Jojo looked at her blankly and she sighed. 'There was this ancient Greek philosopher or mathematician, or something who had a theory that the planets made vibrations, not all mixed up like here, but in harmony, like music. Vibrations only become sounds when your ears sort them out,' she added.

'I know that,' snapped Jojo, recalling the hearing tests a very frightened Davy had endured. Ears were supposed to convert sound waves into noise except Davy's didn't. The tunnel noises grew, bringing memories of Davy's tear-stained face, and Jojo clamped his hands over his ears.

'Are you alright?'

'I just want it over with,' he muttered.

'I'm guessing it soon will be given how cold it is,' said Lee, with a shiver. 'Let's hope we've reached the summit and there's no more climbing.' The plates looked the same which Jojo hoped meant nothing nasty lurked ahead but his foot was so painful he barely noticed the darkness fade. 'Almost there,' whispered Lee.

'We need to be careful,' warned Jojo, and started as the booms and creaks and chimes suddenly ceased. The air was so cold his breath plumed.

'Do you want me to go first?'

Jojo shook his head. 'I've got the dragon plates,' he whispered, took a deep breath, and crept to the tunnel's end.

CHAPTER 66

Jojo stopped and heard Lee's sharp intake of breath behind him. The tunnel exited into a vast circular, snow-encrusted cavern, with walls that swept up all around them to terminate in a small circular opening and, to add to the cavern's symmetry, the opening sat directly above an ice-edged, aqua-coloured, perfectly circular lake.

'Everything's so beautiful,' breathed Lee, her gaze on the disk of sky above.

'And so cold,' muttered Jojo, having to chaff his hands. 'No wonder the Stream tastes of snow.' And given the lake's stillness, the Stream must flow out from its depths and in as well or the lake would empty.

Lee suddenly grabbed his arm and he followed her horrified gaze. Every strange creature they'd ever seen was positioned on ledges in the cavern's deeper shadows. There were versions of Big Talons, dozens of smaller, odd-coloured birds, clusters of countless rainbow butterflies, and the humped shapes of pterodactyls. The serpent's scales glinted green as it wrapped its mighty body around the cavern's curve and a globe of golden light heralded the phoenix, Griffy perched nearby, her feathers red in its glow. The only movement were the spectral figures that drifted about the cavern's margins; all the other creatures were motionless, their attention fixed on Jojo and Lee.

'Griffy,' called Lee softly, but Griffy simply stared at them like everything else. 'They're waiting for the loong,' she murmured.

'Yes,' said Jojo, but the plates were no brighter.

'We should put them in the lake,' suggested Lee. 'A loong needs water.'

'But if it's a dragon, it might drown.'

'You found the plates *in* water, didn't you?' said Lee.

'Only some of the pieces. The plate *you* found was on the beach, remember, and the sickle was in the Store. Let's see what happens if we put them *near* the water,' he said, and keeping a careful eye on the creatures, they made their way down to the lake.

Jojo arranged the plates at the water's edge and they retreated to the tunnel opening and waited. Nothing happened except they grew colder. 'We'll freeze to death if we stay here much longer,' said Lee, teeth chattering. 'Let's put them *in* the water.'

'We'll put them *half* in the water,' said Jojo, as a compromise. They had to break the lake's icy margin first and Jojo was careful to leave part of each plate exposed, but again time stretched away and nothing happened.

'I don't think that's going to work, either,' said Lee, stamping her numb feet.

'You'd think the creatures here would be excited that the dragon's arrived,' muttered Jojo.

'They're like a sporting crowd that's waiting for the game to begin,' said Lee, and blew the fringe from her eyes. 'There must be something else the loong needs. It made us bring it here, so whatever it's missing must be here too.'

'I'm not searching the walls,' said Jojo with a shudder.

'Me either,' agreed Lee, eyeing the creatures warily. 'You don't happen to have another bit of plate in the bottom of your pocket, do you? Or a bit of bottle you've forgotten about, or another sickle?'

'Of course not!' said Jojo, but he patted his pockets anyway and pulled out the mussel shell.

'That's it!' shrieked Lee, making him jump.

'It's just a mouldy old mussel shell I forgot to throw away,' said Jojo. 'And it's probably *really* rotten by now,' he added in disgust.

'No, no, you don't understand,' said Lee, all but dancing with excitement. 'It's a *mussel* shell!'

'I *know* it's a mussel shell. They're all over the rocks where we used to holiday.'

'Mussel shells can make pearls and loongs *love* pearls.'

'Oyster shells make pearls, not mussel shells,' said Jojo, feeling oddly disappointed.

'They can *both* make pearls *and* clams can too! Quick! We need a knife.'

'You should've asked the dragon for the sickle before it took it,' grumbled Jojo, as he struggled with the new turn of events.

'We'll have to use a stone and be super careful not to crush the pearl.'

Jojo doubted there *was* a pearl but at least they had plenty of stones to choose from. He found a flat one and placed the mussel in the middle. 'I'll hold it steady,' he said, but Lee's first blow with a stone was too light.

'You'll have to hit it harder than that.'

'I don't want to hit your fingers,' she muttered.

'Just hit it harder,' he ordered, and flinched as her second blow whacked down. There was a crack and bits of mussel and shell went flying to rain down amongst the stones.

'Oh no!' cried Lee, scrambling after them. Jojo joined the hunt but *if* there were a pearl, it could be anywhere. He grimaced as he picked up a lump of moist flesh but not only wasn't it rotten, it was surprisingly heavy, and he prized it open.

Jojo had seen pearls in jeweller shop windows but nothing like this. It was large, perfectly shaped, and lit with milky fire. 'I've found it,' he said hoarsely. 'You were right. The mussel did have a pearl.'

Lee was suddenly at his shoulder. 'Oh Jojo, it's so beautiful.'

'Let's hope the dragon thinks so. Where shall we put it?'

'*On* the plates, just to make sure.'

Jojo carefully positioned the pearl so it wouldn't roll off and for a moment they simply stared at it. The cavern remained quiet but the air felt like it did before a thunderstorm. 'You were right about it being a loong,' admitted Jojo. 'Dragons don't need pearls.'

'Loongs and dragons have the same hearts,' she said softly, and glanced up at the creatures that lined the walls. 'I think we should wait in the tunnel.'

CHAPTER 67

Jojo was glad to reach the tunnel even though it might be no safer than the cavern below. The plates looked the same but a breeze sent ripples over the lake's surface to disturb the water's icy margin. Ice crystals chimed as they rose and fell, then clashed to release aqua sparks that turned the lake's perimeter into a glittering circle of light.

The chimes were suddenly drowned out by the creaks and booms and organ-like sounds Jojo had heard earlier. Jojo and Lee clamped their hands over their ears as the cavern's confines amplified the racket but it gradually evolved into the sweetest music Jojo had ever heard. He was surprised to feel tears on his cheeks, aware that Lee cried too, but then a great thumping and thwacking erupted as every winged creature in the cavern took flight.

They swept around the circular space, going faster and faster until their shapes blurred and they became nothing more than bands of colour. Gold told of the phoenix, red of Griffy, and green of the serpent which slithered as fast as the creatures flew. Jojo lost sight of the plates but after a while, the bands of colour grew more transparent until it was like peering through a stained glass window. 'The plates are gone!' he gasped.

'And everything's going up!'

Jojo was barely aware he hugged Lee and that she hugged him, as the whirling bands of colour rose up the cavern's walls until, one by one, they disappeared out the opening. It was like watching a sink full of colour-streaked water swirl down a plug hole.

The last of them vanished and Jojo blinked and looked back to the lake. The water was still again but even as he watched, a ripple spread outwards from the centre in a silver circle. The first ripple was followed by a second, then a third, and then a silver horn pierced the water's surface, followed by more horns in silvery blue, then a loong's broad, scale-clad brow, then its sea green eyes, and then a jaw that tapered to a slender snout.

The loong's sinuous neck emerged next, its shining scales coloured every shade of the ocean, from the darkest emerald of its depths to the brightest aqua of its shallows. Jojo could barely breathe but nor could he drag his gaze away. The loong carried the pearl beneath its jaw, but it was many times larger than the pearl Jojo had left on the shore.

Jojo expected the loong to fly straight up through the opening but its sinuous form followed the cavern sides around in a graceful sweep. The snow fell from the stone as it passed to be lit by the loong's blue fire to form a glittering cloud that reminded Jojo of a magnificent snowdome.

Round and round the loong flew, rising in a slow spiral until its head disappeared out the opening, followed by its lithe body and finally the shining taper of its tail. Jojo and Lee remained motionless until the last snowflake drifted to the lake's surface and with a soft puff turned to water again.

It was warmer in the cavern now and the air smelled of damp stone but Jojo felt incapable of moving. The loong had filled the cavern with beauty and he knew that only ugliness waited outside.

'We should get going,' mumbled Lee finally, but Jojo didn't want to release her. She was the only normal thing in a sea of strangeness.

'I don't understand what we just saw,' he admitted.

'We saw a loong and now everything strange has gone. *Griffy's* gone,' she added sadly.

'Back to where she belongs along with all the other things.'

'But what about us, Jojo?' she cried. 'Where do we belong?'

'Here, in this world.'

'Then I hope the Kraken's gone too,' she muttered.

'It probably has, given what's happened,' said Jojo, and took a steadying breath. 'What do you think the loong will do?'

'I don't know but it's wise and powerful so let's hope it's *something*.' Lee sighed. 'We need to eat and then get going. It's late and we don't have the plates for light anymore.'

'No,' agreed Jojo, and grimaced. They were truly on their own now.

Despite his worries, Jojo enjoyed his meal of berries and nuts washed down with the lake's cool water. It no longer tasted of snow and he wondered why the snow had gone along with everything else. At least the empty cavern made it easy to find another tunnel opening. He just hoped it went in the right direction.

The new tunnel was even steeper than the last and went straight up which he hoped was a sign they'd soon be out. But as the dark closed in and his foot throbbed, he worried they simply toiled towards a pile of burning trash. Lee led and the gloom meant he could barely see her but it wasn't long before her voice drifted back. 'We're almost out.'

He forced himself to greater speed and her silhouette appeared against the outlines of bushes. 'They're not thorny,' she reassured him, as she pushed her way through. Jojo followed, relieved to be outside again, even if it were dusk. 'We're almost at the top of the Mountains,' she said, and headed off.

Jojo groaned; he'd hoped they *were* at the top. He hobbled after her but when she stopped, she didn't stare ahead but back from where they'd come, and Jojo reluctantly looked that way too. The thin grey line of the ocean was visible from their vantage point, and the usual blanket of cloud, but then a shaft of the setting sun pierced it as the loong had pierced the lake, and the sky and sea flashed a brilliant blue before the grey closed in again.

Something shifted inside of Jojo and he took a long, slow breath. 'The loong's mending the world,' he murmured.

'It's making a start but it's a big job.'

'The loong's wise and powerful,' he reminded her gently.

'But we're not.'

Jojo pulled her into a hug. 'We've made it this far so let's see what the Mountains hold.'

The descent was steep and as the light faded, Jojo realised that anyone on this side of the Mountains had a very big climb if they wanted to see the ocean. His foot was beyond painful and he was considering suggesting a rest when Lee stopped. 'Do you smell that?' she asked.

'Smoke,' said Jojo, unsure whether to be worried or relieved. 'If it's people, it's best they don't know we're here,' he said, keeping his voice low.

'And if it's trash, we can go back and tell Markus he was right after all,' whispered Lee, but Jojo heard the fear in her voice.

The smoke carried the clean smell of wood and after a while they heard voices too. Jojo gestured for silence and they crouched behind a tree and peered down. The orange glow of a fire was clearly visible below them, as were the group of people who gathered around it, as were the crooked buildings behind them.

'It looks the same as the Town,' whispered Lee in disappointment.

Jojo settled on his backside to ease his aching foot. 'So, we either go down or we go back.'

'Or we go around,' said Lee. All Jojo wanted was to go to bed. 'There's old people there and children running about,' murmured Lee. 'It looks like they're cooking together on the fire.'

A voice sounded, sharp and authoritative, and Jojo tensed as a hush fell on the group, but then the same voice started to sing. It was a man's voice, deep and resonant, and soon joined by other men's voices, and women's, and children's. Jojo was reminded of singing in the car with his mum and dad, and with Davy on camping trips. He couldn't hear the words and the singers weren't always in tune especially the children.

The song ended with hoots of laughter but neither Jojo nor Lee moved. They'd had no choice in where they'd washed up but they had a choice now and Jojo could think of lots of reasons to sneak away. They knew nothing about these people's beliefs, or way of life, or welcome of strangers.

'It looks like a happy place,' said Lee, and Jojo nodded.

A happy place seemed such a small thing, but in some ways, it was everything. 'And if it isn't?' he asked.

'We don't have to stay.'

They got to their feet and for a long moment simply stared at each other, and then they gripped hands, and made their way down to the fire.

END OF

THE DRAGON OF THE

DROWNED WORLD

If you enjoyed Jojo's adventures, you might enjoy those of Jax, a shifter, in *I Heard the Wolf Call My Name*. Here is a peek.

Jax watched the barred shadows fade on the wall. It was the first time he had noticed the light changing which told him the medics pumped fewer sedatives into him, as did his increase in pain. Fighting the straps had not hurt before but it did now. And reducing his medication did not mean they would not return to knock him out for the night and once they had, he would not be going anywhere.

He had not *shifted* since Rua had blown but shifting was as natural as breathing. What made his gut churn was not knowing how birth-form injuries affected a shift-form. If he was just as badly cut up in shift-form, his chances of escape were nil.

There was only way to find out. He needed a shift-form that could shed the drips and catheters, slip through window bars, and get him through the perimeter fence, and assuming he was still at Rilo, he knew the route to take. Rats, moko and snakes came to mind but none could cross moana to Iolana which meant he would need a second shift-form.

Shifting took strength and younger Ahi were warned against *shifting* multiple times without resting in between and Jax was already weak. He would just have to rest when he reached Iolana *if* he reached it.

He took one last look at the ceiling and felt the familiar slide, as if he slipped into one of Rua's cool lagoons, then pain jagged. He had a moment of panicked confusion before his birth-form brain realized the tubes and catheters had ripped from his body, then the pain stopped and as shift-form consciousness grew, he slithered from the bed.

He reached the window, reared upright, and slid through the bars. The window did not lead to outside as he had supposed, but to a corridor, and he cursed his stupidity. No military building had exterior windows open to the weather. He turned along the corridor and set off, flicking his tongue as he went. The floor reeked of antiseptic and he was slowed by its lack of traction.

He craved the cover of bushes but vibrations told of the thump of military boots instead and he took refuge under a trolley parked against the wall. The vibrations dwindled and he went on, hugging the skirting board and seeking deeper shadows where he could but the sense of threat grew and his shift-form consciousness yearned to strike.

Off-islander voices boomed and his muscles bunched but then a sharp drop in temperature told him a door had opened to the outside. He tasted sweat on the air and the vibrations increased but he launched himself forward, the boom of voices like thunder and the air moving as men leapt aside, but there was earth under his belly now and he sped on.

He wove through the bushes at speed, skirted the square, and reached the grass beyond it. Leaves scraped his scales and he slowed as he tasted frog and mouse on the air. His shift-form consciousness urged him to seek them out but his birth-form consciousness hurried him on. The perimeter fence was blurred but its metallic smell was strong and its links rasped his scales as he slid through.

He went on through the trees to the deeper shadows and rested for a moment below the spreading branches of a tree. It was a relief to be beyond the fence but then he sensed movement and looked up. The darkness was smudged by the gold eyes of an owl and then he heard wings scythe the air as it swooped.

Take a peek at other works by K S Nikakis
Non Fiction
Travel and Poetry

Journey: Seeking the Sacred, Spirit and Soul in the Australian Wilderness – For fans of Joseph Campbell's hero journey.

When we set out into the wilderness, what is it we really seek?

Do we seek new sights or do we seek new selves? And are we really on one journey or on two?

Journeying fifteen thousand kilometres into Australia's blood-red heart, Nikakis discovers that every journey is perilous, for travellers risk carrying the clutter of their outer lives with them; a clutter that blinds them to the other journey they crave; that of the inner soul-journey into a deeper understanding of self.

To enter Australia's vast Outback wilderness, is to enter a place of endless horizons; a place doused with brilliant gold dawns and dazzling sunsets; a place silvered by star-encrusted night skies and, most importantly, a place of hidden sacred places in whose deep stillness our inner journeys can at last unfold.

In the spirit of travellers like Robert Macfarlane and Scott Stillman, Nikakis asks what it is we really see, feel and understand when we follow in the steps of those who have gone before us deep into the wilderness.

Drawing on her Ph.D. in Joseph Campbell's hero myth, and using original poetry and novel extracts, Nikakis takes us on this second journey; a journey of the sacred, spirit and soul, where our inner selves finally have the time and space to gift us richer and more fully-realised lives.

In the Company of Birds: Poems from an Outback Odyssey – For lovers of birds and travel (especially through Outback Australia).

What do we lose when we cease to be a child and become an adult? What precious thing do we let slip away and barely notice?

Watch any child in a garden or park or wilderness area as they discover the natural world. Listen to their ooh's of delight at the sight of a caterpillar on a leaf, their excited squeals as a butterfly bobs past, their clap of hands and gap-toothed grins at the gambol of some young animal.

Children delight in the most common and mundane elements of the natural world with a pure and unsullied joy that many of us, somewhere in our journey to adulthood, have lost. We largely remain unaware of our loss, although I recall the exact moment I became conscious that while I saw the beauty of the natural world, I no longer felt it in the deepest parts of my soul.

As adults, we might continue to admire the natural world's beauty on an intellectual level and seek connection with it for our physical, mental, and spiritual health. It's one of the reasons I set out on a 50 day journey through Australia's southern wilderness, but how often do we ignore the sparrows at our feet in our eagerness to admire the eagles that soar above? And when so many things demand our adult attention, how do we even make time to look in the first place?

Beauty surrounds us, as it surrounds a child, but our adult gaze seeks out the extraordinary and so blinds us to the ordinary, denying us the visceral joy that such things deliver. To reclaim this joy, we must suspend our adult judgement and clear our gaze as a child does.

A journey in the company of birds allows us the time and space to do so. Birds require us to search the ground as well as the sky, to delight in the raven's harsh croak as well as the honeyeater's sweet song, to take pleasure in the sparrow's brown plumage as well as the fairywren's blue. And as we still, and look, and listen, we are ultimately rewarded with the return of all we've lost.

And so, let us begin this journey of rediscovery, in the company of birds.

Fantasy Novel Series

Angel Caste 5 book series

Book 1 Angel Blood

Street-kid, thief, criminal: Viv is desperate to change her life.

On day release from jail to attend the funeral of her father, a violent drunk she feared and despised, her real father turns up, the powerful angel Archae Kald. He offers to reunite Viv with the mother she thought dead and, determined to find the only person who has ever loved her, Viv travels through a rift to the male angel world of Ezam.

Kald assigns his protégé, the beautiful angel Thris, to guide Viv to her mother. It is Thris's job to keep Viv safe in the Rynth, the vast tangle of worlds she never knew existed. But Viv is deeply damaged from her life on the streets and in no mood to trust anyone, even an angel with a face to die for. They set out, but as the complications multiply, disaster follows.

Thris might be eons old, but he knows little about females, especially ones who are half human. Like his closest friends, Ash and Ky, all he wants to do is transcend but when he and Viv stumble into the acrid world of Moth Fold, and Viv's latent angel traits emerge, transcendence seems the last thing possible.

After a devastating attack, Viv ends up lost and alone in the Rynth. Will she survive to continue the search for her mother? Or end her days in an alien world?

If you like your female heroes feisty, your male angels glorious, your fantasy worlds filled with brilliant landscapes and a dash of romance, you will love *Angel Blood*, Book 1 in the five book fantasy series *Angel Caste*.

Buy *Angel Blood* today to start your amazing adventure with Viv and Thris in the wild worlds of the Rynth.

Book 2 Angel Breath

Viv can survive on the streets, but can she survive in the Rynth?

Thris is gone, his exquisite body torn apart, and borne away by Ash and Ky. Viv fears she will never see him again, but there is no way she is turning back. She journeys on through the Rynth, narrowly escaping murderous landscapes and worlds full of savage creatures. Her life on the streets might have been a nightmare, but at least it taught her how to run, hide, and out-wit pursuers.

And then, when all seems lost, Thris returns. Viv is overjoyed, but her happiness is short-lived. He isn't the angel he was, and he isn't alone. Ky is with him, and Ky hates Viv. The feeling is mutual, but Ky's terror of the Rynth adds to their peril and they don't get far before they are besieged by savage, long-armed creatures. When Ky is injured, Thris is confronted with a terrible decision, and must abandon Viv to save him.

Viv journeys on but stumbles into a war zone. Desperate to escape, she is determined to take the net rift out, but finds a little girl, the sole survivor of a massacre. Recognizing the chance to make amends for the accident that landed her in jail, Viv delays the search for her mother, to take the little girl to safety.

But in an alien, war-torn world, it is all but impossible to tell friend from foe, and when the little girl falls ill, Viv must take a terrible risk. Will Viv manage to save the little girl? Or will the fighting cost them both their lives?

If you like your female heroes feisty, your male angels glorious, your fantasy worlds filled with brilliant landscapes and a dash of romance, you will love *Angel Breath*, Book 2 in the five book fantasy series *Angel Caste*.

Buy *Angel Breath* today to continue your amazing journey with Viv and Thris through the wild worlds of the Rynth.

Book 3 Angel Bone

Viv didn't abscond from jail to become someone else's prisoner, but that seems to be her fate.

As chance would have it, she resembles a people called the elddra, and that makes her both despised and desired. It also makes friends few and far between. Viv is desperate to deliver the little girl to safety, take a rift out, and resume the search for her mother, but dodging the new world's warring factions proves harder than she thinks.

As they journey on through strange and hostile lands, the little girl's trust and affection for Viv grows, and Viv is surprised by her own feelings of fierce protectiveness. And then, as they near safety, disaster strikes. They are overtaken by fighters and separated. Viv is seized and when the fighters are annihilated by a second force, their leader assumes she is one of the enemy. Prevented from executing her on the spot, the leader condemns her to a slower, more painful death.

In his own world, Thris struggles to care for Ky who is traumatized by his time in the Rynth, and when Ky flees, they end up imprisoned in a maze-like world where the only way out is a death-trap. Their hopes for rescue lie in Ash, but Ash is trapped too, entranced by a world of shining light, and unaware of his friends' plight.

Will Viv survive to be reunited with the child she loves? Or will she lose her too, as she has lost her mother and Thris?

If you like your female heroes feisty, your male angels glorious, your fantasy worlds filled with brilliant landscapes and a dash of romance, you will love *Angel Bone*, Book 3 in the five book fantasy series *Angel Caste*.

Buy *Angel Bone* today to continue your amazing journey with Viv and Thris through the wild worlds of the Rynth.

Book 4 Angel Bound

Viv thought things couldn't get any worse, but she is about to be proved wrong.

To reunite with the child she loves, she must navigate a perilous fold and lethal dangers lie in wait. She comes close to death but aid comes from a man whose kindness is something Viv has never experienced before. He needs her trust but haunted by images of witch-burnings, Viv daren't reveal what she really is. Complications multiply until being with him, and the child she yearns for, seems impossible.

Bound by his pledge to guide Viv to her mother, Thris returns, but his search for Viv ends catastrophically. All Viv's nightmares come true when she discovers his fate but saving him might cost her everything.

In Ezam, Ky and Ash uncover warnings about another trinity of angels who disappeared eons before in mysterious circumstances. The warnings are fragmentary, as if they have been deliberately destroyed.

Can Viv save the angel she loves? Or will she lose him and everything else she has come to care about?

If you like your female heroes feisty, your male angels glorious, your fantasy worlds filled with brilliant landscapes and a dash of romance, you will love *Angel Bound*, Book 4 in the five book fantasy series A*ngel Caste*.

Buy *Angel Bound* today to continue your amazing journey with Viv and Thris through the wild worlds of the Rynth.

Book 5 Angel Blessed

It seems Lady Luck has smiled on Viv at last. Or has she?

When Viv is offered the chance of a home with the little girl she loves, she grabs it but then the child is snatched. To rescue her, not only must Viv battle the little girl's enemies, but those who love the child as well.

The perilous quest leaves Viv horribly injured, and she ends up in a world where she is offered the opportunity to finally heal herself. It means opening herself to terrible new risks but also the possibility of securing the little girl's safety, once and for all.

She returns to the child's world but is pursued by those who believe she holds the key to their deepest desires and, as their threats escalate to violence, Thris reappears. Viv's happiness soon turns to dread, as he reveals a threat that could destroy the little girl's world, as well as his own. Thris joins with Ky and Ash in a desperate fight to avoid the impending catastrophe and as events build to a climax, Viv prepares to sacrifice everything for those she loves.

Will Viv's search finally deliver her the loving home she craves? Or will she, and those she cares about, end their lives in the cataclysm that threatens?

If you like your female heroes feisty, your male angels glorious, and your fantasy worlds filled with brilliant landscapes and a dash of romance, you will love *Angel Blessed*, the final book in the five book fantasy series *Angel Caste*.

Buy *Angel Blessed* today to conclude your amazing journey with Viv and Thris through the wild worlds of the Rynth.

Angel Caste – Complete 5 Book Series

A troubled half-angel, a beautiful angel guide, a binding promise . . .

Viv is on day release from jail to attend the funeral of the thug she thinks is her father, when she comes face to face with her real father, the powerful angel Archae Kald. If finding out she's a half-angel isn't shocking enough, Viv discovers her mother isn't dead after all but lost somewhere in the tangle of worlds called the Rynth.

Determined to find the only person who has ever truly loved her, Viv goes to Kald's angel world where he appoints the beautiful Thris as her guide. Thris is kind and caring, unlike the males Viv has known before, but after living on the streets, Viv finds it almost impossible to trust.

Friendship grows as Thris trains her to travel the rifts, but the Rynth is a dark and dangerous place, even for angels and, as Thris grows increasingly tempted by Viv's emerging angel traits, disaster strikes.

Viv journeys on alone and stumbles into a war zone where she finds a lost child. She pledges to take the child to safety but, as the war rages on, deciding who is friend and who is enemy becomes a deadly game of chance.

Bound by his promise to guide Viv to her mother, Thris embarks on a desperate search for her, but a greater threat confronts them both and, in the end, they must fight not just for their own lives, but for the lives of those they love.

The Kira Chronicles - 6 book Series

Book 1 The Whisper of Leaves

A gold-eyed Healer, a prophecy, two brothers at war.

In seasons long past, twin gold-eyed princes sundered a kingdom. Rejecting his brother's warrior ways, Kasheron led his people away to establish the Tremen community of Allogrenia, deep in the great southern forests. Forgotten by the outside world and protected by the trackless trees, the Tremen flourish for seasons uncounted, upholding Kasheron's legacy of peace and healing.

All Tremen delight in the healing arts, but Kira is the greatest Healer of them all.

To the north of Allogrenia, drought grips the land, and the Shargh suffer. A herding people, they lost their grazing tracts to the Northern invaders years before, through long and bloody wars. As the drought tightens its grip, and their herd animals die, the chief's younger brother seizes on an ancient prophecy to snatch the chiefship for himself.

The prophecy links the Shargh's doom to a gold-eyed Healer, and Kira has gold eyes.

The Shargh attack with devastating consequences, and Kira must fight to save the wounded. But the Shargh wounds rot, no matter her skill, and as the blood-shed continues, Kira faces losing everything and everyone she loves.

Can Kira cure the Shargh wounds? Or will the Tremen community be destroyed? If you love your female heroes feisty, your fantasy worlds with sun-dappled forests, quiet owl-filled nights, and just the right dash of romance, you will love T*he Whisper of Leaves*, Book 1 of the six book *The Kira Chronicles* series.

Buy *The Whisper of Leaves* today to enter the forest world of the Tremen and start your amazing adventure with Kira as she fights to save her people.

Book 2 The Silence of Stone

How can fire quench fire?

The Tremen are dying and Kira is in a deadly race against time to save them. Somewhere deep in the Warens' labyrinth of underground tunnels, lies the answer to a riddle and the cure to Shargh wounds.

To find it, she must defeat the tunnels' unmapped darkness *and* Kest, the blue-eyed, blond-haired Commander of the Protectors. As leader of the force Kasheron established to keep the Tremen safe, Kest is sworn to protect, and everything Kira does puts her at terrible risk.

As she fights to heal, and he to protect, they join in an uneasy alliance to save the people they love.

When Kira is made Tremen Leader, the stakes rise even further. The Tremen are riven by division and Kira must fight to stop the Tremen community from breaking apart. Desperate to find the cause of the Shargh attacks and stop the Tremen's suffering, she goes ever deeper into the Warens' perilous darkness. Kest searches too, his quest in the sunlit forests above.

When he and his men make a gruesome discovery, he realizes what drives the Sharghs' murderous attacks, but then he makes a deadly mistake.

As Kira learns more of her brutal lineage, she is confronted with the horrifying truth that to save her people, she must lose them forever. Can Kira preserve Kasheron's legacy of peace and healing? Or will all he fought for be swept away by the violence he fled?

307

If you love your female heroes feisty, your fantasy worlds with sun-dappled forests, quiet owl-filled nights, and just the right dash of romance, you will love The *Silence of Stone*, Book 2 of the six book *The Kira Chronicles* series.

Buy *The Silence of Stone* today to enter the forest world of the Tremen and start your amazing adventure with Kira as she fights to save her people.

Book 3 The Secrets of Stars

What truths lie hidden in the stars?

Kira is alone, her food all but exhausted, the forest and those she loves, far behind her. When she stumbles on a stranger under attack, she faces a terrible choice: betray everything Kasheron fought for or walk away.

The stranger, Caledon, knows a path over the mountains and has friends nearby who can help them, but Kira's quest is clear: go straight north, gain aid for her people, and return home.

They continue together but the Azurcades are perilous and when a terrible storm threatens to sweep them to their deaths, their journey becomes a battle for survival.

Kira's trust in Caledon grows and his gentleness rouses other, deeper feelings, but Caledon is ruled by forces that pose a lethal threat to her quest. She plans her escape, but new lands bring new enemies and she is taken prisoner.

Fleeing her captors, Kira finds herself with a people under Shargh attack. As the carnage mounts and she joins with their Healers to save the wounded, her stocks of fireweed run dangerously low. Caledon strives to regain her trust and the stakes escalate when he reveals terrible truths that threaten the Tremen's very existence.As the slaughter continues and Kira embarks on a hazardous search for fireweed, disaster strikes and she is snatched by the Shargh warrior who has long hunted her.

Can Kira survive to reach the north and finally deliver aid to her people? Or will her quest end at the Shargh's brutal hands?

If you love your female heroes feisty, your fantasy worlds with sun-dappled forests, quiet owl-filled nights, and just the right dash of romance, you will love *The Secrets of Stars*, Book 3 of the six book *The Kira Chronicles series*.

Buy *The Secrets of Stars* today to enter the forest world of the Tremen and continue your amazing adventure with Kira as she fights to save her people.

Book 4 The Thunder of Hoofs

Who is friend and who is enemy?

When Kira's Shargh captors are attacked, she finds herself a prisoner of those who might prove even deadlier. But then, in a heart-rending twist of fate, their leader is revealed to be the bearer of everything Kira most loved in the world *and* everything Kasheron most despised.

Kira hides her identity but her subterfuge is discovered and the dangers multiply. Her quest is to gain aid from her northern kin, but the forests that hid the Tremen from enemies, also hid them from friends, and there is no help for a people without alliance or treaty. To make matters worse, the northern histories tell a very different story of the great Healer Kasheron.

To aid the Tremen, Kira must turn south again, to where Caledon will bring the Tremen fighters but she and the northern leader share a powerful attraction and he's determined to keep her safely in the north, far from the Shargh. Desperate to learn of Kira's fate, Caledon journeys north too and they are reunited, but his arrival generates antagonisms that threaten alliances and treatiesalike. As Caledon strives to decipher the stars' intent, the stakes escalate, and he fears following his heart could cause the deaths of countless others.

Kira is no slave to the stars and, driven by her duties as leader, sets out for the south.Besieged by squalling winds and icy storms, her escort comes under Shargh attack and she finds herself in a desperate flight through the night in a terrifying attempt to outrun them. But Shargh hunters lie in wait, and in a deadly rain of spears, her mare goes down.

Can Kira survive to finally deliver aid to her people? Or will her quest end in the wind-swept darkness?

If you love your female heroes feisty, your fantasy worlds with sun-dappled forests, quiet owl-filled nights, and just the right dash of romance, you will love *The Thunder of Hoofs*, Book 4 of the six book *The Kira Chronicles* series.

Buy *The Thunder of Hoofs* today to enter the forest world of the Tremen and continue your amazing adventure with Kira as she fights to save her people.

Book 5 The Crying of Birds

Must Tremen healing bow before Terak swords?

Kira's deepest fears are realized when the Tremen are forced from the forests to join the devastating conflict on the plain. To add to her guilt, she can't remain with the people she leads but must go north. Sarnia has no healing, and if the fighting spreads, their wounded will die.

Leaving behind those she loves, she endures the perilous journey back to Sarnia, only to confront powerful forces determined to keep the ways of the despised Healer Kasheron out of the city. As Kira fights to create a place of healing, aid comes from an unexpected quarter, but a healing place without fireweed will save no lives.

Kira's search for fireweed grows increasingly desperate and then her worst nightmare comes true when the person she loves most in the world is mortally wounded. As the fighting drags on and winter deepens, the injured flood in and Kira's struggle to save them takes a deadly toll.

In the south, the Shargh tribes join, and Tierken makes a terrible mistake that puts Sarnia at risk. Distrust weakens their forces and as the bloodshed grows, treachery promises to deliver a Shargh victory. And then, as Tierken and his men fight for their very existence, word reaches him that Kira's life hangs in the balance. Faced with a terrible dilemma, he makes a choice that risks the destruction of his leadership in the north

Kira flees to the healing settlement of Kessom but to reach its sanctuary, she must navigate the raging torrent that claimed Tierken's father. Will Kira survive to reach the healing she so desperately needs? Or will her journey end in the watery darkness?

If you love your female heroes feisty, your fantasy worlds with sun-dappled forests, quiet owl-filled nights, and just the right dash of romance, you will love *The Crying of Birds*, Book 5 of the six book *The Kira Chronicles* series.

Buy *The Crying of Birds* today to enter the forest world of the Tremen and continue your amazing adventure with Kira as she fights to save her people.

Book 6 The Music of Home

What is the price of peace?

With the fighting over, Tierken pursues Kira to Kessom where she is overjoyed to be reunited with him, but neither have escaped the battles unscathed. Kira's health is fragile and Tierken's aggression is honed from months of fighting. To add to the complications, Tierken's enemies in Sarnia have taken full advantage of his absence in the south.

Angered by their scheming and frustrated by Kira's refusal to bend to his will, his arguments with her escalate until Kira realizes the breach between the Tremen and Terak is too large for her to mend. Her hopes for a future with Tierken shattered, she sets out for home, but the Sarsalin is full of dangers and enemies lie in wait.

Caledon waits too as he struggles to reconcile his own want of Kira with the wants and needs of the stars. They travel south together and when they come upon a sick Shargh child, Kira begins to understand the brutal consequences of the fighting, and that bloodshed can only ever seed more bloodshed.

Desperate to prevent future warfare, Kira resolves to offer the Shargh people healing, despite knowing it will likely cost her life. But when she reaches the Shargh settlement, she makes a shocking discovery that changes everything.

There are Shargh women there who crave peace as she does, but she comes face to face with the man who believes her death will deliver him everything he desires, and as the final chilling part of the last Telling unfolds, she realizes for the first time, what is truly precious to her and what is worth fighting for.

Will Kira survive to return to all she loves, or make the ultimate sacrifice as she strives for peace?

If you love your female heroes feisty, your fantasy worlds with sun-dappled forests, quiet owl-filled nights, and just the right dash of romance, you will love *The Music of Home*, the final installment in *The Kira Chronicles* series.

Buy *The Music of Home* today to enter the forest world of the Tremen and complete your amazing adventure with Kira as she fights to save her people.

The Kira Chronicles – Complete 6 Book Series

A gold-eyed Healer, a prophecy, two brothers at war.

In seasons long past, twin gold-eyed princes sundered a kingdom. Rejecting his brother Terak's warrior ways, Kasheron led his people deep into the great southern forests and established the healing settlement of Allogrenia. The Tremen flourished, upholding Kasheron's legacy of peace and healing, and protected by the vast, trackless trees.

All Tremen delight in the healing arts, but Kira is the greatest Healer of them all.

To the north of Allogrenia, drought ravages the Shargh's land, and as their suffering escalates, the chief's younger brother seizes on an ancient prophecy to snatch the chiefship for himself. The prophecy links the Shargh's doom to a gold-eyed Healer, and Kira has gold eyes.

The Shargh attack with devastating consequences and Kira must fight to save the wounded, but the Shargh wounds rot, no matter her skill, and Kira finds herself in a deadly race against time. As the slaughter continues, she makes the horrifying discovery that the Shargh hunt her. To halt the attacks and save her people, she sets off for the North to seek aid from her long sundered warrior kin.

But the dangers beyond the forests exceed even the Shargh attacks. The Tremen detest their warrior kin but Terak's descendants have inflicted a worse fate on the Tremen. Kira's new-found love is torn apart by ancient hostilities and when trust turns to betrayal, it risks everything she has fought for.

As the battles rage on, Kira becomes increasingly sickened by the bloodshed. Desperate to end the suffering once and for all, she sets out on a quest that could cost her everything and everyone she loves.

Fantasy Novels

The Emerald Serpent:

Check out the fabulous book trailer

https://www.youtube.com/watch?v=bGpKxnpCEMg

Betrayal, torture, death: Etaine lives on only to destroy those who robbed her of everything she loved.

Seven years before, Etaine met fellow Ranger Cormac, the he-Eadar she believed was her longed-for true-mate. Emerald-eyed, white-skinned, and black-haired, the Eadar had formed into Ranger bands to fight the Fada, invading religious zealots determined to replace the Eadar's Serpent Goddess with their own gods of stone.

The pure blood of the ancient Eadar runs strong in Etaine and Cormac's veins, and their joining had the potential to open the Emerald and Serpent Ways to them, old worlds only true Eadar can enter. But their love affair goes tragically amiss, with catastrophic consequences.

Etaine flees and as the years pass, slowly rebuilds her life, but as the Fada's attacks grow more ferocious, the Eadar are forced to fight for their very existence. When the Fada mass to commit yet more bloody slaughter, and the bands join in a final, desperate effort to defeat them, Etaine comes under Cormac's command, the very last Eadar she ever wants to see again.

Together they have a weapon that can destroy the Fada, but can Etaine learn to trust again? And Cormac to Remember? And time runs short: the Serpent rises.

Don't miss the enthralling story of Etaine and Cormac's fight to defeat the Fada, reclaim their love, and revive the old worlds of the Eadar. Set in the ancient Caledonian Forest of Northern Scotland, with its misty crags and bright, rushing streams, *The Emerald Serpent* will delight those who love their fantasy with a touch of Celtic.

Buy *The Emerald Serpent* today to share Etaine and Cormac's amazing quest to rid their beautiful worlds of the Fada threat.

Heart Hunter

Fleet is a young Sceadu hunter: skilled, strong, and fast. She hunts deep into the icy mountains, seeking meat for her people, for the rains have failed and plunged the Sceadu into hunger.

Her hunts are hard, but she has much to look forward to. Soon she will be gifted her air-name by the Sceadu's shaman, and then she will be a full adult, and free to marry the man she loves.

But while Fleet is on hunt, the old shaman dies, and the new shaman visions a very different future for her: cross the frozen, ice-locked mountains and complete a perilous quest or lose the man she loves forever.

In a moment of anger and frustration, Fleet commits a terrible wrong and sets out into the frigid mountains to atone with her life. In a journey that takes her deep into the earth's darkest places, into strange new worlds, and even into Death itself, she discovers that only she can save her people. To survive, she must draw on every shred of her hunter strength, and doing the impossible, it turns out, is just the beginning.

If you love strong, independent female hunters, bright snowy landscapes, worlds where truth might lie in the mystical realms of a vision-quest, and a dash of romance, you will love *Heart Hunter*.

Buy *Heart Hunter* today to share Fleet's danger, joy, and discoveries in her quest to save her people and the man she loves.

The Third Moon

Where does the past end and the future begin?

Haunted by inherited memories of his people's dispossession and theft of their children, Warrain is just twelve years old when the nightmare repeats. But Warrain isn't living on Earth in the 21st Century, he is living on the planet Imago in the far flung future.

Five years before, Station One's Mech's got high on the opioid arrash, and in the bloodshed that followed, Warrain's scientific community were expelled from the Station, his father murdered, and his mother and unborn sibling lost to him.

The scientists carve out a rudimentary Station high in Imago's ranges, and Warrain's friends get on with their lives. Not Warrain; he climbs the Tors to stare down at Station One, dream of his mother and sibling, and plot revenge.

And then one day, everything changes. A third moon appears in the sky, one of Imago's life-forms calls him by name, and disease breaks out at Station One.

When the Mechs visit to seek help for their ill, Warrain seizes the opportunity to deal them a blow they will never forget. But the third moon brings changes that threaten them all and, to aid the life-form whose kind is being dispossessed and slaughtered, he must turn his back on the hate that has long sustained him and find another way to live.

If you are fascinated by the power of memory, the excitement of life on other planets, and like your fantasy with a dash of romance, you will love *The Third Moon*.

Buy *The Third Moon* today to share Warrain's life on Imago as he struggles to protect Imago's creatures and make the planet truly his home.

Messenger

In a world made deaf by hatred, who will hear the messenger?

Severine's world ends the day her family is murdered. Being raised in the loving community of gay Travelers always marked her as an outsider, but being female puts her in mortal danger. Women are scarce, precious, and hunted.

When chance brings Severine face to face with the father she has never known, he assigns the son of his murdered best friend to guard her. They soon clash. Severine believes all men are violent brutes and Jeph resents his freedoms being curtailed.

An uneasy understanding grows but Jeph is glad to deliver her to the Enclaves, a sanctuary her father has carved out in the mountains for his women and children. But there is no safety in a world broken by war and sickness and when violence follows her, Severine flees to the northern city of Andhaka in search of a home amongst her mother's people. Jeph follows, bound by loyalty to her father, but the north holds terrible dangers for him.

It's been years since Andhaka has welcomed outsiders with anything but bullets, and to survive and to protect Jeph, Severine must learn to use her enemies' weapons against them. As the stakes rise, she comes to understand the horror of her mother's loss, and what drove her father north seventeen years before. His quest becomes her quest, but she hasn't counted on the savage legacy that war and sickness have left behind, or on falling in love.

Can Severine succeed where her father failed? Or will her fate prove even deadlier than his? If you love your fantasy set in brilliant new worlds, with characters you really care about, and just the right dash of romance, you will love *Messenger*.

Buy *Messenger* today to share Severine's journey as she fights for a home, the man she loves, and a better world.

Fantasy Short Stories

Take a peek at excerpts from my short stories.

The Gift – A Deep Fantasy Short Story #1 – free on my website at www.ksnikakis.com

Thariel sat for a long time, surveying all around her, as if she ate the world that would soon be memory. Then she took the harness from the mare, and with soft words, thanked her and bade her farewell. Her own feet she turned towards the forest, tossing her face-plate aside as she went, so that her hair fell loose to her waist, then she discarded her chest-armor, the sword and dagger, her bow and quiver.

The trees closed in and she came at last to the lake Men call Menios, and stood for a while on its shore. An owl cried and a mouse shrieked, and all around her the souls of the newly dead jostled in their journey to the void. She stepped into the water and the new life inside her quivered.

'Fear not, little one,' she whispered, in her own tongue. 'We are going home.'

The Tale of Prince Anura – A Deep Fantasy Short Story #2 – free on my website at www.ksnikakis.com

I should have been happy, for she was beautiful. Dark rivers of curls, skin as white as moonlight on water, breasts softer than spawn, and she loved me well. But her chamber was small, no matter the comfort of her bed, and the old feelings of entrapment rose, as persistent as gas that bubbles from rot below still waters.

I sat at the casement and listened, as I had once loitered near the watery skin of the second world and waited. The moon grew large and small many times, but it came at last, as I knew it would. The soft lament on the night-time air, the song of a soul as confined as mine. It took me a journey of many days through the depths of a massive forest to find her tower.

Stone it was and sheer, and as remote as the third world's glimmer had once been. I sang to her and she answered with sweet melodies of her own and we made love as frogs do, with our voices. And when trust had built, she let down her shining ladder of golden hair.

Glass-Heart – A Deep Fantasy Short Story #3
Finalist Best YA Short Story – 2019 Aurealis Awards

Geth moved amongst his band, exchanging quiet words while they waited. Some he had fought with since the Tallon's foul ships had first found their shores while others had come later, when the burn of cot and kin had sent them from their valleys.

Hate drove them but hate was no shield against arrow and knife. It was fighting skills that kept them hale, and Geth ensured they had them aplenty. He needed them living, not just for their own sakes and his, but for what would come later. When the Tallon's stain had been scoured away, the destroyed must be rebuilt.

Kyth sat alone and he went to her and gazed about. 'The glass-heart's fled, has it?'

'I sent her to a place of safety. She will come to me when it is over.'

'Safety was what I wanted for you!'

'And what I wanted for Nyar.' Her eyes caught the star-sheen as she looked up at him. 'But you can't always have what you want, can you, Ceannasai?'

Dragon Sprite – A Deep Fantasy Short Story #4

Genn rocketed straight upwards, not just because she enjoyed seeing the limitless blue sky before her, but because a Waiwin's wing shape made vertical flight harder for them. Orin didn't try to catch her but swept in circles around her, gaining height in an ever-narrowing spiral. It was a clever tactic and one Genn didn't believe he had thought of in the instant she had cleared the trees. He had obviously studied her strategies and developed a plan to counter them *or so he thought*.

Genn waited until the spiral narrowed to axeel, the minimum distance a Waiwin must keep from a Velven unless she *accepted* him, then swerved towards him, narrowing the distance between them. Orin's eyes flashed to black, shocked she had accepted him, but before he could act, she folded her wings and dropped.

The strength that had driven Orin's pursuit had surged to his wing-tendrils in anticipation of locking them with hers and he would struggle even to stay airborne until it flowed back.

Ghost Stream – A Deep Fantasy Short Story #5

It rained that day, a mighty deluge and as I watched the water sweep across the ground I wished I had made the water angry earlier. The rain did not last and the next morning the ground was dry as dust but that night I was woken by a roar. Worse still, was the pound of hoofs that told me the cattle ran in panic. The night was thick as I headed out with the stockmen, Billy by my side, to discover the river I had never seen flow, stormed along in full flood. I rode with the men to save the cattle but the water cut between us so that only Billy was with me as we drove the cattle back.

And then the water divided us too. I heard Billy's shout as I spurred after some breakaways, and then my horse was gone, and I was in the torrent, and the night turned in upon itself.

And now I linger here, dead but not at peace, when all I want is rest.

The White Stag – A Deep Fantasy Short Story #6

Tom wiped his shaking hand across his mouth and felt the temperature drop. Colder air settled in the holloway but this was something different and he sensed the start of another mind-tricking episode.

There was certainly nothing natural about the mist that swirled about him or the visitors it brought. At first Tom thought the figure he saw was a poacher with an ill-gotten pheasant slung about his shoulders but then he realised it was the hindmost walker in a line of other walkers. They were skin-clad, their naked backs and legs pale in the silvery light. The men carried small packs and spears, the women hide-wrapped bundles or small children. They went without speaking and then they were gone.

Rite – A Deep Fantasy Short Story #7

My memories have got pretty jumbled over the years.
Sometimes I think I might've been a stockman who
drowned when I chased cattle into a flooded river, refusing
to let a mob of dumb-arsed beasts outsmart me, or maybe
I was a tradie who wouldn't let a bit of water over the road
get in the way of the quickest route home. Maybe I dived
into a river I thought was deep, or likely didn't think at all
beyond beating my mates in, or maybe I did none of these
things. Yet in some weird way, I know I died in water, and
that if there is more than one of me, we all went into the
water and bloody well never came out.

 I mightn't know how I ended up here, dead but
somehow not dead, and a hell of a long way from
anywhere I'd ever been before but I do know exactly
where *here* is, thanks to the sign driven into the rock-
hard ground. Its metal might be a bit rusty but what it
says is still pretty clear to anyone who bothers to read it.
The thing that's caught me, like a cat catches a mouse, is
called a Quartz Blow, but I call it *the She*. The sign has a
whole lot of guff about the chemical reactions that happen
when volcanoes decide to fizz and how Quartz Blows are
formed, but says nothing about how the She keeps me
close.